Torture Porn

Volumes 1 and 2

John Putignano

I dedicate this book to my wife and kids. To my lifelong friend Allison Randall and to all my readers.

Table of Contents

"Our sales were up from last month and our stocks have increased quite a bit; up 2.96. I see a lot of great news coming in and I am sure we all have secured our quarterly bonus."

The meeting room all applauded as Max Rutten modestly held his hands up.

"I couldn't have done it without all of you. Honestly, your hard work and sacrifices have all paid off and allowed me to bring this good news to the table."

He felt the phone vibrating in his pocket. He smiled at his co-workers as he made his way back to his chair. A man next to him gripped Max's shoulder and gave him a thumb up. Once he sat down, he pulled out his phone. He had a text message.

2435 Hazy Creek Edge

8:00 PM Sharp

As his boss continued the meeting, Max obsessively read and re-read the text message. All morning he had been excited about this conference, to deliver this good news, but now he was impatiently waiting for the minutes to count down. Tonight everything was about to change, he just hoped he didn't get cold feet.

As soon as the meeting concluded, Max made his way to the bathroom. With a well-manicured finger, he scrolled through the contacts of his cell phone and dialed a number.

"Hey Max honey, how was your meeting?"

"Baby, it was amazing, nothing short of it."

"When will you be home?"

"Well, we are having a few drinks at the hotel bar so I think it might be a late night. I wouldn't wait up hun; you know how these meetings go."

"Yeah I do; cocaine and hookers."

"Please baby, my days of hookers and cocaine are long behind me."

"I know sweetie. Well, you be good. Don't get too drunk, and if you do, make sure you take a cab home ."

"Ok. Goodnight sugar." Max anxiously ended the call and stared into the mirror. His hair was perfect, parted on the right side of his head in a perfect line. His Versace eyeglasses sat perfectly upon his well-defined face. His skin was flawless with a smooth shave. This was the face of a wealthy, successful, all-American businessman…but the mind inside was far from normal.

He needed to find a way to duck out of this place. He needed to get to that address…he couldn't afford to miss this night. It had taken him months reach out to those who shared his fetish; his obsession. Tonight, he finally got to indulge.

The bathroom door opened and in walked a fit, young man named Clayton Kettler. He was a rising star in the company, a real prodigy at only twenty-seven-years-old. He walked over to the sink and like a magician he revealed a small clear tube full of their favorite white powder.

"Want to do a line, bro?"

Before Max could answer, Clayton already had some of the powder dumped out. He used a corporate credit card to form the small pile into four perfect lines. Max shrugged his shoulders as he reached for the rolled up one hundred dollar bill Clayton handed him. Like a vacuum, he snorted two lines and passed the bill.

"I definitely could use it."

"Hey bro, your hard work keeps bringing me the money to buy this magical white powder. Want to go get a woman in town? My treat."

"Na, I got to leave. My wife is expecting me."

"Listen to you man. I offer free strange pussy and you want to go home to the wife. You're whipped man."

"When you finally get some pubes, you will understand."

With this Clayton laughed as he bent down to snort his two lines. Max made his way for the door when Clayton shouted behind him.

"You don't know what you're missing."

He couldn't help but laugh. If only Clayton knew.

***

As he pulled his car into 2435 Hazy Creek Edge the guard at the front gate checked his ID. After examining the license, he nodded. "They are expecting you Mr. Rutten. At the front door, a valet will take your vehicle and a butler will lead you in. Enjoy your evening."

Max nodded as he drove his silver Mercedes up the curving driveway, his way illuminated by small glass globes of light... As he approached the front door, he felt an overwhelming excitement.

"Mr. Rutten, I will take your vehicle. I assume the title is signed over and inside?"

"Yes it is."

"Very well sir." As soon as Max stepped out, another man greeted him.

"Welcome Mr. Rutten. They are waiting for you. Please, come this way and we will prepare you for the event."

"Very well, lead the way."

They entered the house. The main hall was breathtakingly beautiful. Hanging in the center was a crystal chandelier. The shadows it cast jumped all over the room. The carpet was amazing, a Persian import for sure. He walked across it in his leather Italian shoes and let his feet sink into the soft fabric.

The butler led him to a room. "This is where I leave you, sir. Please get undressed and meet the rest of the guests in the main hall. When you are ready, simply walk out to the left and follow until you see the party. They are anxiously awaiting your arrival, sir."

With this, the butler left and Max walked over to a vanity. Reaching into his pocket he retrieved his phone and searched for his wife's number. He dangled his finger over the call button, but stopped short of pressing it.

He wanted to call her, but knew it would be a bad idea. Hearing her voice would bring him back to reality. He would realize the insanity in all this. He would go home and return to his mundane world wondering what he gave up this night. He loved his wife, but his obsession pushed him.

Instead, he put down the phone. He began to take off his expensive suit. With each article of clothing, he neatly folded it and placed it in a pile. On top, he placed his leather shoes, the ones with the perfect shine. Now, completely naked, he looked at himself in the vanity mirror.

He had muscles, tone, a perfect stomach; he was well-endowed and always had a year-round tan. His wife back home was a gorgeous hard body herself. She was a gym rat and nutrition nut. Their house was full of all the things anyone could ever want…his life was perfect, yet why was he here?

He knew that after tonight many lives would change, including his. He knew this whole thing was insane; no normal person would come here. This fetish, which began as a titillating search on the internet, had developed into an obsession. This macabre fascination drove him mad with sexual arousal.

He knew there was no turning back. He had to commit.

He made his way into the hallway. The air was full of

drunken laugher; people having a good time. He continued on, following the sounds.

In the main hall were nearly two dozen men and women. They were all well-dressed and each one wore a beautifully decorated Venetian mask. They all froze as he entered. Silence fell over the crowd.

"Our guest of honor has arrived. Are our appetites strong?" A man asked. To this they all yelled out in joy. The man approached Max and held out a hand. "Please, take my hand and let me show you something."

Max reached out and gripped the man's gloved hand. He allowed the man to lead him deeper into the room. Many of the guests were licking their lips and one woman nervously sipped her wine to hide her excitement.

The host brought Max to a wall. On it were pictures of good looking men and woman. In each, the person was naked and standing in this exact room.

"You see this one here. It is dated 1923. This is the year our Order of Tantalus was formed. Her name was Natasha Vates. She was a Russian immigrant who worked at a cat house. She was depressed, and one night, she tried to kill herself. Then she met a man who understood her sorrow.

"My great-grandfather, Irwin Leishner was a wealthy man and rather extravagant. He discovered early in life that he had a taste for human meat. You see, during World War One, while in the trenches, he came across a German man. This soldier was a casualty of a flame thrower. Irwin was trapped in the trench for three days. He ran out of ammo, food and water. In an act of desperation, he used a knife to cut away the burn exterior to where it was more…tender.

"When he met Natasha he expressed a desire to eat her. At first, she was disgusted, but after a few days, she warmed up to the idea. My great-grandfather took this picture of her just moments before he laid her on a table and ate her…alive."

Max couldn't hide his erection. The conversations all around proved that they welcomed his arousal.

"So now, this leads to you."

A woman approached them with a camera and took a picture of Max. She smiled as she looked at it in the digital display.

"This came out perfect." She spoke in a soft voice. "You look very nice, Mr. Rutten."

"Thank you." Max responded.

"Max, this night we both will indulge in our fetish. We, the Order of Tantalus, will indulge in devouring you alive. You will enjoy being eaten alive. That is what separates us from criminals. We do not need to force people to fulfill our needs; willing sacrifices are everywhere. We are not criminals; we are not thugs. We are the ones who run this country's corporations, military, government and banks. We are professionals just like you." Max looked at the wall. There was a picture for every month of every year; willing sacrifices. Soon, he would be added to this wall.

"I'm honored. How do we do this?" Max asked. The host could barely hide his smile as he grabbed hold of Max's arm and brought him to a table.

The table was short, the length of a body, and made of African Blackwood. Upon it Max took his place.

"Ladies and gentlemen of the Order of Tantalus; this month, our feast will be Sir Maximilian Rutten. This fine young man will go down in history among the likes of the great and beautiful Natasha Vates. Now get your cutlery in order." With this the masked guests all reached into their pockets and eagerly pulled out silver forks and knives. Looking at Max, the host said, "These forks and knives have been with the order for many years now. This cutlery has cut and pulled apart the meat of men and women and tonight the tradition continues. Mr. Rutten, I ask you to lie down in the center of the table." Max dropped down and spread out upon the table. The guests all gathered around him. "Now, let us indulge."

For the first time that evening he felt guilt. He thought of his wife and children. He imagined the misery and sadness as they wondered what had happen to him.

He felt an urge to flee as he stared at the shiny cutlery. He battled it, fought with the good sense to get up and run from this place. This fetish the internet called Vorarephilia had destroyed his life. And now here he was. He knew there was no turning back.

The group feverishly began to stick their forks into his body. He felt their knives cutting into his flesh. He screamed in both pain and pleasure. He looked down and saw chunks of his meat being pulled away from his body and shoveled into the mouths of those too eager to even chew it before swallowing. All around him were bloody masks as arteries were nicked and blood began to pour heavily out of his body.

A fork jammed into his eye. He felt the metal inside the jelly-like material as the partaker scooped it out like it was ice cream. Max watched with his good eye as the woman sucked it down. All around him they devoured, feverishly pulling meat, and now entrails, from his body... As the room began to fade to black and he began to die, he imagined his meat inside all their stomachs, being digested.

The butler walked down the hall and into the room where Max had changed. He emotionlessly picked up the clothes and placed them in a plastic bag. A vibrating sound captured his attention. It was Max's phone.

The butler picked it up and saw that he had received a picture message. He pressed accept and opened it. In the picture was a beautiful brown-haired woman sitting on a couch with two cute children; one boy and one girl. Below the picture, the text read Daddy come home soon mommy and us miss you so much.

The butler closed the phone and tossed it into the bag. He exited the room and made his way to the front door. Outside he handed the bag off to a man posting security. The man took the bag down a walkway which wrapped the house. He made his way to what looked like a mausoleum.

Inside this stone building there were hundreds of bags containing various personal articles. The man took the belongings of Max and tossed them on the pile, and secured the door.

Ernst struggled against his restraints. He pulled on them and screamed out but it was no use he knew. All this showmanship on his half was simply turning Irma on and he knew it. He heard all about her and her perversities. He knew the stories that she could only cum once she smelled death and he knew that he was her next orgasm.

The room was a dark hellhole. It once was used to house Jewish prisoners but had since been converted into her own private sex dungeon. Along the walls were shelves of tools and sexual toys. She had hammers next to dildos and circular saws next to anal beads.

Ernst had been brought here by a high ranking Nazi Officer. The Officer ordered him to undress and then tied him to this bed. It wasn't until he heard Irma's laugh that he knew she was the reason and by then it was too late. He couldn't fight back any longer. He waited for the torture to begin.

"My sweet little man." The voice came from the shadows and tore through him like a winter chill. He threw his head back and screamed.

"You dog woman, show yourself and get on with it already."

"My o my, aren't you the feisty one. This trait is rare in your bloodline. The Jews are typically so submissive, so docile."

"Well I ain't bitch!"

From the darkness she entered. She wore leather pants and no top. Her hair flowed around her massive perky breasts and on her head she wore an SS Officer's hat. In her right hand she held a bullwhip. She cracked it once to get the man's full attention.

"No, I want to hear you beg."

"I beg to no one."

"You will beg or you will feel agony."

"I won't beg."

"Ok then, be like that. I got ways to make men do as I wish." She approached the wall of sinister gadgets and glided a gloved hand over them. She picked up a medical scalpel and smiled. "Might as well start small."

She swayed her hips as she approached Ernst. He spit and yelled but she ignored him, calm and in control the whole time. She took the scalped and ran it up his thigh.

"You see my legend is spoken in the barracks, I know. I know you know who I am and I know you know what the outcome of our meeting will be. The thing is, the longer it takes me to cum the longer you will be in pain. So you can act the part or you can-"

Irma reached down and grabbed Ernst testicles. She held them tight as she brought the scalpel down. She made an incision on the scrotum which began at the base of the penis and made its way back to the taint. Ernst hollered in agony as he flailed around. Irma smiled and gripped one of the testicles and pulled it from his sack. She then reached for the second testicle and did the same. She placed them onto the table and went back to the display on the wall.

"Or you can make this a lot more fun." She reached for a wad of cotton and then returned to the man. She jammed it into his empty scrotum to prevent bleeding out. "There."

"You crazy fucking bitch!"

"Yeah I heard it all from you parasitic fucks but I could care less what you think of me. I'm Aryan and you are Jewish scum."

Irma returned to the tools and returned with a spoon. She smiled at Ernst and asked him if he knew what it was.

"Fuck you."

"Wrong answer." She leaned in and placed it at his eye. She pressed down as the metal entered his socket. She continued to push as blood secreted all around the spoon. She gave it a scoop and then pulled out the gelatinous eye. She placed the spoon down and reached into her pocket. She retrieved a pack of cigarettes and lit one up. Returning to the testicles she picked one of the grape like fleshy balls and plopped it into Ernst's eye socket. This made her giggle like a child. "Can you now see a little clearer? Are you going to beg now?"

"Fuck you; sadistic fucking whore!"

"God you are making this so much fun." Again a trip to the torture tools and when she returned she had a hammer and a long nail. She rolled the nail in her hands. "Did you know your people nailed Jesus to the cross with nine inch nails?"

"Slut, whore, skank!"

"Yes; it's true. Now I hold this nail and I wonder what else a person could do to a Jew with nine inch nails. Wait, I got it!" She gripped Ernst's penis into her hand and began jerking it. "Come on and get hard already. It will hurt less if you're hard."

"Just kill me."

"No sir, we are just engaging in foreplay now. The sex comes soon. Now get your dick hard." After a few minutes of rubbing Ernst's penis became half way erect. She nodded and shrugged. "Well that will have to do."

She took the nail and began sliding it down his urethra. Ernst convulsed in agony as the nail slid down the inside of his penis. When it wouldn't go any further Irma grabbed the hammer and began hammering it. The nail punctured through his penis and into the wooden table. Irma screamed out in joy and let out a little moan.

"My god, that got me hot!" She cried out and ran like a child toward the torture wall. She scanned the shelves like that same child in a candy store looking for the perfect sweet. She found it. This is the one which will do it for her. It was time to cum. She picked up the funnel complete with a tube and the bottle of acid.

Ernst was quiet now, losing consciousness. Panic ran through her as she placed the objects onto the table and knelt down next to his face.

"No, not yet; stay with me. We are almost done now." She got undressed and climbed onto of the body of Ernst. She used the hammer to pry the nail out of the table and slid the tube of the funnel into the man's anus. "It has been a long time since I did this. I almost forgot about it."

She backed her ass up as she plopped her pussy onto Ernst's face. She reached for the bottle of acid and opened the top. She held the funnel in her hand and moaned.

"Get ready baby…make me cum." She then poured the acid into the funnel.

Ernst's screams were muffled under Irma's thick ass. He flailed in agony as she rode his face, breaking his nose during the ride. The acid ate Ernst's insides as Irma threw her head back and let out a loud moan of pleasure.

"I'm cumming, I'm cumming baby." And as she climaxed her pussy spilled her juices all over the dying man's face, down his throat. He gurgled as the acid ate his insides and as he drowned on the liquid she squirted out.

A few moments later Ernst lay still, dead. Irma climbed off his body and leaned down to kiss his dead lips. "Thank you for not begging, I hate a pussy."

The car cruised down the dark highway; carrying on somewhere around eighty mph. Valerie groggily glanced over at her husband, shaking her head as she studied the speedometer.

"You know Tim; we're already late by a whole day. Let's not push it and get pulled over." She groaned, stretching her arms above her head. She cracked her neck. "Or killed."

"Oh come on Val, where's your sense of adventure? Are you going to keep that pebble in your pussy all night or will you let it out just long enough to have a little fun?" This insult grabbed her attention. She turned to him as she expressed an exaggerated appearance of shock.

"Oh, I'm sorry but when I think of going to visit your aunt in California I visualized palm trees, beaches, and drinks with tiny blue umbrellas served to me by some cute boy who barley speaks a word of English. I didn't expect this vast and empty desert, this complete desolation."

"Yeah, but don't you know all those guys in California are fags." She looked at him, shocked at his ignorance.

"Oh listen to yourself, what are we in high school? Not every guy in California is gay?" She rolled her eyes as she turned her head to the window. She gazed off at the hills of sand and the endless stretches of nothing. "I miss trees."

"Whatever. Anyway my aunt does live near the beach but we need to cut through this patch of desert first."

"These little towns we keep seeing, these people actually choose to live here?"

"Ah it is not so bad, all heat but no humidity."

"No civilization either."

"Jesus Christ, unless there is a strip lined with clubs and late night hot dog stands you are uncomfortable." She closed her eyes and day dreamed.

"Hell, forget the clubs and hotdogs; I'd kill for a Starbucks; cinnamon dolce latte."

Tim rubbed his eye as he yawned. He reached down for the radio dial but Valerie slapped his hand away.

"What the hell is that for?" he asked defensively.

"All that comes in over here is that religious horseshit. I would rather hear the motor hum than more of that ancient garbage."

"But the lord almighty said to hate the fags and the niggers!" Tim yelled in a mocking preacher voice. Valerie tried to hide a smile.

"Come on Tim, I know you're kidding but I don't like that word."

"I am the Lord and I sayeth that there be death to the kikes, the Sodomites and those who worship false idols!" Tim fishes into the breast pocket of his button up shirt and pulls out a marijuana cigarette. "He sayeth that there shall be death to those who indulge in drugs."

"Well preacher man, let's light up that joint to brighten the mood."

Tim placed the joint to his lips and reached for his lighter. He raised the flame and lit it, inhaling deep. He passed it to Valerie as he exhaled.

"I never inhaled." Tim said in a Bill Clinton impression.

"You fucking dork." Valerie said before taking a drag from the joint. She exhaled as she sat up, pointing out the windshield. "Look at that. That car in the other lane has his headlights off. What a fucking idiot."

"Maybe they're drunk, trying to get home before the cops see them."

"Yeah, god forbid they hit a cactus, or a coyote."

"Or a roadrunner."

"Roadrunners aren't real."

"Of course they are."

"Hell if they are! I'm telling you with certainty that the roadrunner is a made up bird. Invention of Warner Brothers, or whoever the fuck made that cartoon."

"Well I will have to prove you wrong tonight." Tim reached down and flashed his headlights at the car. It did not respond as it whizzed past him, headlights still off. "Well fuck you too amigo."

"Maybe his headlights are broken, you know like a daytime driver."

"Perhaps, I'm leaning more toward a drunken asshole." Valerie leaned back in her seat and adjusted her body.

"God I cannot wait to crawl into a real bed, right after I take a real shower." She took another puff off the joint before passing it. Tim shot a disapproving glare at her. "What the fuck is that look for?"

"You took two puffs."

"So what?"

"Well that's bad pot etiquette."

"Excuse me?"

"Bad pot etiquette; there are rules to smoking weed." With this response she shook her head.

"I am sorry; there are rules to indulging in an illegal substance?"

"Listen to yourself are you some hedonistic fucking hippy? Should we indulge in orgies since we fuck?"

"Orgies? Seriously?"

"I am making a point. We indulge in sex right? There are rules though."

"Yeah like you better not fuck anyone else besides me."

"Well sex has unwritten rules, and so does pot."

"By who, who the fuck wrote the rules?"

"They are un written rules; are you even listening? In this situation I began to session, thus I set the pace. Are you following me so far?"

"Yes, so far. Please go on oh great Weedologist."

"Ok, so the pace I set was puff pass. You took two puffs off the joint before passing it, thus you are in direct violation of the rules of pot etiquette."

"What? There are no rules. Puff, puff pass has always been the way, since the movie Friday." With this Tim burst out laughing.

"Listen to yourself. Anything with Ice Cube in it must instantly be disregarded."

"And this is because?"

"He is a Hollywood gangster, not a real gangster. He came straight out of Compton with NWA just to star in the family friendly, and awful movies like Are we there Yet? How do you take pot etiquette from such a sell out?"

"Listen, I am not here to debate the poor career choices of a half talent rapper and no talent actor like Ice Cube, but while we maintain this ridiculous debate the joint is burning and no one is puffing, I am sure that must be a violation of your pot laws." Tim smiles at her and puffs once and exhales. Before he passes it he puffs again. "Hey?"

"I changed the pace."

Suddenly from behind flashed headlights. Both Tim and Valerie jumped and Valerie screamed.

"Is it a cop? That son of a bitch is right on my ass? Where the fuck did he come from anyway?" The vehicle suddenly began to blow its horn repeatedly as it road up a few inches from their bumper. The blinding headlights began to swerve hectically from right to left as the engine revved.

"That's not a cop. Oh my god, I think that's the car that drove past us with the headlights off."

"Asshole should be thanking me for trying to help him; instead he is riding my bumper."

The horn continued to blare as the car abruptly jerked far to the left and sped up. Now the car was side by side with Tim's. He turned his head, trying to look in the windows but they were tinted so dark.

"What the fuck do you want?" Tim hollered. Then the car swerved to the right and collided with their car. Tim gripped the wheel desperately trying to keep it on the road. For a second they hit the hard packed sand but Tim got it back on the road. Again the car swerved and hit, this time sending Tim's car careening off road and into the desert.

Instead of breaking it Tim slammed on the gas. They didn't go far for soon they hit soft sand and sent the wheels spinning but the car remained stationary.

"Tim! There's-"

A baseball bat smashed against the windshield causing a network of spider webs in the glass. The bat came down again, this time smacking against the driver's side window. The glass shattered sending shrapnel into the car slicing up Tim's face. Before he could react a hand reached through the window and in one motion pulled Tim right out of the driver's seat.

"What the fuck!" Valerie screamed as she pulled open her door and barreled into the desert. She heard Tim screaming as she forced her legs to pick up speed. Her lungs pumped with the cool desert air. Then she stopped. Standing in front of her stood a man with a hooded sweatshirt and jeans. He held in his hand a baseball bat and some rope. "How the fuck did you get in front of me?"

The figure walked up to her. Valerie turned to run but tripped and as she fell her head slammed on a rock, knocking her out cold.

***

Valerie's eyes opened to Tim's screams. The first thing she saw was that her husband was tied to a wooden pole. They were in some sort of room. Tim screamed for help and from the hoarseness of his voice Valerie knew it had been going on for hours.

Hours and no one heard him. We are doomed.

Valerie tried to move but she was also tied to a pole.

"He brought us to some cabin."

"A cabin?"

"Yeah, in the middle of nowhere; we are in the middle of the fucking desert."

"How long have I been out?"

"Oh geeze I don't know I can't reach my fucking cell phone."

"Ok, ok…stupid question. Did he say what he wants?"

"No, he hasn't said a fucking word. A goddamn mute, we have been kidnapped by a goddamn mute!"

Valerie struggled a bit but it was pointless. The shackles and chains would not make for an escape; this wasn't some cheesy horror film in which the actress uses a bobby pin to pick the lock. No, there was no escape. They were at the mercy of their kidnapper.

But why did he do it?

Because he's going to kill you!

No, there's more to it than that. You need to find out.

A door opened out of Valerie's view as a light filled the room. A shadow of a man stretched across the wooden floor as footsteps entered the room.

"Son of a bitch let us go!" Tim hollered. Valerie shot a look at her husband to shut up.

"Mr. What's your name?"

The footsteps continued. They got closer to Valerie and were coming up to her rear.

"My name is Valerie and this is my husband Tim."

The footsteps stopped behind her. She gulped.

"Why did you-"Something smashed against the side of her face, knocking out her front teeth and shattering her jaw. Tim hollered as the kidnapper dropped the hammer onto the floor. Valerie cried out in agony as the kidnapper came into the limited light in the room. He held in his hand a saw and a blowtorch.

He approached Tim. The terrified man kicked and flailed as the kidnapper approached him and knelt down next to him. He still wore that hood concealing his face. He reached out with the saw and held it to Tim's throat. The kidnapper said nothing but Tim understood that he was being asked to be silent or he would get his throat slashed.

He watched as the saw blade was lifted off his throat and the tip of it ran down the front of his shirt. It ran down his belly and to his crotch. Here it stood for a second before lifting. He then ran it to Tim's right left and stopped.

"No!" Tim kicked but the man came up quick with a knife and held it to Tim' throat. Tim calmed and understood. It was his leg or his throat.

Valerie was crying as he broken jaw slacked and hung to the right. She was unable to close her mouth fully. She watched as the saw blade moved back and forth, among the screams of pain and the sound of saw cutting through bone it was unbearable. When the leg was completely severed the kidnapper took the blow torch and immediately began cauterizing the wound. The smell was atrocious, burning flesh and fresh blood, not to mention the smell of piss and shit from Tim vacating his waste during the amputation.

The kidnapper rose with the leg in his hand. He turned and walked across the room, shutting the door behind him.

Tim passed out. Valerie calmed herself as she quickly saw that the saw and blowtorch were left behind. She kicked out her legs to try to grab the saw. No use. She kicked out again. This time she not only touched it but kicked it further away. It was pointless. It was now obvious that they were going to die. Her only hope was that someone would find them.

***

Valerie tried to sleep but it was pointless. The pain in her face was throbbing. Tim was no awake and blubbering like an infant about his leg.

"He took it; he fucking took it with him."

"Listen, we need to figure this out."

"How? There's no way."

"I don't know but I refuse to see this as the end. I am not going to die in here." Valerie began tugging on her cuffs. She stained and pulled. She tried to break her hands so she can get her wrists out of the cuffs but despite putting on her strength on it the cuffs wouldn't budge.

"We never saw his face." Tim laughed. "This whole time and I don't know the face of the man who did this to me."

"Tim you're stronger than me, try to pull your hands through the cuffs."

"It's pointless."

"Tim, stop being a little bitch and try."

Tim yanked hard. He pulled with all his might. It was pointless. If only there was some way he could reach that blowtorch, maybe he could weaken the chains with heat and break them. It didn't matter; the torch was far away from reach. Then they heard the door open. The footsteps.

"Let us out of here!" Tim hollered. "You fucking pussy let us out!"

The kidnapper entered the room holding a chainsaw. He placed it on the ground and removed some nails from his sweatshirt pocket. He walked over to Valerie and picked up the hammer he left behind earlier. He knelt down and grabbed Valerie's foot. She kicked but when he dropped the hammer and raised that blade to her throat she stopped.

You need to stay alive. You need to not give in.

The kidnapper took the nail and placed it on her foot. He put the blade back and retrieved the hammer and in one motion swung it down, hammering her little foot into the floor. Blood poured out, filling her sneaker. She cried out as he grabbed the other foot and repeated the act.

"Son of a bitch!" Tim hollered as he spat. The spittle hit the back of the man's hood. He stood and turned toward him. He grabbed a nail and turned toward the scared man who hid behind a false bravery. He quivered with fear as the kidnapper grabbed his foot and nailed it to the floor.

The kidnapper reached for the chainsaw and grabbed the pull chord. With a pull it came to life in a roar of the engine and the screams of the two prisoners.

"You fucking coward, let me see your face. If you are going to kill me at least let me see your face!"

Engine still running the kidnapper placed the chainsaw on the floor. He knelt down so his head was at the same level as Tim. The kidnapper reached up two hands and pulled the hood back. There was no head. It was missing right at the base of the neck. All one could see was a grey neck and a clean cut where his head had been severed.

Tim panicked and tugged his chains. The kidnapper grabbed the chainsaw and let the thing roar. He lowered it a little so it was level with Tim's neck and began to cut. It took only a couple seconds of screaming for Tim to go silent with his head falling to the floor and rolling into the darkness.

Valerie watched as the bloody stump where Tim's neck ended poured blood. She pulled on her foot, tugging it with all her might. She pulled it free and as the headless man approached her with the chainsaw she kicked. He swung the chainsaw and cut off her leg at the knee. She cried out for help as the headless man lowered the chainsaw to her neck. He revved the engine and glided it through her neck, severing Valerie's head from her body.

Torture Porn

The sun shines through the window. I close my eyes and feel the warmth upon my face. It feels magnificent. I let the rays penetrate my soul and at this very moment I am the Zen master. Nothing will ruin this instant for me. All chakras are in perfect alignment, all is centered and I'm the focal point of my own universe.

She screams…maybe I should have sewn her mouth shut first.

I'm pulled from my relaxation and back into the hell I love so much. I was at Zen, I'd given in to nature and accepted the fact that I am but a morsel within the cosmos…not now. Now I am god almighty and I control this domain of death before me. It is nothing short of awesome.

This is a little whore is laid out before me; a smorgasbord of tender flesh and wondrous organs to explore. This pathetic slut bag tramp was just hours ago slinging pussy to buy crack rocks. The cunt had a stem in her purse which was still hot. Now the naked and busted bitch was tied down tight with an expensive leather bondage set I purchased online. It is amazing the things the internet provides for you.

I once bought a book on cannibal cuisines.

I once bought a shrunken head, authentic.

I have heard it all so many times it makes me sick.

Please mister, let me go and I promise not to go to the police.

I swear, women these days have no pride and no dignity. Granted, I've never been at knifes edge on the verge of losing my very existence, however, I wish to believe I wouldn't be as pathetic. The fact is they are going to die regardless, and they know this. This little slut whore hasn't begged much yet but she did give me the sob story about kids at home. News flash for you sweetheart, your kids are better off in foster care.

I run my hand down the right side of her face. She's crying, my skin soaks up some tears. I feel her pain, her agony enter my flesh and run throughout my blood like heroin. I feel my legs get wobbly as I close my eyes. When I do this I'm at peace, I feel all is in control. Order has been restored and soon all will be synched with perfection. I have solved all problems within my life and the world has been fixed. I am god and-

With my other hand I bring the hammer down hard. It's not really a hammer, more of a rubber mallet. The impact on her jaw is quite severe nonetheless. I feel the mental foramen turn into bone rubble as the coronoid process of mandible breaks off the zygomatic arch on the left side. Three incisors, a canine, and a bicuspid tear from the gum and shoot like a bullet down the back of her throat. She gags and gargles as the shards of teeth rip gashes. She vomits and spits out the teeth as she saves herself from choking to death.

Stupid bitch, you could have gotten out of this easy.

I once bought a chemical called 5-methoxy-dimethyltryptamine online.

I once bought a series of medical books online.

She is trying to ask me why I'm doing this. When I was

younger explanations really got me hot. That was nearly three decades ago now and how I have I matured, thus I ignore her. Now don't get me wrong, I still see the artistic integrity within the mind fuck and can appreciate the impact of psychological torture; but it just doesn't get my dick hard anymore. I am a physical kind of guy now. I love to get my hands filthy.

I walk away to my record player. I always liked vinyl. This new age of digital music, it lacks greatly. When I drop the needles upon the record I feel bliss throughout my body as every sense is awakened by the classical work Orpheus in the Underworld. This wonderful work was written by none other than Offenbach. I hear the string instruments, the brass, and the screams of my victim and one word comes to mind...grandeur.

I once bought a embalming kit online.

I once bought a dildo with a knife attached to the end online.

I turn with an diabolic grin upon my face. She sees this and I see panic throughout her body as she pisses all over my table. She's terrified for she knows that I'm truly getting off to this. And now the song is picking up it pace and I feel the energy throughout my own body. My mind is flooded with images of Roman gladiator battles, burned corpses in the trenches of World War 1 and the bloated bodies floating around in the flooded streets of New Orleans after Katrina. I reach down and grip hold of her lower jaw, my thumb tucked within her mouth and my other fingers now pressed hard against the mental protuberance. It takes very little effort as I yank it free from her face.

Her tongue flaps around like a fat slug, and her eyes begin to roll around like a slot machine. She unleashed a grotesque sound of gurgles and distorted screams. Denying her a second to react further I took the jaw and began to beat her with it. Each strike made fresh gashes into her skin. After a few jaw whippings the little bones crumbled to nothing and now my raw meat mitts were pounding away at her face.

I once bought a book on Jeffery Dahmer online.

I once bought a snuff video online.

Beneath my force her right supraorbital process cracked along with the ethmoid bone. This caused that eye to now float a little within the socket. I jammed my index finger over the top of the eye, thrusting it down into the jelly of the retina, tearing through the choroid, and felt for the optic nerve. Once I felt a good grasp on it I tugged, tearing her eye free.

She went into convulsions as her tongue flopped wildly in her mouth. This was it. This was the end. She had enough and her body was going into shock. My god it is so beautiful.

I once bought a knife set online.

I once bought a hooker online…and now she's on my table and dying.

I fucking love the internet. That's why I do this, that's why the camera in the corner is connected to a live feed. Somewhere in Japan a man in a business suit is jacking his cock and watching me destroy this fucking broad. I am someone's internet purchase.

As she dies I imagine my bank account increasing by six figures. When she goes silent I slowly walk over to the camera and shut it off.

My work day is complete.

"Come on, keep up baby." Pete called out to his girlfriend. Breathing heavy she stopped and rolled her eyes.

"We can't all be a soldier hun; I can't keep up. You need to slow your roll." Clarissa responded. This made Pete laugh as he dropped his pace a little. As she struggled to catch up she puffed, lungs burning from the torture. The sweat poured down her face and between her breasts. Pete loved the look of a worn out woman tired and stinking from a good hike "I thought hiking was supposed to be relaxing. This is far from it."

"Please baby, in Fort Benning I hiked many miles with full gear on." He responded sarcastically to take a job at her pride. It didn't work.

"I work at a clothing store in the mall; I'm not in the Army. Sorry, we don't have the same punishments." Still she knew this was important to him and they needed this. God they needed this for the sake of their marriage. It had been crumbling since he returned from Iraq. Isn't this what the therapist meant when he said spent quality time? She didn't know it would be so much torture though. Her idea day off was to sunbathe in the back yard, lounging by the pool while other soldiers gawked at her beautiful body. If only Captain Pete Anderson knew who he was on the verge of losing.

And she had someone in mind. Sgt William Torch; a real man who had an eye on her. She didn't really cheat on Pete, while he was in Iraq she did have a drink or two with him and they had kissed but never had sex. He tried, but she said no. She didn't want the marriage to work but had to try.

"Punishment huh? Wow. Well let's-"and Pete screamed out in agony as he fell to the ground. The sharp pain tore up his leg in excruciating agony. His right foot spilled blood and Clarissa saw he had stepped in a bear trap.

"Oh my god." She hollered, prancing around unsure of what to do.

"Fuck me! Shit!" Pete hollered in agony. He huffed and tried to hold back his shouts but the pain was unbearable.

Return from the war without a scratch and step in some fucking rednecks trap in North Carolina. Good job asshole. This may be a career ending accident.

Clarissa reached into her pocket for her phone. She signed. "No signal. Fuck. Fuck. Fuck."

"Clarissa you need to get help."

"Can you move?"

"No babe, I can't. Every moment we waste we risk losing my leg now please, just go. Get help."

"Where?"

"Baby, do you remember that small cabin we saw." She did and already didn't like the thought.

"The creepy one?"

"Yes the creepy one baby. You need to reach it and get me help." She was hesitant. The house didn't sit right with her. It looked like a horror movie scene. Still, she didn't want Pete to lose his leg. He would blame her and although he never raised a fist to her he had been acting weird since his friend Woody was blown apart overseas. She saw what happened to Rachel when Danny returned. Black and blue and a broken arm and why; because she drank the last beer. This is the life she feared but wouldn't it toss her into Will's arms? Be the last straw. Still, she didn't want a broken limb in the process. And it's not like she hated Pete, her feelings just changed.

"Ok. Just don't move."

"Is that supposed to be a joke?" He laughed a little. She managed a frightened smile and took off. Her legs were pumping, every muscle strained as the burn set in. She tried to ignore the cramps. The cabin was ten minutes away. When she got to it she stopped to catch her breath.

Just some backwoods yokel; and that's all. Nothing to be afraid of. Don't think about the horror movies.

Ignore the horror movie? How could she? This place creeped her out. Maybe it was because it was hard to imagine the type of person who would live so far out, away from society. She would find out her fears were true soon as she descended upon the house.

***

"Clarissa? Where the fuck are you?"Pete cried out as he wrapped his other sock around his leg like a tourniquet. He knew he couldn't save his foot. It pissed him off but still, beats dying.

Stay calm soldier.

The pain was agonizing and he could only pray they Clarissa would make it back. The sun would be down soon and when this happened he knew his time on this planet would be short lived. His blood has filled the air for a while now and he knew that predators were just waiting for the perfect time.

***

"Hello? I need help! My husband has been hurt!"

The old cabin was far from welcoming. In the distance she heard what sounded like a bottle wind chime. The porch was littered with old beer cans and whiskey bottles. Tanned wolf fur lay over the rails. Next to an old chair sat a nasty bucket of tobacco spit covered with flies. In the walls light escaped from within as the cracks gave a glimpse into this person's filthy little world.

Clarissa stepped over the remains of a dead cat, trying to hold her stomach in place. As she got closer to one of the holes she smelled a rank of putrid decay.

My god, smells like a pile of dead cats inside.

The inside was eerily lit. The furniture was moldy and nasty. The walls and ceiling were a nightmare of grime. Surely no one-

"The lord he told me, for I now know it's true. Kingdom of heaven, Jesus always comes through." The music sang softly; the crackle of an old record on a turn table with a filthy needle. This raised more fears as she wondered what kind of religious fanatic lived here.

Well unless a ghost haunts this place someone is here.

She pulled back from the hole and made her way to the door. Three gentle knocks. The sound of movement inside. As the door swings open a giant man with rotting teeth and devilish smile stands there.

"I need help; my boyfriend got his leg in a bear trap."

***

The room seemed unbalanced, like a sloppy construction work done without any regard to building code. The big oaf led her inside as he disappeared into a back room without further conversation. Still the record played.

"Jesus Christ, lord of earth. Open your arms to me."

"Like I said, my husband is about ten minutes up the road. If you got a phone or something."

Of course he doesn't have a phone. Just look at this goddamn place.

There was a rumbling in the back room like pots and pans. She slowly made her way into the living room, taking one

look at the disgusting couch and deciding it was best to stand. The TV was on but the volume was on mute, pornography of course. She watched the slutty girl getting rammed from behind by some hairy guy stuck in the seventies with a push broom mustache.

"My god, even his porn is old and filthy."

Something caught her eye. It lay on the table next to the couch. As she got closer she saw it was something she recognized from anatomy class. It was the bones of a human hand.

Get out of here. Get out.

Suddenly she felt something hit the back of her head. Everything went black.

***

When she came to she felt restraints. She quickly realized that she was tied to a pole, bound by her wrists to iron shackles and chains. She tugged and nothing happened. She was about to scream until she saw Pete. He was also tied to a pole across the room. He was asleep or dead.

"Pete, Pete honey wake up." She whispered. She figured this was a basement and feared to get the man's attention. Her shoes were off and she saw lots of little rocks in the earthen floor. She wrapped her toes around one rock, picked it up, and tossed it. She missed. She tried again. Miss. "Pete."

The subterranean hell was dark. It stunk of wet earth and as her eyes adjusted fear overwhelmed her. On one wall, hanging by hooks, were various bladed instruments intended for yard work and construction. These had been mis-used for nefarious intentions. Each item was stained with old blood. Her fears about this cabin were real.

"Help! Help me!" Pete suddenly began screaming.

"Pete, shut up!" Clarissa whispered, looking up as she listened for footsteps. "Stop yelling or you will get him down here."

"Where the fuck are we?"

"The cabin. I was assaulted and woke up here."

"I don't remember much. I was in the road and a pickup truck pulled up. Next thing I know I am here. My foot! My fucking foot is missing!" Clarissa didn't see it at first but he's right. His foot had been amputated and a tourniquet was tied around the stump.

"Stay calm."

"Calm, some fucking hillbilly kidnapped us and-fuck is that blood on those saws and shit. Fuck."

"Honey, you're a soldier. Get your shit together. We need to-"The basement door opened. An ominous hum filled the room as the descending footsteps filled the nearly empty cellar. "He's here."

"Face me you coward fuck!" Pete yelled, his pride suddenly kicking in. "Un chain me and we will fight man to man."

The man entered the center of the room. He was wearing an apron over his nasty clothing. The apron was once white but now was yellow and stained with blood. He smiled a broken grin and laughed.

"Stupid little man, I'll crush your skull."

"Un chain me and find out big boy. Country fuck."

"I will."

He walked over and pulled a key from his pocket. He leaned down and unlocked the shackles. Before Pete could do anything the oaf picked him up with ungodly strength and smacked his head on the pole. Dazed, Pete hung there trying to cling to consciousness.

"I show you." He spoke in his simple language as he tossed Pete down on his belly. He reached and pulled down his running shorts, exposing his bare ass. He gave it a slap with a filthy hand. "Nice."

He unzipped his pants and pulled out his massive erect penis. He spit on his hand and stroked it a bit and then knelt down in position. With a hard thrust he shoved his dick up Pete's ass. This tore Pete back to reality as he screamed out in agony. The oaf grabbed Pete's arm and snapped it back, breaking it with a sickening sound. With the working arm Pete tried to spin around but the oaf jammed his finger into the bloody stump where his foot once was.

"You motherfucker!" Pete cried out. Clarissa cried as she strained on the chains until she through her wrists would break.

The skin broke and began to bleed through.

"Leave him alone."

The oaf stands up with his dick still hanging out of his pants. He grabs Pete and drags him back to the pole and quickly chains him up.

"Faggot." Pete screams as he spits at the oaf.

"No faggot. Saving nut for her." He smiled as he descended upon Clarissa. She kicked at him but he grabbed her legs and pulled them apart.

"If you don't relax ill jam a knife up your cunt." Terrified she relaxed as he pulled her shorts and underwear off. He massaged her pussy with his nasty fingers and then pulled them back to his nose. He sniffed deep. "Love stinky pussy."

Pete watched in horror as the oaf raped his wife. She cried but let him violate her out of fear of what else he might do. When he unleashed a thunderous climax into her he took his balled up fist and punched her in the face, knocking out three front teeth.

Pete stared at the man with hatred and anger. He didn't move. The oaf turned to him and smiled. "What?"

"I will kill you. I swear to this."

The oaf walked over to the wall of instruments and picked up an ice pick. He rolled it in his hands as he walked slowly toward Pete. He saw the terror in the chained man's eyes and his erection grew. Without a delay the ice pick was jammed into his eye.

The oaf dug around and scooped the gelatinous goo from the man's socket. He then reached down and grabbed Pete's penis and positioned the ice pick. He jammed it down his urethra. It didn't take Pete long to pass out. Clarissa soon followed.

***

Her eyes opened as a smell of cooked food filled her nostrils. For a second she forgot where she was until she saw the giant rapist standing in front of her. He shoved a plate in her face.

"Eat."

The plate was slop but she was starving and weak. How long could she hold out without eating? She eagerly opened her mouth as the monster spoon fed her the slop. It reminded her of chunky soup and she wasn't sure if it was because she was so hungry but she enjoyed and eagerly sucked it down.

"You like human sludge?" He asked. The words in her mind jumped around. She looked at him curiously. She looked over to check on Pete but he was gone.

"Where's Pete?"

"You like human sludge?" He repeated with that dump, uneducated backwoods voice.

"Where the fuck is my husband?"

"He is human sludge." And like that it dawned on her what she was eating.

Immediately she vomited all over the front of the man's

bloody apron as he laughed. She pulled tight on the chains, drawing more blood. She wanted to kill him. She kicked at him but he deflected the blows and laughed. His fist came up and let three blows smash her nose. It exploded like a grenade as she slumped back, crying manically. He smiled and stood up.

"Guess she don't like." And with that the oaf disappeared upstairs.

Clarissa screamed and cried. She felt bad suddenly for what she did to her husband while he was in Iraq. "I'm sorry baby."

Her sadness quickly left and now she was fuming with hatred and anger. She wasn't going to die here. No, and if she did she would kill this motherfucker trying to escape. She tugged and pulled on the chains as blood began to pour from around her chaffed wrists. She screamed in pain as she jerked. The blood lubricated enough for her to pull one hand free.

Astonished she immediately tugged on the other but wouldn't budge. She scooped up the vomit from the dirt and slid it between her wrist and the cuff. She continued to pull, knowing full well it was bits of her cooked husband and stomach regurgitation in there and after a few agonizing moments she pulled free.

Quiet now. We must plan.

***

The monster made his way down the stairs, humming that ominous tune again. When he got to the bottom he stared in shock at the empty pole. He scratched his head dumbfounded.

"How?"

He felt the hammer hit his head and everything went black.

***

"Wake up." Clarissa whispered as the oaf came to. He saw her dripping with insanity and hatred.

"Hello gorgeous." He tried to reach up for her but couldn't move. He pulled tight. Nothing

"Oh, did I tie you up? I found this nice bed deep in the cellar and figured I'd put it to good use."

"Bitch." He muttered and spit in her face. She wiped the snot and laughed.

"Yep." She raised her hand to reveal a set of garden shears. "And first things first."

The shears were brought below his belt and his penis was put between the blades. She smiled at him.

"Don't-"And he cried out as she snipped and his penis fell to the floor.

"Sorry about that baby. Clumsy me." She stepped on it, grinding it into the dirt with her bare feet.

"Fucking bitch!" The blood was gushing from the hole

where his penis was. He began to tug and Clarissa could only hope the ropes would withstand his strength. Clarissa put the shears down and returned to the wall. She surveyed the tools of destruction.

"I wanted to take my time with you, make you really hurt. I'm not a monster though. No, I'm not like you so instead I think I'll just finish you off."

Then it caught her eye. It glistened in the sun which poured in from the cellar window. It looked like Excalibur ready for the taking. She reached out for the chainsaw.

"But first I am going to introduce you to a whole lot of pain."

She took her time sawing him apart, showing him his body parts. It wasn't until he was a limbless that he went into shock. As he shook and convulsed she then took the chainsaw and positioned it at his ass.

"Let's see how you like it." She then jammed the chainsaw in. He jerked and puked as the chainsaw tore a hole into him. The blood sprayed her body as she screamed out. Not a scream of pain or anger but a battle cry. And when the chaos cleared she dropped the tool. He was dead.

She made her way up the stairs and opened the door. She crossed the filthy kitchen where her husband's butchered carcass still lay on a table. She stopped at it and said a prayer.

"I love you baby." She said as she kissed his head.

She turned and made her way into the living room and stopped. Standing before her were three more filthy hillbillies and each one had the same inbred appearance as the monster she had just killed.

"Hello there gorgeous."

A putrid reek filled the aura of the room. A network of ancient pipe work dripped slowly into overflowing pails of water. The wood was swollen and water-logged, bowing from the excessive moisture. The ground was made of cracked and tarnished concrete. The walls were covered in mold and grime, adding to the filthiness of this cellar. This was a revolting, all-encompassing atmosphere of woe; a woman shrieked.

Her extremities strained as she pulled tight against the ropes that bound her. Like a fish she flopped and flailed, her naked body smacking against the old wooden table. She cried out. "It's coming!"

He emerged from a dark corner in the cellar, appearing devilish in the light of the swinging hook lamp. He wore a filthy white undershirt tucked into old blue jeans. He was whistling a soft tune as he approached the nude and pregnant woman. At the base of the table he bent and picked up a large leather apron. He put it on.

She continued to push and strain, hollering out as sweat poured down her face, neck and breasts. "Help me!"

"Shhhh, breathe sweetheart." He whispered as he ran his fingers through her soft hair. He pulled up a metal stool and positioned himself between her legs.

"Daddy, it hurts so much." She managed to get out before more screams took over. He held back tears; he hated seeing her in agony.

"I know hun, I know." He reached a hand out and gripped her knee. She continued to cry as the labor pains shot throughout her body. He reached down into a toolbox which rested next to the table. He rustled inside it a little. "Ok, I need you to push sweetie."

"Daddy…"

"Push darling. You need to push."

"I want to go to a hospital."

"This is not an option sweetie. You know what the hospital will do. We take care of our own, now I need you to listen to me and push."

"Oh god!" She pushed. Her wails pierced his eardrums. He felt his brain rattling inside his skull. The head began to crown. A smile plastered his face. He positioned his hands in place as the birth continued. He allowed the child to fall into them.

The baby cried out. It flailed its little arms and legs as it sucked in its first breath. She raised her head, desperately trying to see the baby. "Daddy, let me see."

He ignored her, reaching into the tool box. He pulled out some garden sheers and snipped the umbilical cord.

"It is a boy. Your first child is a boy." He said excitedly. His daughter leaned up and smiled at her father.

"You mean our child."

"That's right baby…our child."

"You can do it if you want, I know how much it brings you pleasure."

"No baby, you should do it." He shook his head. "It is your first. With childbirth come great responsibilities."

"We should do it together." He didn't need any more convincing, and like a child in a candy store he nodded.

"Ok." He stood up and carried the baby over to a small steel table. He placed it on the cold surface as he returned to his daughter. He reached down as he began to cut her ropes. "It is amazing to see you on this table. Your mother has given birth countless times on this exact table, as has your sister. Now you have become a woman, my sweet little girl."

When the restraints were gone she pulled her sore body off the table. She eagerly walked bare foot to the metal table. Her father was right behind her, his arms wrapping around her. She reached a hand back and rubbed his face as he kissed her neck. They looked at the little crying infant.

"He's so beautiful." She tried to hold back her tears.

"He is." He wrapped her hand in his as he slowly pulled it across the table. They rest on a metal hammer. She smiles as she runs her fingers over the small metal object. She felt a jolt of excitement throughout her body, similar to sexual arousal.

"I am wet." She whispered as he blew into her ear.

"It is your first time. You will remember this forever."

She wrapped her hand around the handle of the hammer as she raised it. She felt his hand still wrapping hers. Together they raised it high in the air above the crying infant.

"I love you daddy."

"I love you baby."

And with this the two of them slammed the hammer down, onto the baby. Its cries instantly ceased as the skull cracked open. Blood and brain matter spilled out from the hole and onto the table. They raised the hammer again and when it came down the abdomen burst like a piñata. The blood sprayed all over her nude body as she laughed hysterically. They brought the hammer down a few more times before dropping the weapon. She turned in his arms and looked excitedly into his eyes.

"I did it."

"You did. And next time you can do it yourself."

"I can't wait for my next child." He held her in the dark cellar, kissing her beneath the glow of the hook light.

Upstairs, in the kitchen, the mother hummed a soft tune. She was cleaning dishes when she excitedly turned to the cellar door.

"It's done. My little girl is now all grown up."

"Tell me when you first developed an interest in cannibalism." Dr. Tara Shields inquired as she jotted in her notebook. As the pen glided over the paper Luke smirked at her. He found her to be very pretty, a rare conservative beauty in an age of flash. Those stunning eyes nestled behind designer glasses; that long red hair straight; soft as silk with a glimmer of blond in it. He began to wonder if the rug matched the drapes. What appealed most to him, however, was her soft pale complexion. Without a visible blemish he wondered how she tasted.

"No slow descent into my madness today doctor; right to the point?" Tara turned back to her notebook. Truth was that she was also very attracted to him. His flowing collar length hair and blue captivating eyes, his physical attraction was irresistible, but his mind was the source of her real attraction. She found him mis-understood, labeled defective by a biased mental health community. This condition of falling for one's patients was not unheard of, but she knew the taboo of it. So much complication comes from it and it could easily be avoided if she would just turn him over to a different psychiatrist. She couldnt. No, she cared for him too much.

She had looked forward to their bi weekly meetings; obsessed was a more appropriate word. At first she chalked it up to morbid curiosity but soon she found herself day dreaming of him. Her mind would wander as she envisioned the man with the perfect physique and charming smile lying her down in a bed. She would undress him as she ran her soft hands over his perfect sinew, felt those muscular arms wrap around her thin frame and position her as he slid his hard erection deep inside. She found her mind drifting as she listened to her other patients. Gregory Sharp talked about his sexual attraction to his daughter as Dorothy Lain babbled about suicide idealization. Meanwhile she daydreamed of Luke Peirce, drew pictures of him on her note pad and thought of his voice.

"Just decided it is time to get to the middle of it all."

"The meat and potatoes…no puns intended." God she loved his wittiness. "It began in High school. I did a sociology report. My topic I chose was a South American tribe which indulged in human flesh consumption. I guess my draw was immediate and it was only a week later I sought out my first meal. Like all of them this one was stolen from the morgue. It, like all of them, was a woman."

"Why women?" She asked, trying not to make it too obvious that she watched his full lips as they moved.

"I find them attractive."

"So you link sexuality with cannibalism?"

"Don't most cannibals?"

"Clinically speaking yes. Jeffery Dahmer is a good example; homosexual male who hunted other males. He got a sexual satisfaction from devouring them."

"I never sexually molested the corpses. This was not my intention at any time. I'm not a necrophiliac. In fact I have a healthy sex life, even now." A healthy sex life; at the thought her pussy moistened.

"So your conviction for cannibalism doesn't hamper your dating?" She asked, slightly disappointed.

"Doctor, do you know how many women out there are turned on by my acts?" And to this she turned red and she knew Luke took notice. He smiled as he positioned himself in his chair. "You want to know if any of these women ask me to eat them?"

"The question did cross my mind. Have you?" She asked like a mindless school girl lost in conversation.

"No, I have not. If I did I would be foolish to admit it however now wouldn't I? Most of them simply got their rocks off at the rush of even asking. No, the only part I eat is their pussy, so to speak." Tara felt her loins moisten more. She crossed them to tell them to behave.

"Tell me-"

"How about you tell me something?" This stunned her and she grabbed her composure with desperation.

"Like what?"

"Like why you look forward to seeing me."

"I look forward to seeing all my patients."

"But you refer to me on a first name basis. I listen when you talk to Mr. Sharp on the phone. You refer to me as Luke, like we are old time friends or lovers. Why is that?"

"Luke we are here for you."

"Are we now?"

"Court ordered therapy. That is part of your release."

"But part of your release is to analyze me, except our terms are different. My release was from prison, yours is from your mundane life."

"Ok I think this is enough for today." Luke stood up and walked over to Tara. She felt the desire to jump up and kiss him but restrained. He gently pulled her notepad from her hand. She went limp and let it go.

Drawn were crude pictures. One was of a big dicked man resembling Luke as he penetrated a woman that looked like Tara. The other was him blowing a load in her face. The third one was her with a fork. On the end of the fork was some meat which was removed from her own arm. She was feeding Luke in the drawing.

"Nice art work." Red with embarrassment she watched as Luke walked out of the office.

It had been three long days of waiting. She needed to see him. In the meantime she listened to Gretchen Fuller talk about her boring eating disorder and how Brian Callahan was molested by his father. For three days she was lost in her mind until finally it was Luke's slot.

He sat across from her, handsome as ever.

"So let's talk about the last time you were here." She put on her fake doctor voice as she forced herself to confront the elephant in the room.

"The drawings."

"I'm sorry, that was unprofessional-"

"I liked them. I thought of them when I went home and drew some myself."

"You drew some?"

"Want to see?"

Before she could answer Luke had reached into his backpack and pulled out a sketchbook. He opened it up, handing it across to her. Their hands met, and as his fingers brushed hers she felt it again, her pussy quivered.

They were a beautiful charcoal drawing of a woman which looked like Tara. She was naked on a platter as a handsome Luke held a knife and fork. He salivated in the drawing while she lustfully looked up in anticipation.

"These are…amazing talent." She tried to contain her excitement.

"I know my drawing skills are good but what about the subject."

"I…" She was at a loss for words. She decided to just give in. "I…like it."

"I thought you would."

"So after the High School paper you-"

"When did you develop the idea of cannibalism?"

"Me? I have no desire to eat flesh." She laughed a little at this and shook her head. "No desire at all."

"No, not to eat, to be eaten."

"Excuse me?"

"When did you first want to be eaten?" And he figured it all out, saw past her. She felt violated, felt dirty. She shook her head and threw her hands up.

"Luke we need to end this session."

"Hide all you want, but you know my words are true."

Luke got up and went for the door. She watched him and something came over her. She knew she couldn't wait until their next meeting. She wanted him.

"Wait." With a nervousness in her voice. Luke turned to her.

"Yeah?"

"I want to see you tomorrow."

"Tomorrow; why so early?"

"Just be here."

***

Luke entered the dimly lit office and closed the door. The room was lit with candles. He smiled as he dropped his backpack. Sitting on the desk was a naked Tara. She was sprawled out on a platter.

"I bought this on my lunch break at Peir One Imports. It comes from China. Did you know in China they call humans they consume long pig?"

"I did. You have done some research."

"So, come closer to me." Luke approached her. The light glow from the candles lit up her perfect body. No shadows could conceal her excitement.

"What do you want? Sex?"

"More." She moaned.

"You want me to just eat a chunk of flesh?"

"No, I want you to eat as much as you can."

"I got quite an appetite."

"I imagine."

"You wont survive."

"I don't expect to. That's what the drug is for. Put me under first. It is enough to ease my pain but I want to be conscious during it. I want to watch you eat me."

Luke approached her not like a hungry lion or a wolf stalking prey, but more like a lover. He placed a hand on Tara's face and looked her in the eyes and saw that this is truly what she wanted. He reached down and took the needle from the table. He placed it against her soft skin and injected it into her arm. Blood emerged from the hole and the sight drove him nuts. After fifteen minutes she felt blissful.

He made the first incision as he cut a piece of her arm, like in her picture. She watched with dreamy eyes as he chewed, the meat swishing around in his mouth. She played with herself as he continued to cut pieces of her and eat them raw. It wasn't until he opened her abdomen up and forced his hands into her guts did she feel this world slipping away. She felt, on the cusp of death, pure ecstasy.

Virginia's Nissan Altima pulled into the gravel driveway. Anxiously she hummed an upbeat melody to divert her mind. It wasn't working. The small rocks which made up the driveway crunched beneath the weight of her slow moving tires. She continued to hum, a desperate attempt to hide her angst from both herself as well as Jeff.

She put the car in park and killed the engine. With her hands gripping the steering wheel she closed her eyes tight. She shook her head and let out a deep breath while whispering to herself "He'll be fine. It's just three days. I'll be gone and when I return things will be fine."

She briskly shook her head as if somehow this would empty her mind. She imagined her fears and insecurities falling free like dandruff from her hair. She imagined an overwhelming sense of calmness flowing over her body like water from a shower head. She took a deep breath and let out an exaggerated exhale. She then reached a shaking had to her car door handle and jerked it open.

Jeff watched from the window. He watched Virginia's queer behavior. Thoughts began to develop in his paranoid mind. He knew something was wrong and being as sick as he was he expected the absolute worse.

Cancer, Sickle Cell Anemia, Multiple Dystrophy, AIDs

He decided it was better to wait the four or five seconds until she reached the front door. Maybe it isn't that bad? He shook his head, disappointed with himself. He hated acting like this, hiding in the shadows and watching. He wished he could greet her at the door like before. Greet her with a smile, meeting her halfway. He imagined the world as it was before, before his mental breakdown.

It seemed like forever to him but it had only been three years since his agoraphobia isolated him from the rest of the world. Three years since he lived a somewhat normal life as an average man with a decent job making decent bank. Three years since he would smile and be the social epicenter among peers. Three long years have passed since the day he couldn't get out of bed.

He remembered that day well. Had it been two days before someone noticed? He was catatonic, lying in bed muttering incoherent sentence fragments. He was unable to move. He urinated in his bed, and lay there in his filth for two days, that is until a concerned Virginia came to his rescue.

She called the paramedics, and they took him away to the hospital. He spent a week there before he would be released back to his home. His home; this turned out to be a prison sentence. It was here he remained since, not so much as stepping out the front door. He segregated himself from the world and it was within the confines of this house where he found solace. This was his world, and the only outside influenced allowed was Virginia.

Virginia was a true friend. She made sure to visit him every day and bring him groceries once a week. The love he had for her was strong, an unbreakable bond like brother and sister. Jeff was ignorant, however, of Virginia's feelings.

She saw their love in a much different light. Where Jeff saw sibling love, Virginia saw a potential for long, everlasting romance. She understood he was unable to commit to any relationship right now, but in time. He was ill, damaged yet salvageable. His vulnerability amplified her feelings for him as she set a foundation to build passion; one day when he's finally healed she would be there.

And they lived happily ever after…

She knocked softly on the door, careful not to knock to hard. To knock with aggressive force would set Jeff into a panic, and he would retreat to a safe spot in the house. Days would go by before he could be convinced to come out. Batting her lashes she cleared her throat before calling out in a soft voice "Jeff, It's me Virginia."

Now came the routine; the deadbolt would open giving Virginia her cue to open it. Jeff never opened the door. His phobias wouldn't allow him to. He would retreat from the door to the entranceway of the kitchen as he awaited Virginia's safe entry.

"Hey Jeff, how are you?" She called out, closing the door behind her. He emerged from the shadows timid yet excited to see her. She had a calming effect on him, sort of like a drug.

"Oh, you know how it is. It's just another day in my mental little world." He joked. Virginia forced a laugh although she was uncomfortable with it. She understood that his jokes which made fun of his ailment were a defense mechanism to help cope with the situation. She didn't have to like it though.

He led the way to the living room. It was bare with the exception of a couple leather couches, a coffee table, and a television sitting on a stand. As always his house was immaculate.

Of course my house is clean I'm locked in here every goddamn day. Even a shut-in is capable of developing cabin fever. If it wasn't for the cleaning surely I'd have fallen off the deep end a long time ago.

Jeff motioned for Virginia to take a seat. She followed, obeying the laws of Jeffery's World. Jeff decided who entered his world, as well as how they behaved in it. He always led the way from room to room and gave permission to sit, lean, eat and drink; or whatever else. Virginia only one time in the past sat down without permission. For the next two weeks Jeff sat in a mind shattered catatonia because he lost control of his world.

"I was watching an amazing documentary earlier." Jeff took a seat in the couch opposite of her. He leaned back sinking into the cushions. "It was on string theory. Are you familiar with it?"

"Yes I am. It involves a lot within it but the bulk of it is the theory of extra dimensions."

"Yes. I found the documentary very exciting yet frightening. It sure is terrifying to know privacy is an illusion." Jeff could read the puzzled look in Virginia's face. He smiled. "What I mean is that in this theory there are other worlds overlapping our own. We share this space with others in another world. I might be next to another being right now or inside one. Perhaps those strange feelings we sometimes get, that sensation that we are not quite ourselves, is because we fused two beings together. Our worlds separated by a thin ethereal fabric. I may not like it but I cannot deny the compelling evidence."

"As I recall many scientists consider it junk science." Virginia responded shaking her head. "I mean it is a theory not a law."

"Yes, but hasn't all science at one time or another been called junk science; Witchcraft or back magic sometimes? Before something becomes law it must first be theory." It wasn't what he said that troubled Virginia but how he expressed himself. He was getting more eccentric, wilder in his expressions. His hands madly flailed with his eyes as his tone took erratic jumps and dives. He looked like a conductor leading an orchestra.

"Well that's real interesting." Jeff could tell she was distracted. He studied her and noticed she refused eye contact. She looked at her feet as if somewhere in that general direction was an escape for her; a back door where she could slip out.

"What's wrong? I can tell something's wrong."

"As usual you're right. I do have something to tell you. I got a promotion at work."

"Well this is fantastic news, but why the sullen look? There's more isn't there?"

"Jesus Jeff, I swear you should become a psychologist when you-" She looked up at him. She didn't want to finish the sentence. She made it a point to not mention his condition. He held a hand out letting her know it was alright. She continued. "I'm now the regional assistant director of marketing research."

"Wow, quite the title but I don't see why the

melancholy."

"I need to take off for a few days" She shot her hand out in a stop motion to prevent Jeff from over reacting. "Don't worry, it's only three days and I'll be back. I'm going up to New Hampshire."

Jeff twitched slightly, forcing a giant smile as a pathetic way to hide his disappointment. Fears and sadness overwhelmed him. "Ok. Then go."

"Oh Jeff, don't be upset. I wish to god I could call or email you."

"No way are you getting one of them goddamn computers or phones in this house. They carry cancer and allow the CIA to listen in on your conversations."

"I know Jeff, I know you don't trust them I just worry about you and wish I had the means to check in on you."

"Listen, you go. I'll be fine. Christ it is only three days, you think I'm that crazy?" Jeff laughed. This time Virginia also laughed. She had to. He motioned for her to stand and she did. He hugged her tight as he whispered. "Now not another word about phone calls or emails."

***

After Virginia left Jeff quickly dashed off to the kitchen and reached for the drawer. In the drawer he keeps a collection of pills. There were bottles of paroxetine, diazepam, clonazeopam, buspar; and then he found it hiding in the corner, alprazolam. He pulled off the top to his favorite little anti-anxiety and popped two into his mouth. He shook his head.

"Three days. Three days and she'll come back. She has to. But what if she has a car accident? What if she's kidnapped or raped? If she was raped she could develop a major phobia of males, thus she would stop seeing me altogether." He shook his head as he softly hit himself with a closed fist. "Stop it, you are doing it again. The what ifs always make you lose control. TV! Got to watch TV!"

He stumbled back into the living room and plopped himself down on the leather couch. He reached for the remote and turned it on. It was the news. The newscaster looked into the camera with a stern look.

"A young woman was found today murdered in the Raintree Village projects in Brockton. The woman was believed to be a police informant responsible for a raid on a drug house on Winthrop Street last month. The woman was found execution style with four gunshots from a .22 caliber handgun. Her hands were tied behind her."

"And I'm the crazy one for not leaving my house. Terrorism, shootings, gang banging; the whole world goes to shit but still people flock in record numbers to buy more bullshit, yet I'm the disturbed one." As he talked to himself and the pills began to take hold he heard from upstairs the patter of small feet running across the floor. He shook his head, ignoring it as a side effect from the pills. It was the undeniable laughter of a child which made him shoot up. "What the fuck?"

Terror overwhelmed him. He felt his heart speed up considerably. He pulled himself from the couch and slowly made his way toward the staircase. The sounds of the feet ran back and forth accompanied by the laugh of a little girl.

"Hello? You're not supposed to be here." And the running stopped just like that. He gripped the railing with a shaking, white knuckled hand. There was nothing now, nothing but empty silence. He shook his head letting out a nervous laugh. "These fucking pills, I'll tell you-"

"You're not fun anymore Jeff." A girl's voice yelled behind him. Spinning around he lost his balance and fell to the floor. He scanned the area but saw nothing; no girl.

"It's the pills; don't freak out. There's no one in this house, especially not some child. You're tired. It's been a long day and you just took two real strong pills."

Of course it's just the pills you dumb shit. Look at you.

Jeff laughed as he pulled himself up. "These fucking pills will-"

Suddenly something whizzed past his head at a high velocity; smashing against the wall into a million pieces. Jeff spun around to see no one behind him, just an empty end table where there once was a ceramic vase. Jeff walked across the room and looked at the broken object.

"Just the pills? How the fuck can you blame the pills on that?"

***

Don't worry Virginia, you're almost there. Check into the hotel; take a shower and then crash. A good night sleep is all you need to get you through tomorrow.

She desperately tried to trick herself into thinking that the source of her worries stem from the class; anxious over the promotion. She could be nervous over the economy, the war, terrorism, fucking aliens…but she could not admit that she was worried about Jeff. To admit this would raise panic. She cared too much for him.

The mountains of New Hampshire were overwhelming. They looked like massive sculptures carved by the mighty titans in Greek Mythology. The sun had already begun to sink behind them. As the daylight began to disappear and make way for the night, a sense of dread tore through her. She felt the hairs on her body stand on end as her mind began to race.

As she struggled to stabilize her thoughts the radio went to static. Startled, yet annoyed, Virginia immediately reached down and turned the station. More static is all she got. She got a collage of broken notes, chopped voices and ominous static. Frustrated she turned the radio off.

Silence. She could deal with silence.

"Mountains must be blocking-" but before she could finish the radio turned back on. Static, noise and voices.

"You…can't save…dies along…Jeff…will you try…collapse." A voice spoke between the static. Suddenly the static dropped and the song "In Dreams" by Roy Orbison played.

Panic ran through her body as she stared at the radio. Did she hear that right?

A horn honking pulled her attention back to the road. Headlights were barreling toward her and she jerked the wheel hard, narrowly missing the head on collision. The car spun out in three complete circles before coming to a stop on the side of the road. Virginia sat there with shallow breaths, her hands cemented to the steering wheel.

"A candy colored clown they call the sandman, tiptoes into my room every night, just to sprinkle stardust as he whispers, go to sleep, everything is alright." Roy Orbison sang as Virginia sat there, still in shock of the radio message as well as the near death experience she just had. She beat her hand off the steering wheel.

"Fucking goddamn it Virginia. Get a grip on yourself. You're nervous, you're distracted and fucking exhausted. The hotel's close. Let's just focus in order to get there." She sat up tall and put her car back in drive and pulled on. She cut through the New Hampshire night as she listened to Roy Orbison and tried to forget what she heard on the radio.

***

Jeff, in a desperate attempt to distract his mind, ran his finger across his record collection. Although he loved all his records, among his favorites were those from the 1950's; the golden age of rock. He read the titles. The Mad Lads, The Platters, Buddy Holly, The Spaniels, The Duprees, Dion and the Belmonts; each record was like a time machine to an era he wished he could live.

He picked up a record by The Duprees and placed it on the player. He dropped the needle as the song Have you Heard dreamingly slipped out his speakers. He lay down on the couch and closed his eyes.

He lost himself in the song as he placed himself in the 1950's. Here he wasn't some insecure shut in, nope. He even owned a Chevy Fleetline. The color was black with red interior, no blue! The glow from the dash lit up the cab as she stared into the eyes of a high school sweetheart. They were at a secluded area, lost beneath the endless stars and intoxicating moonlight. The girl had beautiful green eyes and her black hair was all done up, she was…

"Virginia." Jeff whispered as he let Virginia's face enter the blank canvas of his fantasy girl. He ran his hand through her hair as he intoxicated himself in her perfume. As the gentle breeze creeps into the vehicle Jeff runs his hand down her shirt and cups one of her ample breasts. As he kisses her neck he hears her moan. When he lifts his head he catches a glimpse in the rearview mirror out the corner of his eye.

In the back seat is a little girl. She's no older than nine. The long haired girl is wearing winter clothing which certainly was from a more modern era. The girl's soaking wet and her skin is blue. Her dead, glassy eyes stare up at the ceiling of the car.

Virginia turns to see what's distracting her lover. She sees the dead girl in the back and laughs. "Oh come on Jeff, she is dead and that was a long time ago. Don't let her spoil our evening."

Jeff's eyes shot open. Standing over him and only an inch from his face is the girl from his dream. Jeff froze, unable to move a muscle in his body.

"Who the hell are you?" He asked in a small, broken little voice. This had to be a hallucination, a side effect of the medication. What was it his doctor had told him once?

These pills, they might make the world a little funny. You may see, from time to time, things that simply aren't there. You may even hear things that aren't there. Keep telling yourself it's just side effects from the drug. If need be, just go with it. Sometimes it's ok to trick the brain.

This certainly seemed like one of those moments. He tried to tell himself it wasn't real but still she remained, staring at him with those dead eyes. He will just go with it and play the game.

"Will you play with me Jeffery?" the little girl asked. Her voice was distorted and sounded almost like a cassette tape in a player, one in which the batteries were running low. Her breath stunk like mold.

"How do you know my name? How did you get in here?"

The needle pulled across the record as the music stopped. His living room began to melt away all around him. The windows, the furniture, the walls, the ceiling; it all melted like the Salvador Dali painting with the clocks. When it was done a new world emerged like a mist. As it came to existence Jeff saw that he now stood in a playground during winter. Snow was everywhere and the cold icy New England wind tore through him.

"Ok Lydia, I'm coming!" the voice of a little boy called out. Jeff stepped back, barefoot in the snow, as a child in a thick New England Patriots winter jacket ran past him toward the little girl. The girl no longer looked dead, but full of life as she ran as the boy who playfully chased her.

"My god, that that's me." Jeff shook his head laughing. "I've truly gone insane; fucking insane. I've finally gone off the deep end."

He knew this park from his youth. It was in Middleboro, near the town pool. Of course the pool was closed for the winter, but the park was open. He played here plenty but didn't know the little girl.

A headache tore through his brain as he clawed at his skull in a desperate attempt to release the pressure. He closed his eyes but his brain suddenly flooded with images, memories of birthday parties and recess with the unknown girl; the girl the boy-he called Lydia. Lydia. He saw his mother picking her up in their 1988 Honda Accord. She laughs. She's at school with him. They are in the same class. They play at recess. They swim in the pool during summer. She hands him a note in class. He reads. It says Best Friends.

"I don't know this girl!"

He heard his record playing again. He opened his eyes to see that he was now back inside his living room again. There was the couches, the television, the table; it was all here. He sighed with relief but his relief was short lived. Standing in the corner of the room was a figure.

The figure defied all logic and reason. It combated science simply by existing. It was an ash or granite colored, hulking figure; a towering six feet of sinew. It had not features, just a silhouette like a three dimensional shadow. Upon the face of the figure was not a nose, not a set of eyes nor a mouth. All that existed was nothing but a dark, black void. The creature was surrounded by a red aura that intensified and dulled. This aura seemed to be feeding the creature as it siphoned from the aura which came from Jeff's own body.

Gooseflesh covered Jeff's body as his jaw quivered. He swallowed as he tried in desperation to control his breathing. As his fear increased the aura grew a deeper red. Jeff closed his eyes tight.

This isn't real. Get your shit together.

When Jeff opened his eyes the figure was now in front of his face and he saw himself staring directly into the dark void. He saw himself staring at endless, eternal emptiness that sent a chill throughout his bones. Jeff screamed out but all audio went mute. He collapsed to the floor as the aura turned to the deepest shade of red he ever saw. The shadow creature didn't move, just fed off Jeff's fear.

Get the fuck out of here. Get upstairs!

Jeff scrambled to his feet and fell backwards as he knocked into a table. The vase which sat upon it fell onto the floor. It shattered in silence; no sound as the vase smashed into a million pieces. Jeff clawed up the wall to get back on his feet. He turned and ran up the stairs. He looked back once and saw that the shadow figure didn't move. As soon as he reached the top of the stairs he took an immediate left into his bedroom and slammed the door shut. As the door slammed he could hear again and screamed out.

"Help me! Fucking Christ I am losing it! Help me Virginia!"

***

She checked into the hotel around nine and immediately crashed onto her bed. Her mind was anxious, swimming with worries but she was also burnt out. Within minutes she was asleep. She dreamed of a little girl from her childhood. It was Lydia Hull. She was standing on a hill holding in one hand a red balloon. She giggled as she brushed her long brown hair behind her ear.

"Hey Virginia." She called out to her waving. Virginia waved back, shocked to see her hand had shrunk and fit into a small Barbie winter glove. She looked down and saw a Barbie shirt beneath a pink winter jacket. She was a child again.

"Hey Lydia" a child's voice escaped Virginia's mouth. She approached Lydia. "I thought you were dead."

"That's not funny at all." Lydia let go of the balloon as she placed both hands on her hips and crunched her face in disapproval. The balloon climbed higher and higher until it was lost in the vast sky. "You don't joke about death Virginia."

"Your balloon!" Virginia pointed. Lydia looked up and laughed.

"Don't worry Virginia, it will come back down. They always come back down eventually." Virginia looked around. All around them were endless grassy hills. There was not a tree, not a house; nothing as far as she could see.

"Why are we here?"

"Jeff."

"What about Jeff?"

"He is in peril Virginia. If you are a friend you'll help him, but disappointment is the only ending regardless." Lydia spoke but now her voice was distorted and watery. Her skin began to change and took on a wet, blue look. The wind began to pick up. It was gentle at first but soon took on a hurricane force. She began to shake as water leaked out of her pores. Crying she collapsed to the ground.

"Lydia what's wrong?"

"Mommy, he put me in the barrel. I was alive. I'm dead now. Jeff, please help me!" From the sky fell thousands of black balloons. They fell all around them. Lydia's eyes sunk into her head. "I told you they all come back down eventually."

Virginia shot awake and sat up so fast she almost gave herself whiplash. She was back in her hotel room. On the television screen was an infomercial about some state of the art new vacuum. The man was a fat guy with a bad comb over stuffed into a cheap suit. He bounced around with energy a man of his girth rarely exerted.

"This vacuum will suck up water, oil, dirt, grime and it doesn't even require the use of a bag. Simply rinse in your sink and use again and again."

Virginia pulled herself from the bed and walked over to the little desk where she had her laptop. She rubbed the sleep from her eyes as she sat in the chair, lost in the glow from the screen.

Lydia Hull. What does she have to do with Jeff?

Virginia pulled up a search engine and typed in Lydia Hull Middleboro MA 1986. She pressed enter and suddenly the screen filled with websites discussing the young girl. Virginia clicked on a link and pulled up an old news article.

Young Girl found Dead in Barrel

The body of nine year old Lydia Hull was discovered inside a metal drum full of water. The drum was located in the back yard of a house belonging to a factory worker named Daniel Phillips. Phillips claims he has no idea how the girl got in the drum.

Evidence from the medical examiner report states that Lydia was hit in the head with a rock or other similar object and lost consciousness. She was placed into the barrel of water and the top was put on. The top had fasteners which locked it shut. It was in this water which Lydia drowned.

David Phillips has been arrested and charged with murder. A young boy said he witnessed Mr. Phillips walking off with Lydia. The boy said he never saw her after that.

"A boy?" Virginia shook her head. "Who was the boy? I don't remember."

"This will be the last vacuum you will ever need. Just three easy payments of 29.99; but wait! Call in the next fifteen minutes and receive this Big Toms Carpet Odor Eliminator absolutely free as our gift to you." The man with the bad comb over continued to holler as he bounced around the screen.

Virginia scrolled down the page until she saw another article.

Boy's Testimony Delivered, Dan Phillips Convicted of Murder

> *A young Middleboro boy's testimony was all the evidence the jury needed to convict Daniel Phillips of First Degree murder in the death of nine year old Lydia Hull. The boy, ten year old Jeffery Peterson, told jurors how he watched Daniel Phillips lure the girl, Lydia, with promise of candy. Jeffery states she went with him to his house just across the street from the park.*

The infomercial guy continued to yell about how amazing his vacuum was as Virginia stared at the computer screen in disbelief. She put the pieces together and laughed a little.

It makes sense. That is why he's suffering. He watched Lydia walk off to be murdered. He must have suppressed the memories of that day and years later it came back.

She began to cry as she imagined how horrible Jeff must have felt after Lydia's death. She figured this was it; this is what she needed to pull him out of his fears. Once she forces him to face the suppressed memory he would slowly get better. In time the possibility of romance would now be within her grasp. Her happy ending was now within reach.

Or maybe it will make him worse. He suppressed the memory

for a reason. Don't you think to bring it up might send him over the edge?

"This vacuum will not let you down!"

"No I need to see him now. This is it, the key to help him. I can help him now. I've been looking for a way to help him and I may finally have it."

Don't be silly, you got the workshop in the morning.

"It even comes with an extendable hose for those hard to reach areas."

"Fuck the job. I'll tell them I had a family emergency. This is more important."

"There's no point; he's already gone over the deep end you stupid cunt." The voice was that of the fat infomercial salesman. Virginia turned to the television and saw the fat little man continue to jump around. "I'm so excited to show you this amazing deal, available only on TV.".

Virginia pulled open the drawers of the bureau and threw clothes into her suitcase. She packed everything into her Nissan, got behind the wheel and drove into the night.

***

The house was unnaturally silent. The normal noises, the sound one expects from a house, were absent. He strained his ears in a desperate effort to find evidence of the world outside, a world he feared yet yearned to hear. There was nothing; no sounds of automobiles, no sounds of barking dogs. There wasn't even the sound of the wind.

It's the meds. The meds are fucking you man. This isn't real, this makes no sense. It's all in your mind.

He didn't believe it though. Sure he experienced side effects from time to time but this was different. There was something real, supernatural, but real about all this. He ran his fingers through his hair as he yanked on it. Tears streamed down his cheeks as he battled with conflicting thoughts in his mind.

This is not real.

This is real.

This is not real.

This is real.

Not real.

Real.

Not real.

Real.

I'm losing it. Here comes that deep end and I'm falling over. I'm finally breaking. I was slightly damaged but now I'm fucked, my mind is fucked and there is no turning back.

Deep end, here I come.

"Virginia! I need you!" He hollered and then stopped.

Virginia. Of course! She's been here every day and that's what changed today. My mind is lost without her. It is true, I'm insane. None of this is real I am insane. Give me pills and lock me away. I am insane but safe!

"Denial." The little girl's voice filled the room. It surrounded him. Desperately Jeff swung his head looking for the little girl.

"You aren't real, I am insane. I know now you're just in my fucking head!" Jeff hollered as he squeezed his eyes as tight as he could and shook his head violently. The truth was he was trying to convince himself that this was not real. "Get out of my head bitch!"

"You really tried to forget it, didn't you Jeff? You did a good job but memories do not stay suppressed forever. The time has come to remember."

Jeff opened his eyes and the world around him was gone. He now sat in an empty, dark room on an old rusty metal chair. It looked like the snowed in remains of some old cinema which hadn't been used in decades. Suspended in the darkness was a giant video screen. Jeff slowly rose to wobbly knees as he watched in tranquil amazement.

On the screen he saw the little boy from earlier. It was him again, as a child. He wore a knit hat and that New England Patriots pull over winter jacket. He sat on a swing at the playground.

I...remember this.

"Jeff let's go on the slide" The voice came from behind the boy off screen. The girl ran into view past the boy with her long hair flowing behind her. "Race you."

Suddenly the view switched to a first person view from that

of the child Jeff. The boy ran after her, both laughing uncontrollably. Finally Jeff tackled her and both collapsed in the snow.

"Lydia…do you have a boyfriend?" The boy asked shyly. She shook her head no. The boy smiled as he saw this to be his chance. "Could I be?"

"Jeff you're a friend, a good friend, but just a friend." Lydia's cold response left Jeff shattered. The room's temperature dropped dramatically; his breath was visible. She closed her eyes deep in fantasy. "Besides I am waiting for Timmy."

The boy's thoughts raced. Rejection was alien to him, and he didn't know how to take it. He shook his head as an overwhelming anger developed.

Just a friend? What's that supposed to mean, I'm not good enough to be anything more?

Just as his anger continued to boil he saw a rock the size of a softball sitting in the snow. He reached out a hand and picked it up. He rubbed his gloved hand over the edges as he watched Lydia out the corner of his eye, still lost in her day dream. Jeff sat up still facing her.

"No, I remember this now. No more!" Jeff hollered at the screen. He turned around and reached for the chair behind him. He tossed it at the screen but it didn't break, it seemed to just absorb it.

You're in pain. She caused the pain and she is joyous. A little skank lost in her mind, thinking about people other than you. You're not good enough for her, so make her understand hurt.

He brought the rock down with all his might. Blood exploded from a gash in her head. Besides a quick yelp she didn't do anything else. She was still, not moving. That's all it took.

"I killed her." The boy said. He stood up. He turned his head in every direction to see if anyone saw. Not a soul was around.

"She's breathing you fucking idiot. Get help!" Jeff screamed at the screen like a frustrated audience member watching a movie; a movie where the main character did something outside what the viewer hoped. "What are you doing?"

The boy was now dragging the unconscious Lydia by a leg. She made a trail in the snow; but light flakes fell and already began hiding it. All sorts of conflicting thoughts went through his head. He felt sick, he felt strong, he felt guilt, he felt pride, he felt what he did was wrong but most importantly he feared Juvi.

I'm not going to Juvi. The kids in jail are rotten and will kick my ass every day. Some killed parents or raped siblings. I don't belong there. I didn't mean to kill Lydia.

"She's not dead you fucking asshole, get help before I come through that screen and kick the shit out of you!"

The scene changed to the boy dragging the body up onto a back porch. The hair collected later from this scene would be used in evidence wrongfully convicting Daniel Phillip. Once he got to the top he saw the bucked was the same level as the porch.

They will never find her. This barrel has been here forever. They wouldn't open it, it would make no sense.

The boy hesitated for a moment as he thought further into his decision. Feeling that there was truly no other option he pushed the girl into the barrel of water. Quickly he reached for the lid which locked into place by three large winged screws. Once the lid slid over the top the boy secured it. Inside there was suddenly a violent struggle. He heard Lydia flailing and hitting the walls of the barrel.

She wasn't dead.

Frightened, the boy turns and runs away as the screen fades to black; the only sound was that of a projector running an empty reel. He could not believe he forgot the memory for so long, nor could he believe his hands were capable of such a horrible thing.

A glow made Jeff look up as he saw a soaking wet Lydia standing before him. Next to her was the shadow man. His empty void stared at Jeff making him uneasy. He began to cry as he looked at her blue skin and her body shaking. How could he be such a monster over something so ridiculous?

"You took two lives Jeff. You took mine and Mr. Daniel Phillips, that is who stands next to me. Two years after being incarcerated he took his own life. He died because of your crime." Blood ran down the walls. At first it was a small stream or two accompanied by drips, but soon the wall was covered in it. The blood collected on the floor as it began to form pools.

"Please, you need to believe me Lydia, I'm sorry."

"That's all we ask for, but there is only one way to make this all stop; you must admit your guilt to the world. You must admit you are responsible for the deaths of both Daniel Phillips and I; then we will be released into the afterlife. If you do not admit your guilt we will be here all the time, until your mind finally does go over the deep end."

Jeff looked at the shadow man. He thought of the boy in the video. "I'm not him anymore. I'm not that boy."

But he knew what he had to do. He wanted a shot at a normal life again. He wanted a job; he wanted to go out to dinner or to the movies. He wanted to find a woman and settle down. He wanted a normal life. If this is all it took, to admit to something he did wrong when he was ten years old, then so be it.

He rose from the bed and stood before Lydia and the creature that once was Daniel Phillips. "Alright. I will confess."

***

Virginia pulled the car onto Limewood Ave as the sun showed slight evidence of its presence. Her heart pounded in her chest as she anticipated the best from this great mess.

You will rescue him. How could he not fall in love? You have been with him every day for the last three years and now you might hold to key to reverse his condition. He couldn't find a better woman.

Virginia guided the car onto Jeff's street. She turned the steering wheel into his driveway, pulling in faster than usual. She couldn't help her excitement. As she put the car in park and turned the key she saw the front door fly open. To Virginia's shock, Jeff ran out for the first time in three years.

He flew down the porch stairs and collapsed onto the concrete walkway. Her eyes swelled with tears of joy as she pulled the handle to her door. She could hardly believe it, to see him outside his house. Her emotions overwhelmed her as she cried, cried in absolute joy for this triumphant step toward recovery.

"You did it Jeffery, you finally did it."

Jeffery turned toward her with an upsetting, serious look on his face. He looked lost, distant, aged…worse. She expected a healed man to be standing there, instead he was beyond broken…he was demolished.

"What's wrong Jeff?"

"I killed Lydia Hull." He mutters, laughing a little. He repeats it a little louder, and again even louder. Soon he is screaming between the hysterical laughter of a lunatic. "I killed Lydia Hull."

Virginia was at a loss. She didn't know what to do, how to react. She stood there as the sun rose and neighbors flocked to their windows to witness the commotion outside the home of Jeffery Peterson. She was reminded of what Lydia said to her in her dream.

Disappointment is the only ending regardless.

Barry hated the warehouse. It smelled like sweat and oil. It was full of Mexicans and although a minority in the country, in the warehouse Spanish was the main language spoken. Maybe it's the deep rooted hillbilly in him but he hated the wetbacks. During break times he would loath the smell of burritos cooking in the microwave. He hated their laughter at jokes he couldn't understand. He hated spending his break eating ramen noodles and wondering how many of these fuckers were illegal.

He hated the power jacks he used to fill orders for the grocery store. When he got to the rice section he had to pick up fifty pound bags of rice and hated the Mexicans for it. White people don't buy rice and if they do it's a small bag. A fifty pound back of this shit would last him a couple years. The most rice he ate was when he ordered his honey chicken plate at the Chinese restaurant.

When the clock struck three he felt relieved. He felt a sense of joy flow throughout his aching body as another brutally hellish day had come to an end. He clocked out and made his way to the car. In the parking lot the spics were already pounding beers and speaking their gibberish. They drove their pimped out 1994 Civics and blared that obnoxious music with all those horns.

Barry lit a cigarette and stopped when he got to his truck. Sitting on the front seat was a cigar box. It was strange because he locked his doors, he always did. He didn't trust the brown skinned co-workers to not steal his cd player. How did this box, sitting neatly on the driver's side seat, get there?

Barry unlocked the door and leaned in. He opened the box. Inside were ten human fingers. They had been severed where they met the hand. They didn't bleed; they had been cauterized or something. Normally a person would freak out and scream but not Barry. He knew this was a practical joke and he didn't want to give the fuckers the satisfaction. The damn things were probably fake.

Barry took the box and tossed it in the passenger seat. He started up his truck and began to pull out. As he did he saw Mario and Juan looking at him with smiles. Those bastards had set him up after all. No, he would not give in. He smiled back and headed home.

The house was empty. His son, Jared, was off probably getting some girl pregnant and his wife worked until four. No, he was by himself and it was this alone time, although brief, he loved. He took the box of fingers in with him and made his way to the living room.

He placed the box on the coffee table and turned on the television. He planned on returning the box tomorrow to Mario and Juan and lie to them by telling them it was a good joke. He planned on them laughing hystically as they ask if he thought they were real. He planned-

"Hey, let us out."

The voice was high pitched, almost cartoonish in nature. Barry looked around the room but didn't see anyone. He shook his head, blaming the heat from the hellhole warehouse when he heard the voice again.

"Down here idiot, in the box."

Barry looked at the box in fright. If this was a joke it was a pretty fucking good one. He reached down with a shaking hand and opened the box. The fingers were inside but now they all flipped up as if they were standing on the nubs where they had been severed. They seemed to look at him even though they had no faces.

"Barry, it's us." A different voice now; this one was more normal. Barry chuckled to himself.

"Must be a tape recorder in here or something."

"No, there's no goddamn tape recorder, it's us."

"This is impossible."

"No, what is impossible is that you can't understand what your eyes see and ears here. We are talking to you."

"How is this-"

"How is the grass green, how is the sky blue-who gives a fuck but you? Now we don't have much time before that bimbo gets home so we need to get to work."

"What do you want?" Barry asked, now a little frightened. Then to lighten the mood he suggested "nail clippers?"

"Fuck off with your jokes." A new voice emerged. "Get some flour."

"Sorry, flour; like baking flour?"

"Yeah, are you dense?"

"Listen I have had enough of your insults." And with this he felt suddenly real stupid. Here he was arguing with a box of severed fingers about flour. This was getting more ridiculous by the moment. Barry, trying to decide if he had lost his mind, played along and got the flour. "Got it."

"Take us into the kitchen because we will need perform this ritual there."

"Ritual?"

"Candles; we need four candles. We will also need rosemary and sugar."

"What if I decide not to help you?"

The room got cold, so cold in fact that Barry developed goose bumps. On the television were his wife and son. They appeared to be in some kind of Hell setting full of fire and demons. The demons were short and stabbed the two with long knives. Then the image faded as the television went off and the room temperature returned to normal.

"Now you know we're not fucking around."

Barry ran to the kitchen with the box of fingers and gathered all the things he needed. They instructed him to cover the kitchen floor in flour and make a circle with the sugar. Around the circle he placed the candles as he was instructed. The fingers began to chant.

The chant was low and ominous. It was hypnotic in a foreign language. The house lights flickered and in the flour Barry saw footprints manifest in thin air. They were large and moved slowly toward the circle. Once within the circle the chanting got loud and there was a flash of light. Standing in the center now was a demonic entity.

It stood a towering eight feet tall. Upon its head were horns and it's face was similar to a bull. The body was the build of a strong body builder. The monster huffed as the front door opened.

"Baby, where are you?" It was his wife.

"Audrey don't come in here."

"Barry, what's going on?"

The beast huffed as the fingers chanted. Barry could hear Audrey's approaching footsteps but he was frozen in place. He couldn't move.

"Whats with the music?" She asked as she entered the kitchen and let out a scream. The demon lunged forward and grabbed Audrey. He ripped her head off her shoulders in one motion, tossing the head across the room.

"Son of a bitch!" Barry yelled as he ran for the box of chanting fingers. He grabbed them and tossed them into the sink. The demon hollered in anger as Barry quickly pushed them down the drain. He then reached for a switch and hit the garbage disposal. Blood erupted from the sink, so much blood in fact that one would swear a dog was shoved down there.

The demon faded and screamed as it disappeared. Barry laughed with insanity as the blood shot up from the sink, spraying all over the kitchen along with the scream of ten dying voices.

***

Jared opened the front door with his ear buds in. He listened to the death metal music as he approached the kitchen. When he got there he dropped his iPod. Sitting on the floor was his father. In his lap was his mother's severed head. On the floor was a hack saw and where his father once had a right hand was now just a bloody stump.

The clouds thickened and the daylight was dwindling over Plum Island. Dennis watched as all the spineless filled their cars with junk and scrambled to the mainland. They wanted protection from the storm. Every year this happens and every year Dennis stays behind. He hated the yuppie bastards of Newburyport and even more importantly, he loved the emptiness of the island.

He knew Cody would stay behind like he did every year. Cody operated the only store on the island. It was a convenience store/bar/restaurant and every year it flooded. He kept swearing he would do something about it but every year the middle aged neo-hippie wasted money on marijuana and magic mushrooms.

As Dennis stood on his porch, smoking a cigarette, Cody waved to him from the store. They were too far away to actually converse and for this Dennis was grateful. He hated talking to a man who wore tye dye shirts and hair longer than most women. No, he planned on a quiet evening of silence and watching the storm roll in from his sun room. No use in being rude so he returned the gesture and made his way inside. And as darkness descended upon Plum Island Dennis found his seat, drink in hand, and watched the tide roll in.

***

He found the storm relaxing. The snow fell like kamikaze pilots against the glass walls of the room. It was now too dark to see but the surge had reached the wall by now. He listened as the wind howled outside. Then, near the wall line, he saw a light.

It bounced around as if a drunk was swinging a flashlight but it was too dark to even make out a silhouette. He knew Cody was a dumb hippie, but he was a veteran of Plum Island and certainly not careless enough to act so foolish during a storm, even if he was tripping balls. Terror formed in his gut and quickly spread like a cancer throughout his body. Was it a child? Had a family stayed behind? Had careless parents been so self-absorbed in their bullshit that they didn't see their offspring jut out the back door to explore the storm outside?

"Son of a bitch." Dennis muttered as he pulled on his winter jacket and reached for his LED lantern. "I swear to god, if that is a child I will beat its father's ass."

Outside the wind had really picked up. The wet wintery mix of snow and rain was suffocating him as he made his way down the street. He trotted as fast as he could through the slush mix, making it to the wall. He hoped that if it was in fact a child it hadn't already lost its balance and fallen into the sea.

And there it was, now heading up to the Nature Reserve trail. Dennis cursed as he climbed up the dirt trail where it disappeared beneath a tree. Aggravated, Dennis called out as he got closer.

"Child, you are in for a world of trouble. Don't you know how dangerous it is out here?" But when he turned around the tree he simply froze. What stood there was beyond all logic.

It was no more than seventeen inches tall and covered in a green scaly skin. It stood on two legs and wore a white shirt and brown shorts. Its eyes were like coals and where hair would be were large red fins. The glow came from an oil lantern which it held in its left hand. It turned to Dennis and held its right index finger to its lipless mouth.

"Shhhhh, you're all mine and I don't want to share."

The little creature stared at him, no inside of him. He looked devilish in the limited light from his lantern and nightmarish images flashed through Dennis' mind. He saw people dying, axes smashing open their skulls and knife plunged deep into their abdomens. He heard screams. He saw children beat with hammers and a quick newspaper article flashed. The headline read MASS MURDER ON PLUM ISLAND.

"You're mine." The creature disappeared. Dennis stood dumbfounded and seemingly lost as he struggled to wrap his rational mind around what he had just witnessed.

"What the fuck?"

"Dennis!" He turned his head to Cody's voice. He was so terrified and Cody could see this clearly in his flashlight. He made his way down, off the trail toward the pale, scared old man.

***

"So what in the hell were you doing down there?" Cody asked. He had helped Dennis back to his house and fixed him a hot coffee. Dennis continued to stare out at the beach. "I have never seen you like this."

"I never felt like this." He replied, lost in his mind and obviously troubled by what he had seen. Cody frowned.

"Well…" Cody took a seat in the couch next to Dennis' chair. He sipped his own coffee. "I'm a good listener. Tell me what frightened you."

"You wouldn't believe me if I told you."

"Try me."

From upstairs there was a crash. It sounded like furniture was being turned over. Both men shot up from their seats.

"Do you got visitors?" Cody nervously asked.

"Cody, have you ever known me to have visitors?"

"Well someone is up there."

"Or something." The concept of a non-human making the noise caused a chill to run down Cody's spine.

"What did you see out-" The crashing of dishes cut him off as both men hurried to the kitchen. Dennis flipped on the light switch to the unfolding chaos. All around the kitchen dishes flew out of the cabinets and smashed on the floors and walls, some unseen force guiding them. A mug nearly hit Cody in the head as he moved just in time.

"Dennis." The eerie voice of the creature he confronted earlier echoed throughout the house. The two of them turned back to the living room and as if it had been rehearsed ran to the door. Dennis tried the knob but it wouldn't turn. It was no use.

"Smash the window." Dennis yelled. He ran to the sunroom and reached for a lamp on an end table. He picked up the object and hurled it through the air. As it came in contact with the glass the surface seemed to absorb it; a slight ripple and the lamp disappeared. The glass remained intact.

"What in the hell is going on Dennis?" Cody hollered.

"I honestly don't have a fucking clue but I know we need to get out of this goddamn house."

***

Outside the wind howled like a demon as the trees ached against the harsh conditions. Cody stared out the window as he took a rest. His thirty minutes were up and he was exhausted. Had it been three hours already? Three hours of taking a sledge hammer to a simple door and nothing, not even a fucking dent. His hands hurt and his arms echoed the pain throughout his body. He watched the old man swing with all his might; nothing.

"Dennis, this isn't working."

"Well what the fuck do you suggest we do?"

"Dennis, I want blood." The creature growled, still nowhere to be found.

"Show yourself coward!" Cody yelled. "Show yourself now!"

"I don't want to see it again." Dennis hollered as he turned to Cody. "Never again."

"Again? You saw something by the shore didn't you? Tell me."

"It's nothing." Dennis tried to shake the fear but it was impossible.

"Tell me Dennis, this involves me now and I got the right to know."

"Do you believe in demons?"

"No." Cody responded with full confidence but a little worried where this was going.

"Neither did I."

The house began to shake violently. All around them objects fell from the shelves. After a few seconds it stopped. There was a breaking sound from the concrete floor as a massive spider web of cracks formed.

"Dennis look out!"

The floor began to open up. Smoke bellowed from within.

"I told you to be quiet, I didn't want to share!" The demon's voice howled. A light filled the basement as the heat began to rise. "Now you will deal with us all."

"Cody, what I saw was not of this world. Be ready. The're coming."

***

When morning came and the storm passed Plum Island was full of life again. People were in their homes assessing the damage done or relieved that all was as they left it. Children laughed and played outside in the snow as parents dialed their insurance agents.

The front door of Dennis' home crept open. Cody and Dennis walked out into the light like zombies. Dennis held an axe and Cody held a knife. Confused, their neighbor Darlene approached them.

"Mom let me call you back." She lowered her phone and approached the sweating, filthy men.

"Dennis, Cody is every-" Dennis' axe crashed through her skull. She didn't have a moment to scream as her head cracked open. Emotionless the two men turned and walked to the next house. They entered it, greeted by ungodly screams as the two men butchered the residents.

Bloody weapons in hand they continued to the next house.

Then the next house.

Then the next house…

Diana stared at the lake. She loved the tranquility, the calmness. George put his arms around his wife and smiled.

"Beautiful isn't it?"

"It is. To have such a thing in our own back yard; it's like a dream."

"We are living it." And they were. Both of them had good jobs, two kids and now a house. By the looks of George's profit margins the house will be paid off in only ten years. He prided himself in providing so well for his family. If he only knew what horror the lake had over Diana he would have never bought the fucking thing.

***

George parked his Escalade and strolled up to his home. As he walked into the kitchen he was smacked in the face with the smell he was sick of. It was fish again. He loved that his wife enjoyed fishing but it was getting ridiculous. He smiled as he kissed her on the cheek.

"Hungry baby?"

"Yeah…fish again?"

"It's good for you."

"Yeah, but so it beef."

"Beef will kill you hon."

"Where's the kids?"

"Upstairs."

Trevor was playing a video game when his sister Rachel entered his room.

"I told you to knock before you enter." He muttered. Trevor was a typical fourteen year old boy, rebellious in nature and territorial. Rachel was only five and loved pushing her brother's buttons.

"Afraid I'm going to catch you jerking off again?"

"Keep it up and I will decapitate your Barbie dolls."

"Mom said dinner is ready."

"Fish again?" Trevor asked already knowing the answer.

"Yep."

"Fuck."

"Don't swear or I'll tell mom." Rachel exclaimed. Trevor turned in his chair to face her.

"You know what, you keep ratting me out you will turn into a rat."

"Will not." Her face suddenly filled with fear.

"Will to, happened to my friend Freddie. He turned into a rat."

"I don't want to turn into a rat." She innocently responded.

"Easy enough, stop ratting."

Rachel swore to herself to stop ratting from that point on, even when her mom began to act crazy, she promised never to tell anyone out of fear of being turned into a rat.

***

A noise awaked George. He bolted out of bed and grabbed his gun. He slowly exited the room and to the hallway. He heard squishing noises and a voice. It was Diana.

"No, I never imagined it would taste so good."

George put his gun in his waist band and descended the stairs. As he got to the bottom he heard a slithering noise. When he turned the corner he found Diana sitting at the table. She was soaked and wet. She looked up at her husband and smiled.

"You want some eel?"

"No thank you baby…who were you just talking to?"

"Tefnut; now take a seat and-"

"Who the fuck is Tefnut?"

"She lives in the lake."

"Like on the lake, like in a house on the lake?"

"No she lives inside the lake. So does Daucina and Ahti. They were busy this evening so only Tefnut could come over."

***

"I don't need a psychologist."

"Fuck if you don't, you were wet cooking eel in the middle of the night talking to imaginary people."

"They are not imaginary and they are not people."

"Well then what the fuck are they?"

"I'm not telling you with that condescending tone."

"Sorry baby, what are they?"

"Mermaids George, real mermaids." Her eyes lit up and George saw only madness in them. He shook his head.

"Listen, I know it has been stressful with the move and all but adjusting takes time."

"I am adjusted George."

"I want you to see a psychologist."

"Ok. I will see one for you."

***

George was at work getting reports together when his cell phone rang. "George."

"George, it's Dr. Lee."

"Hello Doctor, how can I help you." George looked up at his secretary Megan and shook his head. "File these in the W345 file not that one."

"Sorry to call you at work I know you're a busy man I am just concerned about your wife."

"Oh yeah, she tell you about the mermaids?"

"No, in fact I haven't seen her. She never came by."

"Son of a bitch; ok doctor sorry for wasting your time I will pay for the session."

"No need George but please, get her in here. It sounds like she is quite confused."

***

George rushed home and parked his SUV. He barreled into the house screaming. "Diana!"

"She isn't here." Trevor hollered from the living room. He was sitting on the couch watching TV. "Keep it down I'm watching this."

"Where did she go?"

"Off to the lake with Rachel."

George stormed through the house and out the back door. He ran across the yard and stopped at the lake. He saw Diana and Rachel in the water.

"Honey isn't it amazing?"

"She's swimming." George laughed. "Oh my god you taught her how to swim."

"Yeah; she's pretty good to."

"Come on in I want to talk to you."

"Ok. Say goodbye to Ahti."

"Goodbye Ahti."

***

"It's not healthy, you're not healthy and now you're taking Rachel down into your looney head."

"That's why you haven't met them yet George. They don't like your attitude. You should have seen Ahti playing with our Rachel. He is only ten years old himself. They play so good together."

"Enough of this shit. You are going to the doctor tomorrow or I swear to god I will divorce you."

"Ok baby. I will go for you."

George stormed off. "And no fucking fish tonight!"

***

"Honey wake up." Rachel opened her eyes with sleep still in them. "Mommy?"

"Yes. Let's go play with the mermaids again."

"I don't want to." Rachel had played along with her and her game about mermaids but she didn't feel like playing now. She was tired and certainly didn't want to go into the water.

"Come on, Ahti likes to play with you. Get your swim suit on. Tonight you will see their home."

***

George was awoken in the middle of the night again by a soaked and wet Diana. He ignored her and went back to sleep. The next morning he woke up late so he quickly got dressed and made his way out the door

"What about your breakfast hun?"

"I'll get something on the way. Don't forget to see Dr. Lee."

"I promised and I will."

George spent the morning fixing the problems all his co-workers had made. He met clients, shuffled papers, responded to emails and made phone calls. At around

10:30 his phone rang but he was in a meeting. On his lunch break at 12:15 he saw the missed call was from Dr. Lee. He dialed back.

"Dr. Lee."

"Hello doctor it's George calling you back, sorry I missed your call."

"Yes. I wanted to tell you I saw your wife today."

"Great. So is she crazy or are there mermaids in my back yard."

"Well she certainly is confused about something, but she said something that raised concern for me."

"Oh yeah, what's that?"

"She said your daughter Rachel was staying with the mermaids, and that she slept there last night at their house. Now it might be all in her mind but."

"I understand. Thank you doctor."

"No problem. I will see her again in a few days."

George hung up the phone and dialed Rachel's school. The principle said she never showed up. George, now in a panic, called his wife. She wasn't answering. He felt a dread in the pit of his stomach and panicked.

"Meghan!"

"Yes George?"

"I got to go, just cancel the rest of my appointments."

"Is everything ok?"

"I hope so."

***

The house was empty and George rushed down to the lake. He found Diana naked in the water. She waved to her husband.

"Come on in honey."

"Diana, where's Rachel?"

"Come in the water is great!"

"Where's Rachel?" He hollered. She looked at him puzzled.

"Oh don't worry, she's safe. She's at the mermaid's house playing with Ahti. Really, take off your clothes and feel this water."

George was fighting back tears. He reached into the holster in the back of his pants and pulled out his gun. He pointed it at his wife.

"What the fuck do you mean my daughter is at the-where do the mermaids live?"

"Why are you pointing a gun at me?"

"Where the fuck do the mermaids live?" He screamed. Diana shook her head.

"They live at the bottom of the lake. I brought her there last night. Be quiet, she's probably still sleeping. I assume they were up all night swimming."

"You fucking dumb bitch!" George hollered as he put his finger on the trigger of his gun. "You killed our daughter you sick bitch."

"No, I can get her. She's just sleeping at the bottom of the lake."

"You crazy bitch, you drowned her."

"No George listen-" The gun went off. The bullet hit Diana in the chest. She reached up and touched the hole. "George?"

"You made me do this."

"George you shot me."

"You made me do this." George cried out and collapsed to the ground. "Oh god my daughter; why?"

"George…your daughter is fine." And with these final words Diana fell back dead. George cried on the bank of the lake as the water took her body, floating away.

As he sat there crying something made him stop. It was a laugh. It was the laugh of Rachel. George jumped up and screamed out.

"Rachel! Where are you?"

"Over here daddy."

George stood up and walked to the edge of the water. Sitting on a rock was Rachel except where her legs once were was now a fish tail and fin.

"They made me a mermaid daddy."

"Baby? What is going on?"

"Why did you shoot mommy. She was Tefnut's friend. Tefnut won't be happy."

From the water, close to George, began to raise a figure. It was a man of muscular build. His skin was blue and his hair was green. He swam toward the shore and when he got to the beach he used his forearms to pull himself up. He slid on his tail and fin as he made his way closer to George. The look on his face let George know he was angry. George stood there as the mermaid rose up, standing on his fin. He towered over George, standing ten feet tall. He looked down at the man who had again collapsed to the ground out of fear.

"Tefnut?" George asked. The beast reached out his massive arms and grabbed onto George. He then opened a fanged mouth and lunged forward. He dug deep into the screaming man's head as the water beast ate his face. There was the sound of bones cracking as his skull collapsed in on itself. Within seconds the headless body of George fell to the ground, blood pouring from where his head once rested.

The beast turned to Rachel who was smiling with a smaller one as well as a female. They waved to Tefnut. Tefnut nodded and hollered in a booming voice.

"Now where is Trevor?"

Dorothy Bane was a widow who lived alone in a tall house; a house which sat tucked away deep within the woods. A cloud of mystique surrounded the weak old woman. The odd behavior she had developed after the death of her husband alienated her and drove her into seclusion.

Countless nights she spent by that creek just out back of her southern home. She spent these nights wishing to the Alabama gods that they would bring her someone or something to help her pass these last few years. She prayed for someone whom would understand her and not judge her; someone who simply would accompany her. Her plea for a companion fell upon deaf ears, until one hot and humid night.

"Please lord, I wish to be alone no more. Just bring me something to help a dying, lonely woman" And as if on cue a drum was heard coming from behind the back yard from within the forest. It was distant and continuous; a slow and low beat. She shook her head in disbelief.

It certainly wasn't from a neighbor; her nearest one was four miles away. As she wondered with disbelief the sound of a violin followed the drum. Both were distant but could not be mistaken as a mind trick.

Dorothy didn't know how to react to this strange phenomenon. Suddenly there was a piano. The music grew closer every second, almost like an invisible marching band in the woods. Then to top off the weirdness she heard a voice. It was beautiful and masculine as it sang. "All in all you're just another brick in the wall".

Finally unable to cope with it any longer the old woman stood up, leaning over the railing she hollered out, "Who may you be, what do you want with me? I am a poor old woman, who has nothing to offer. I got no money, and I don't have the body for the taking. I got not a pot to piss in, nor window to throw it out. Please show yourself, and join me for tea, less you mean me harm. If this is your intention I beg you to kill me now, and take me from this misery the lord has cast upon me!"

The music stopped. No longer did she hear the drum, the violin, the piano or the voice. The music ceased abruptly like a record being yanked from the player. There wasn't a sound, only the natural noises of the Alabama woods. Dorothy was alone, and in silence once more.

"Oh Dorothy, you truly are losing your mind." Quickly she disregarded the incident, rationalizing that what she heard was not real; nothing more than her old mind playing tricks on her. Then she hears a guitar and a voice.

"I got my first real six string, bought it at the five and dime, played it till my fingers bled; it was the summer of sixty nine."

The music was closer now; the guitar, the drum, the piano, the violin, the voice and then suddenly the low heartbeat of a bass guitar. Dorothy was becoming overwhelmed with fear as the music got even closer, and her fears reached their peak when she saw a rustling in the bush. Whoever was playing this music was no more than a couple yards away, and Dorothy had never been so afraid.

"Show yourselves! This game of playing with the old woman's mind has gone too far. You are on my property, and I demand you show yourselves!" She needed to say no more. The music stopped as the culprits stepped out from the shadow and into the moon light.

Standing before her were six beings. They were no taller than toddlers, but they were not humans; they were frogs. They stood on two legs and dressed in colonial American attire complete with sheathed swords. One carried a small drum which fastened to his body. One had a violin in hand, another bass and another one held a guitar. The piano player wheeled his instrument. Holding a microphone was the lead singer. Six frogs stood before Dorothy Bane.

"This, this cannot be real. You are the devils work aren't you, why else would you carry those little swords less you plan on cutting me up real good" The woman hollered as she pointed a wrinkly old finger at the frogs. The lead singer of the frog band stepped forward and spoke in the most soothing voice any living creature could make.

"Sorry to have startled you my fair lady, but we come as a gift. We are not from the devil, but from the Alabama gods. You wished for company all these years, and now we have arrived. We are dreadfully sorry if we frightened you, for that was hardly our intentions. We are here simply to be alongside you these last days of your life." And then the frog motioned with his eyes down to his sword, "and these are simply for show my lady and I could never imagine using them to harm a fly let alone a little, lonely old woman."

Dorothy had trouble accepting that the Alabama gods wound

send a band of six musical frogs to keep her company, but she couldn't complain. For the first time in a long time she had company. A smile broke on her face as she realized that they had indeed listened to her pleas.

That night, in her back yard, she had the time of her life. The frogs played classic rock ballads, blues, jazz and the pianist ended the night with a little Beethoven. When all was done, and Dorothy grew tired, the frogs packed up and headed for the creek.

"Wait, where are you going?"

The lead singer turned to the woman and smiled. "Did you not have the time of your life?"

She looked young and energized. She smiled the way she smiled for so many young men during her prime. Her body still old, but her soul rejuvenated. "Yes but where are you going I must ask? Why abandon me like a lover? Why leave me here, begging for more? Why put me through the pain of watching you leave? Why frogs, must you go? Did you not say that you would stay with me until the Alabama gods decided to remove me from this earth?"

"Yes ma'am. You are correct. So do I understand you right? Are you asking us to stay with you, live in your home and spend the last days of your life with you?"

"I would be more than honored. I will cook for you as well as clean and tune your instruments. The rent will only be one song a night."

"Are all utilities included?" He asked and they all had themselves a good laugh.

All day the frogs entertained the woman with impersonations, political humor and musical ballads which filled Dorothy's soul with utter ecstasy. She loved the frogs. Then one night, while the frogs slept, Dorothy returned to the chair she sat in by the creek where she first met the wonderful creatures.

As she sat there she heard a song in the distance. She heard a piano, a sitar, a banjo… three banjos. There was another drum, four bass guitars, a tuba; all these instruments continued to play as they made their way closer. They all played a totally different song, blending together. As they got nearer the numbers grew.

There were now seven drums, ten or eleven different flutes; could that really be twenty, thirty, even forty different saxophones? The pianos were endless and there were around fifty different singers all singing different ballads. Old Beatles songs mixed with Crosby, Still and Nash. Somewhere in the mix was Jefferson Airplane with "Don't you want somebody to love". When the music reached its pinnacle of ear bleeding torture, they all started emerging from the shadows. They were playing their own songs as they gathered on Dorothy's lawn.

There were hundreds of them. Each one had their own instrument, dressed in colonial attire with sheathed swords. It seemed more and more arrived every second, all adding to the musical mayhem. Dorothy was overcome, infuriated with the nerve of these frogs.

"Please stop playing that racket!"

The frogs grew silent. Now all one could hear was a natural sounds of the creek. Then one of the lead singers, the one who had been bellowing out Helter Skelter just moments earlier, spoke up. "What's wrong Dorothy?"

"What's wrong?" She hollered, flailing her little arms in the air, "what's wrong you ask? How about you answer this question; what on earth are you doing in my yard playing that racket? Why are you here?"

The entire assembly of toddler sized frogs stopped and looked around at each other. Some were sitting in the trees, others had climbed up on Dorothy's house; all had a look of confusion.

"We were sent here by the Alabama gods just like you wished." One of the pianists called out.

"You said you wanted company during your last days, someone or something." A drummer called out.

"So here we are, and here we will stay until your dying days." A Guitar player called out. And with this they all cheered. "For our fair lady, Dorothy Bane!"

"No, this is not what I wanted; this is not what I wanted at all. I want you all to leave. Get off my property now!" Dorothy hollered.

"But we were told by the Alabama gods to stay with you until you die, and so shall we remain!" A frog hollered to more cheers.

"Well I want you gone right now! I don't' want you here anymore. Leave this very minute!" She shouted. The frogs put their instruments down. They stood in silence at the position of attention. They looked like they were standing in a military formation. From inside Dorothy's house the original six emerged onto the back porch with their instruments. Dorothy turned and fell to her knees. "Please, oh please frogs make them go away. I can't stand the racket."

The lead singer frog looked at her. His black eyes showed no emotions as he spoke. "You want us to leave? Well this puts us into a position, for you must understand that we are under contract with the Alabama gods. We were told to remain with you until you die, you want us to go… if that is your wish then we got no choice but to speed up the process."

The frogs that surrounded the house quickly pulled their little swords out from their sheaths and approached the house. They opened their little amphibian mouths and revealed rows of sharp teeth. Their eyes now burned a fiery red. The original band of six played the Pink Floyd song "Wish you were here" as the old woman hollered and screamed out for help.

The frogs closed. They climbed onto the porch as she ran to a corner and jumped up onto a table. She screamed and kicked at the frogs but they came in endless waves. They began to sink their teeth into the meat of her legs. One crawled up her flailing body and sucked out an eye. The empty socket poured blood as another frog sliced open her throat. She gagged on her own blood as it sprayed like a geyser. She turned around as she tried to scream but the stabbing and slicing came from every direction. And while this orgy of death played out the original six played their instruments.

Her clothing was sliced off as her old and wrinkly body as she was ripped open from the neck down to her crotch. A steaming mass of entrails hit the porch as the army of frogs, sent by the Alabama gods, continued their assault of hacking, slicing, stabbing and ripping.

And as the body of Dorothy Bane was torn to shreds, and her pieces scattered all over her house by the frog army, the original six played on. When the murder was complete, and the house walls were repainted with Dorothy's blood, the frog army marched back into the creek. Deep into the heart of the woods they marched like little green soldiers as the band played on.

And the sounds of their wonderful music carried on throughout the night. In the morning their songs were replaced by that of early morning birds, the sound of running water in the stream and the soft croaking of the countless frogs which reside in the Alabama wilderness.

"Come on Bucky, this is bullshit!" Phil yelled to me as he stood at the top of the playground. I smiled at him and shook my head with full disapproval. He looked like a fool; standing there in a ninja Halloween costume. I couldn't be seen with this dip shit.

"Are you kidding me? What the fuck is that?"

"It's a ninja suit."

"No shit Sherlock, but why?"

"We're going to steal that Nintendo game from Craig; he won't see me in this."

"Dude, what he'll see is a total douche bag trying to steal his shit. Then he'll kick your goddamn ass. Get that thing off or I'll just steal the game myself. If I do that though, I won't let you play it."

Phil sighed for a second but then went down the slide. When he reached the sand below he immediately began pulling the ridiculous Woolworth's costume off. I swear. I know we're the same age but for thirteen years old he can be a complete moron. When he was back in his normal attire he ran over to me with the rags in hand.

"Bucky, what am I supposed to do with this?"

"Toss it away for all I care."

"My mom will tan my hide."

"Well hide it for now; we'll get it later when we return with the game."

"Ok." He hesitated but quickly ran to a rock where he tucked the costume with hopes that it would be still be there upon return. I know he hated me but I couldn't care less. I wanted that game more than anything at this moment. It came out a few weeks ago, Super Mario Brothers 3, I almost had a heart attack when I heard and almost died when I realized that I didn't have the money for it... We were going to get that game.

Craig is a rich kid. His mom will probably just think it got lost in his massive room of shit, the kind of shit spoiled little rich bitches accumulate but never even use. The son of a bitch barely used his Nintendo anyways now that he owns a Neo-Geo and a Sega Genesis. Boy, I wish I could steal those but it would be kind of hard to hide those from my parents.

I hated my parents. My dad was a loser who worked at Levitz Furniture. He was an awful salesman who was always on the verge of being unemployed. Mom was a real up and comer at the Food Pantry. She was a head cashier. The two brought home measly pay checks and obviously they couldn't part with the $39.99 that Super Mario Brothers cost. It wasn't my fault I was born to a poor ass family. So, I decided to take it.

Now I know I got this little fool with me but Phil is alright most of the time. He let me watch his mom undress one time, showed me a secret place where she wouldn't catch us. Says he went here a lot to watch her. I know it's a little creepy but fuck it; I got to see some boobs. She really ain't too bad looking either.

Now that we got the whole ninja costume out of the way I tell him it's time. Well it was less of a statement and more of an order. We jump on our bikes as we tore down an old bike trail behind the school. We're riding fast, pedaling hard as we whip around corners and jump overturn trees. Branch ahead, I duck. Small hole, I swerve. I am the master of my art and as I take the lead I see Phil catching up. Everything is a challenge to show I'm the best.

"Come on you slow fart, try to catch up…unless you're scared."

"I ain't no wimp Bucky. Watch this!" Suddenly his speed increases as he frantically pedaled. I can't let this little punk win so I pedal harder as well. My legs are really pumping blood now as my muscles burn and ache. I feel the adrenaline rush through me as my breathing becomes labored. Now we are really tearing down the trail at break neck speeds.

"Come on baby boy! If you can't hang you can always go home and suck on your mommy's titty. Better yet, how about I suck that titty and you take your daddy's dick!"

"Fuck you, you're the faggot you-"Before he could finish I heard his bike smash. I slammed my brakes. My bike did a perfect donut in the sand as I jumped off and toward my friend. Phil was lying on the ground, crying. He'd hit a branch and went head over handle bars. I already had the insult ready but as I got closer I saw that his arm looked broken.

"Oh fuck man."

"Bucky, it really hurts. I think I-"

There was a blinding glow from the woods. Before I could react I felt a violent tug at my ankles and I was suddenly being dragged. I felt the branches and stuff tearing up my skin as I struggled to grab hold of a tree. It was pointless; whatever had me was pulling me too fast.

I looked forward to see what it was. I made out what looked like a naked man with a thin frame. His long arm was grey and the skinny hand wrapped around my leg. I, for some reason, thought about my bike and hoped no one would steal it. Here I am being dragged by some naked pervert and all I can think about was my bike.

He is naked. The thought suddenly became reality. A naked man kidnapping a thirteen year old boy could only amount to one thing. Was he going to try to force me to suck him? Was he going to try to stick things into my ass? The panic was setting in and the branches and rocks I was being dragged through were really tearing my skin up something nasty.

We stopped in a clearing. I could hear the man talk but it certainly wasn't English. What a strange dialect. It reminded me of old movies in which they discover some African Pygmies who talk that strange talk full of clicking sounds. It wasn't the same but similar. The man turned toward me and I nearly shit myself.

His eyes were large and round, a solid black. His head was oversized and sat upon a thin neck. The skinny frame, the grey skin, the strange language; these were aliens and I'm not talking about Mexicans from over the boarder either. These were actually extra-terrestrials!

"Bucky! Help me for god's sake!" I heard Phil scream as one of the grey aliens had scooped him up into his arms. A beam of light shot from the sky and within seconds they were gone. Before I could make sense of it my abductor scooped me up as well.

"Let me down you faggot alien fuck!" I yelled, punching at its big head. It opened its mouth to reveal rows upon rows of sharp teeth. Terrified, and with a crotch full of fresh urine, I stopped my pathetic assault just as a beam of light fell from the sky. Within a second I was gone.

***

I opened my eyes. How long had I been out? I didn't even remember falling unconscious. As I pulled myself from the sleep fog I took a look around. It looked like something out of Star Wars. Everywhere I look I could see blinking lights and other electronic gadgets. I lifted my body but when I tried to stand I felt a strange disorientation. The word drunk came to mind, although I admit that I have never had a drink in my life. After a few seconds of trying to keep my stomach down I sat up.

This room was certainly used for medical research. I've seen enough movies to know what this was. They were studying us. The thought of anal probes enters my mind and I shudder. Besides the endless walls of switches and buttons I see blood, and a lot of it. I knew this wasn't going to end well if I didn't do something. Although Phil was a pain in the ass I needed to find him.

I needed to stand up. Alright, on three; one, two…three!

I collapse to the floor. What the fuck? My legs were like

jelly. Whatever those things did to me I could barely move my legs. For what seemed like an eternity I sat there trying everything and finally I could move again. The whole time I kept thinking that at any minute those thin grey men would come in and get me. They didn't. Was this an experiment? Were they watching me?

When my legs decided to work I ran to what I perceived must be a door. No handle, of course. That would be too fucking convenient. Look around, look around; fuck someone was coming this way! No place to hid. Think. Table! I rush to it and I find the jackpot; surgical tools all lay out before me. I grab a really nasty looking knife and hide under the table.

I wait. I can hear their gibberish talk. I wait and then opportunity hits. The door opens.

I don't give it a second. I rush the first body I see and plunge the blade into its abdomen. The penetration is squishy as the blade moves around freely inside the torso. It's as if there are no bones to stop it. The screams are ungodly as red liquid spills out each time I stabbed. It sounds like a pig squeal. Fuckers bleed just like us.

The second one was a coward. He ran and I immediately dashed into the hallway. An alarm sounded and I knew my time was now limited. I must find Phil and get out of this place.

The hallway is a fucking nightmare. Blood, guts, bones, skulls, clothing, personal effects; for an advanced civilization they lived no cleaner than a savage. To my left I heard the noise. It was Phil. Of course the door was closed and I had no idea how it opened. Think…

The alien I killed.

I run back to the small room and rush to the corpse. Looking at his body I see nothing attached to him to open doors. There must be something. I look at the door for a means to enter and I find it. There is a pad on each side of the door, almost like a lighted welcome matt. This device must read their feet! How it worked I could care less; I need the right feet.

I rush to the table. Knives, scalpels, drill like devices and then I see it. A hacksaw! I grab it and rush to the alien. Now being the sick kid I am I have mutilated my fair share of cats (what the fuck else is there to do in Eutaw Alabama?) so to cut this things feet off wouldn't really upset my stomach at all. So I saw away.

There seems to be no bone as I slice through him like butter. Now with the two severed feet in hand I hear Phil's screams growing as I rush back to the and place the feet onto the small mat. It glows with a blue light. There is an electronic hum and the door slides open. Without a second to spare I rush in with that knife raised high.

I see Phil on a table, an alien doing god knows as his blood is pouring off the table. I rush and start stabbing. The alien screams in agony as I stab the shit out of him. He stumbles, loses his balance and when he collapsed to the ground I take the knife and plunge it down into one of those big fucking eyes. Green goo leaks out as I twist the knife deeper and deeper until the fucker finally gives up and dies.

Phil is still screaming. The alien had chopped his arm off. It looks bad. The bone near his elbow is exposed along with what looks like lose meat. "Come on Phil we got to go! You need a doctor!"

"Bucky, why are you doing this?" What a weird question.

"You're my friend."

"You killed me!"

"No you moron, I'm saving your stupid ass. Come on!"

I look around for a weapon. There is none. I find it odd but perhaps these things are pacifists. They seem to be doing this in the name of science and perhaps they never expected anything to get this out of control. This was obvious by the fact that not a single alien showed up for the alarm. They must be hiding, waiting for it all to end.

Even in space there are pussies.

Now Phil is bleeding bad and seems to be on the verge of going into shock at any moment. He babbles about how I murdered him, about how I'm going to hell and I know this is a bad sign. He's delusional. I know he's going to die but not here. I'll get him home. We run through the hallway until we see a room full of lights, the same colored lights that brought us into this place.

"See Phil, we're almost there."

"Why?"

"Come on, we're going home!"

I knew it was too good to be true. Nothing is this easy.

Before the door stands the only brave alien on this damn ship. He's holding a screw driver looking thing and waves it at me; no laser guns or light sabers…nothing these sci fi dorks dream up every day. This was just a ship full of pussy pacifist aliens and common tools found in a redneck's tool box.

I'm still holding my knife so I take my chances. I rush the motherfucker and slice open its soft throat as it slams the screwdriver down on my shoulder. It hurt like a motherfucker but didn't even break the skin. Their bodies are so weak; it amazes me that they die so easily. He's too busy holding his neck together to bother with us so I grab Phil and rush toward the light.

For a second we seem to float in this room. The light surrounds us and numbs us. I see a picture on a screen of the area where we last were. It was still programed for the spot where we were abducted. This seemed too easy. And before I knew it we were shot back down.

We slam into the ground hard. I stand up, knife in hand and laugh. I can't believe we're actually back in Alabama, and can't believe I'm so happy to be here. I see the police are here to. There are three of them and also a group of frightened people gawking with terrified faces. One officer pulls a gun out and tells me to drop the weapon. I look at him puzzled and do so.

"We were abducted." I shout. He ignores me.

"Get down on your knees."

"I saved us from the aliens."

"I said get down on your knees."

"Tell them Phil."

I turn my head to Phil and see he's dead. Then something strange happens. He was mutilated. How did this happen? His throat is slashed, his abdomen is stabbed, his arm is cut off along with his feet. All around me there is blood, I'm fucking drenched in it. I see the saw I used to cut the alien's feet off.

"I cut the feet off." I mutter. "The alien…why?"

"On your knees! This is your final warning!" The officer had a shot lined up on me. The people muttered amongst themselves. I heard one call me a murderer.

"I killed the aliens! By the Alabama Gods you got to believe me!" I shouted to the cops. I looked around and suddenly it all came back to me. There were no aliens, there never was. There was no light beam, no space ship, no abduction…I did this. I cut the feet off, but the feet belonged to Phil. I killed my best friend.

I look at the cops, at the people and in the crowd I see my mother. She looks embarrassed. She don't look concerned, just mortified. I shake my head and laugh. I laugh because I don't know what else to do.

My psychologist is right. I need medication.

The Incident at Bleak Ridge Lake

I remember the tales from when I was a child, and now I believe that behind every tale there's truth. You must understand that the town of Eutaw has always had its legends; we even had our own quasi-religion. We called them the Alabama Gods. The residents really ate this shit up. It was kind of Christian, kind of Voodoo mixed with Paganism I guess. There was talking in tongues and even snake rituals. When I was young it was normal but must admit now that it was pretty weird.

The legends were strange. I remember what happened to Bill Stokley down by Bashful Swamp. He was as white as a ghost when they pulled him from the muck. He spent the entire night submerged up to his neck in a state of catatonia while the leeches sucked his blood. The Sheriff said that there were four alligators nearby. It was a goddamn miracle that they hadn't eaten him. It took weeks for him to die from infection, and before he passed away he babbled a mad tale to the Sheriff that a lizard humanoid and his lair.

The town got wind of this and people talked.

"I always knew that boy had a screw loose in that noggin. He got real weird after Vietnam." Margery Tierny said one Sunday afternoon after church. But despite this, many thought there was truth in what he said. Even the local newspaper The Eutaw Tribune wrote an article on the subject. It told a tale of a mud hut filled with alligator corpses and dog cadavers. The Sheriff was curious if there was some validity to this tale and asked if he saw any human remains, especially of any children. You see, in

Eutaw we have always had a missing children problem. It seems children just up and disappear around here, never to be seen again. People blamed witches, serial killers, and now they could blame the lizard man. Bill shook his head however and later that night died.

I always believed in the tale. I was no older than eight at the time and remember when they discovered old Dorothy Bane butchered in her house. She also was a firm believer in the Alabama Gods, and we all thought her to be a witch. We figured she was killed by her coven during an argument. I thought at one time she was taking the local kids, but when she died they just continued.

Now I am sixty three and have spent the last thirty eight years trying to make sense of what I saw that night when I was only twenty five. I had spent the night fucking a passed out Gretchen Ball. I know by today's standard that is considered rape, but back in 1975 is was just something we did. Hell, Terry Wilson was fucking his sister Rachel every night, and no one batted an eye at that even though he was twenty and she was fifteen. It was a different time.

Anyway, I was sniffing my fingers and tossing back beers as I walked down the path to Bleak Ridge Lake. Today you all know it as Tanner's Lake. I was lost in my head, reliving the events of the night when I heard a faint song. I couldn't understand the words but I could hear that it was a woman, and by the sound she was beautiful. What kind of woman would be out here this time of the night?

I, in my drunken and horny state of mind, made my way deep into the woods and toward the lake. I tried to picture the face of this woman. I imagined her with brown hair at first, than blond. I soon realized that I imagined her to be a white woman because that's all that lived in Eutaw. She's speaking another language, so surely she must be foreign. She could be Asian or Indian; Brazilian maybe. I wasn't too educated then, nor am I now by any means, but I didn't know what any of these kinds of women looked like so I just pictured white women with brown skin. The song, although I didn't understand it, seemed full of sadness and loneliness. Was she depressed, did her boyfriend leave her by the lake during an argument? Had the Alabama Gods blessed me to become her knight in shining armor?

As I closed ground on the voice I saw a dark silhouette in the distance. It was indeed a woman. I couldn't see any features, just the dark outline. She seemed to be sitting on a small island of earth in the center of the lake. How did she get there? She had to swim, and if she swam there she had wet clothes on. Maybe she had no clothes at all.

When I got close enough I started to walk to my right so I could see her in the moonlight. My jaw hit the floor. She was stunning. Her skin was brown. It wasn't the normal brown color of human skin but more of an earth tone. It was full with hints of red. Her hair was long and flowing. Its color was a bright mossy green.

She was naked. Her breasts were big and perky. Lost in her cleavage she wore some sort of necklace which I couldn't make out from where I stood. I got closer, so close that I came to the water's edge but still had trouble seeing her. She stopped singing and turned in my direction and I froze.

Her eyes were blue, but not the blue of any girl I had ever

seen. They were icy, frozen as she stared at me. They seemed to glow in the night and even give off a light mist. Her lower body was lost in the shadows and I wanted to see more of this exotic beauty. For some reason I kept thinking she must be from Iran or something. I never seen an Iranian at that time but I thought they might look like this. Then she spoke clear English.

"Come closer handsome." Her voice was beautiful but sounded dreamlike. Did her lips even move? I could've sworn they didn't. It didn't matter, I wanted her. I tore my shirt and pants off. I stripped down to my underwear. She motioned with her finger for me to remove them. I did. I now stood there, completely naked and then she motioned for me to come to her. I ran into the lake and swam toward the little island.

Once I reached land I quickly pulled myself up. I was an attractive man in those days and my hair was a little long. I pushed the brown strands from my eyes to behind my ear. As I allowed my eyes to adjust to the night I gasped as I saw the woman up close and almost fell back into the lake. You see, from the waist up she was human. Sure she had unusual skin and hair color, but this was nothing compared to the waist down. She looked like a lake trout. She had no legs, but a massive greenish colored fin. It was coiled beneath her as she sat on the little bit of land.

"By the Alabama Gods, are you a mermaid?" I asked stupidly. She didn't answer, just giggled. This had sobered me up. I felt something in her presence. I felt comfort, I felt safe, and I felt as if everything in my life would be just fine from this point forward. She brought a beautiful feeling I had been searching for my entire life…inner peace.

Her ice cold hand gripped my naked arm and before I could realize what had happened I was being pulled through the lake. I descended and as I looked around I saw hundreds of fish swimming past me. Who would have known so much life existed in this tired old lake. Then it struck me. How was I seeing this? It was night, but somehow my vision was able to see everything. I could even see the bottom of the lake, something I couldn't see even during the day from the surface. Then I realized another oddity, I could breathe. I was underwater and could breathe!

The mermaid continued to pull me toward the bottom of the lake where we approached a cave. She pulled me inside and we barreled through a long tunnel. After what seemed like ten minutes we suddenly pulled up and we were in a pocket of air. As we came to the surface I saw dry land. Here she let go of me and climbed ashore. I pulled myself up as well and stood before the exotic beauty. She smiled at me and giggled as her icy hand reached out to my genitals. She slowly massaged it. Here I was, underwater and with a real mermaid and all I could think about was where her pussy was?

She moved toward me and dropped her head below my waist. I felt her wrap those beautiful lips around my dick. My eyes closed and I remember wondering how on earth I would explain to my friends that a mermaid gave me a blow job. They wouldn't believe me, so this would be my secret, a beautiful mermaid all to myself.

And then a smell hit my nostril that I didn't notice earlier. That stink, it reminded me of the trash outside the butcher shop. The trash cans that were full of rotting pig heads and other spoiled meat. The stink was similar. I opened my eyes and looked around me.

Everywhere I looked I saw small bones. Some were in little piles while others were tied to strings for decoration. The stink originated from the half decayed bodies of children. They had been gutted as little piles of gore collected at their feet. How many were in this little subterranean cave? Then one dead face caught my eye. I recognized it well for she had gone missing not more than a week ago. Then I recognized another, and yet another. I looked down at the mermaid as she continued to perform oral sex on me and realized that it was she who was responsible for the missing children in Eutaw.

It had to be her song, like the Siren's in ancient Greek lore. The enchanting song attracted them to her, much as it did for me. She then pulled them down and ate them. Did she plan on eating me to? I suddenly felt ill and reached down, pulling her off me.

She looked up at me confused. I shook my head. "These children, I know them. I know these children. You've killed them."

I explained this rather calmly, afraid of what she might do. She just looked at me seemingly emotionless, but then I saw the tear running down her cheek. I hurt her feelings. My rejection, it hurt her. I realized at that moment that I was judging the actions of something I didn't understand. Maybe this is how she ate, much like me and my Pa would hunt deer. She was obviously lonely, and I must have given her something she hadn't in a long time…attention.

Now I hurt her. I began to fear how she would react. I stepped back and she looked up at me. "Go then."

She grabbed ahold of my arm and before I knew it we were

tearing back through the tunnel at absurd speeds. We pulled out of the cave and back into the vast open water. She pulled me to the surface and before I knew it she was gone, lost beneath me. I remained there for a bit, floating in the lake. Then I saw her floating nearby.

I felt bad that I hurt her. She killed those children I knew so well, but who am I to judge her for that. She's not human, so she isn't a cannibal, just a hunter. How many times have I eaten veal? That's baby cow. Maybe to her, human kids are like veal.

I had insulted her and wanted to apologize. I wanted to explain my insulting behavior. I approached her and reached out. It wasn't her. I felt my hand wrapped around the small naked corpse of the little girl who disappeared a week ago, the girl I saw in the cave. Her eyeless face looked up at me in the moonlight. I felt ill as I stared at the little girl's corpse. Then I heard small splashing sounds all around me. My initial fear was that the mermaid had friends, other mermaids and my insult made them all mad. I figured they would take me below the surface and tear me apart.

There were no other mermaids. What had been splashing all around me were the small bodies from the cave surfacing. All around me I was surrounded by the missing children of Eutaw.

"What the fuck?" The voice came from the shore; it was a voice I knew well. It was Sheriff Jack Tanner. "Boy, I suggest you come to shore and surrender yourself or I'll shoot you dead in the water. Let the gators eat your fucking ass up."

That night I was arrested and charged with the death of forty six children. I told them the story about the mermaid. They obviously didn't believe it. It wasn't until a few weeks later that police realized that some of these children had been killed when I was no older than an infant, others before I was even born. I was released from the town jail and a dive team entered the lake.

I waited ashore and watched for hours. They came up with nothing, didn't even find the cave. The report read that I discovered a dumping spot to a serial killer. My mermaid story was removed from record.

To this day I return to what is now Tanner's Lake and wait for the mermaid. I haven't seen her since. I sit out there and wait, straining my ears to hear that enchanting song which I can still hear in my head on quiet nights. Even after all these years, I still wanted nothing more than to apologize.

"Suck down that drink bitch!" Britney hollered in a drunken stupor. She flung herself onto Jeff's lap as Lawrence handed another shot to Amy. Amy took the drink and threw it back. She then shook her head and fanned her mouth.

"Goddamn, goddamn that drink."

"Ah, we're just getting started baby." Lawrence laughed. Amy leaned over and started kissing him. Britney playfully slapped Amy on the shoulder.

"Slut, don't go fucking we're in the middle of a party."

"Nobody's fucking nobody." Amy said rolling her eyes.

"Not yet." Lawrence smirked.

"Not tonight, I got church in the morning." She patted him on the chest as he made puppy dog eyes at her.

"Ah, good Catholic girl; sin all week and absolve on Sunday."

"Shut up." Amy reached up for her crucifix necklace and kissed it. "Jesus protects me."

"No doubt baby; I didn't mean offense."

"You don't understand. Amy should be dead right now." Britney paused for a second to let it sink in. " Last year she was in a car with a bunch of drunks and they hit a tree. She was the only survivor."

"Well then I will lay off tonight."

"I actually gotta get home, Britney will you walk back with me?"

"Sure doll." Britney stood up and looked back at Jeff. "No drunk bitches while I'm gone. I'll be back soon."

"She never said no drunk men." Carlton laughed as he plopped on Jeff's lap. He looked up at Jeff and batted his eyes. Jeff pushed him off.

"Fucking faggot."

"Well he is drunk and he is a bitch." Lawrence laughed as Carlton trotted off to flirt. Amy looked at Lawrence and smiled. She kissed him.

"Goodnight babe."

"Goodnight."

Amy's apartment was only a few blocks away. She walked with Britney, or stumbled, as they laughed and talked.

"So you and Lawrence are doing good."

"Yeah, he's a good guy."

"It must be hard getting over Brett." Brett was Amy's ex who died that night in the car last year. They had been out all night hitting the bars before hitting the tree. She remembered the last words Brett said to her was that he loved her and that he was sorry. He died in the ambulance. She looked up and smiled at her friend.

"It was hard but I care for Lawrence a lot. I'm glad you set me up with him."

"Oh I just love a happy ending."

The two girls made it up the three flights of stairs to the hallway where her apartment was. Out of breath and panting Britney laughed.

"You need to find a place with less fucking stairs." Britney playfully pushed Amy who fell into the wall laughing.

A door swung open from across Amy's apartment. It was her neighbor Carla. She was an old woman, very religious. She shot a look of disapproval at the drunken girls and their antics. She scorned at them. Britney, full of drunken courage, stuck her tongue out at the woman.

"Jezebels are gonna burn in hell."

"Fuck's your problem you old bitch." Britney hollered. Amy grabbed her friend and shushed her.

"I'm sorry Carla we just had a little too much to drink."

"And you, I know about you and your accident. You escaped once, but Satan will collect his toll." These words struck hard at Amy. She stumbled back a little as Britney gave her the finger.

"Sit and spin you old crow. Close your fucking door." Carla went back into her apartment as Amy fished in her purse for the keys. Once she got inside she said her goodbyes to Britney and collapsed onto the couch. She couldn't stop thinking about what Carla said. Satan would collect his toll.

She heard the church bells ringing. She bolted up from her sleep and rushed to the bedroom to get dressed. "Fuck. I can't miss church again."

She threw on some deodorant, a dress and her Sunday shoes. She bolted out her apartment door and down the steps. She threw open the front door and onto the street. It was still dark out. She looked for her cellphone to check the time but she forgot it upstairs. She had no idea what time it was but it was winter so it wasn't unusual to be dark. Still. The church bell rang again and she took off running.

The church was only a block. No one was outside, they were inside already. She had to quietly sneak in so not to disturb the service. She opened the door and slid in. The church was full. She eyeballed for a seat and found one halfway down the aisle. She rushed down the aisle and took a seat. Everyone was in prayer and didn't even notice her coming in.

"Heavenly Father, forgive us sinners for we are but human." The priest said. It wasn't the regular priest, he must have been sick. Amy hoped Father Anthony was alright. She reached for her bible and spied on the bible next to her, opening up to the same page.

Amy didn't recognize anyone from the congregation. It was weird. Maybe she was early and they had two masses now. She had no way to tell the time so she decided to just sit there.

"There is a heretic amongst you. There is a Jezebel." The word tugged at Amy's insides as she recalled what Carla had said last night. She began to feel strange. She looked up and saw the priest was looking right at her.

"She is here and she doesn't belong here. She infiltrates our sermon with the stink of alcohol on her breath and fornication on her body. The harlot is here right now in this very room."

Amy began to feel sick. She felt watched. She took a look around and saw now that all faces were looking at her. The priest was calling her out. She began to stand up.

"The harlot stands defiant of our law of understanding. She has no respect for us. She feels she doesn't have enough that she has to come to our service."

"I'm sorry, I'll go." And as she turned to make her way to the aisle she stopped. Was that Joyce Carter? There was no mistaken it but she died a few years ago from a drug overdose. Then she saw Tyrone Spencer, a friend of hers that committed suicide. Then there was Frank Willis, he died last month from heart complications. He lived a few doors down from her. Then she saw him…she saw her ex-boyfriend Brett. He stood up and walked toward the aisle. As he did others began to stand.

"Brett? You're dead."

Brett rushed up to her and took her in his arms. She hugged him tight and cried. He then whispered in her ear. "We are all dead. This is a service for the dead. You got to go now."

Blown back by all this Amy stumbled backwards and fell onto the floor. She saw others now gathering in the aisle heading in her direction. She screamed as she pulled herself up and turned toward the door. It was no use. It was blocked by more of the dead.

"This living being interrupts us as we try to mend our broken souls, as we try to patch our spirits, as we try to right our wrongs. This harlot must not leave."

She was grabbed from behind by two women. They held her arms as others gathered around her all with faces of wrath. Amy screamed out.

"Brett!"

"I'm sorry Amy."

Then she lost sight of him. She fell to the floor as the dead piled around her. They reached down and grabbed at her body and yanked. She felt their dead fingernails ripping into her skin, felt them drawing blood. They pulled chunks of meat off her body. Amy continued to scream as the priest stood over her with a knife. "We shall strike her down!" He plunged it into her gut.

Amy felt the world around her fading as the priest ripped down with the knife. She watched as the dead began scooping out her innards. They took chunks of bloody organs and danced wildly in prayer. With her intestines they looked like those people who dance with snakes at church. They spoke in tongues as the priest yelled praise Jesus. As everything went dark the last thing she heard was Carla's voice.

"Satan will collect his toll."

"Son of god, you're a fucking fraud!" The crucified man shouted. Jesus turned his head and looked at him tiredly.

"I am dying for you."

"You're dying because you're a big mouth and a liar." The thief on the other side of Jesus shouted. "We all know your story. Born of a virgin; mother was probably a whore!"

"Father they know not what they say."

"I know damn well what I say and I say that you're a fucking idiot. If you're the son of god get us off these crosses and let's all get an ale." As night descended upon Golgotha the people left and surrendered the three men to their fate. A raven dropped down from the sky and landed on one of the thieves head. "Get this damn thing off me."

The other thief laughed. "You got a little friend."

The raven pecked into the man's eye. It scooped it out in one peck and the screaming thief hollered in agony. He flailed on the cross as more ravens approached. They now surrounded the second thief and began pecking at him. Blood fell down the crosses as the two men died. Jesus remained untouched.

He wept. He cried for the men. As he did he looked up at the moon. "Father, forgive these men."

"Shut the fuck up!" A voice called out from the ground. Jesus turned and saw a demon looking up at him. The little red creature was nothing much more than a blob with extremities. He laughed hysterically as more little red demons appeared from just outside of Jesus' eyesight.

"Demons be gone!" Jesus hollered.

"Look it's the one who calls himself the Christ."

"Christ huh? I never heard of him." One of the demons responded while scratching his head.

"Just some looney who thinks he's the son of god."

"I am the son of god." Jesus proclaimed. To this the demons all laughed.

"You are the son of a whore and that's it." The demons scrambled up the cross and sat on the horizontal part, three on one side and two on the other. One demon reached down and stuck his finger in Jesus' wrist wound.

"Does it hurt?"

"Yes demon."

"You really think you are the son of god?"

"I am the son of god."

"Listen to this guy, he's hysterical. You are one hell of a head case. We would know if God had a son."

"Lies, you all are like your father." Jesus hollered. He dropped his head in prayer.

"Well my father is Belphegor but I assume you mean Satan."

"It's all the same." Jesus muttered.

"Listen to you. I thought you were supposed to be all understanding and shit and then you sum all us demons up as one thing; the nerve of this guy." One of the demons said as he pointed at Jesus. The others shook their fat little heads.

"Demons are pure evil."

"You can't talk to this guy. Next thing you know he will be bashing people of a different color and writing books promoting slavery and condemning homosexuals."

"Homosexuality is a sin." Jesus said as he turned to face the demon. The demon laughed and spit in his face. Jesus hung his head.

"So gays can't be Christians?"

"They can if they forsake their sin."

"What about Buddhists, are they going to Heaven?"

"They follow the wrong path."

"They existed long before you did. So people should listen to some bullshit carpenter and follow him?"

"I'm the Shepard."

"You're the moron is what you are."

"Father please-" Jesus suddenly screamed out in agony as a demon bit into him. He tore the fresh from his body and swallowed it. He then drank the blood that spilled out.

"You did say to eat your body and drink your blood." Said another demon.

"Blood drinking, doesn't god condemn that? Drinking the lifeforce and all." One of the other demons said with a hint of sarcasm in his voice.

"My body and blood brings salvation."

"So it is the way into heaven?" Suddenly the demons eyes all lit up.

"Yes."

"Well why didn't you say so sooner."

The demons began eating the man on the cross. They ate him as he screamed in agony and drank of his blood. When they were done there was nothing but bones. The fat little demons sat at the bottom of the cross and laughed.

"Don't know if this will work but at least I got a good meal."

As old age sets in, and I near the end of my life, I question all that I thought I knew. We all try to ignore death, for this morbid thought quite often is the killjoy. It will surely cast you in its shadow, and you will run for cover. When you are as old as I am you realize that hiding is no longer an option. I had not only acknowledged it, but accepted it. People often have the misconception that old age is synonymous with darkness. Many believe that our days are dismal as we stand on the horizon of death. This is just not true.

Admittedly, my positive outlook on life has deteriorated. The reason for this, however, is not my aging perception. I blame it on my orphaning of a gift, one that all of mankind received upon its conception. We have not only disregarded it, but often challenge it. Ignorance is bliss, and much unappreciated.

What I would do to regain ignorance.

My existence forever fell into chaos one evening, two years earlier. It was ritual of me to take evening walks in the placid, hallowed grounds of Swan Point. This was a wonderful graveyard in which one of the greatest writers of all time rests. I am talking about none other than Howard Phillips Lovecraft.

The monuments of stone and the statues of angels looked so lovely in the accumulated snowfall. The moonlight cast down upon this graveyard and pulled all the beauty to the foreground. The dead never have bothered me. I saw peace, and closure, within the fields of bodies, those planted by loved ones. Even those who were torn from this life at such tender ages were now brought comfort, sleep, and we survive them with remembrance.

I let my mind wonder as I read the epitaphs. So many lives in which I never got the joy or burden of meeting. I intoxicated myself in the chill air as I surveyed the land of silhouette angels and crosses. And what did I see, in the distance, none other than movement.

I remember thinking that the moon must be playing tricks on the mind of an old man. Night trickery, that evening chicanery which will bring the most level headed individual down to the level of a fool. I knew it was all in my mind, yet the movement intrigued me and demanded investigation.

I felt rather silly being, me being a man of rational thought. It was quite unusual for me to engage in such queer behavior, yet like a curious child I pursued the mysterious movement. Was that fear in me as I got closer? The tightening of muscles, the closing of a parched throat, and the blast beats of an old man's frail heart? There was no denying any longer, for a man of wisdom and a man of science was brought to his death that day. I was lost, left to stare at the ghoul whom sat on a grave marker.

How could this thing exist? Had I lost my mind, has mental illness befallen me? It had a rubbery, shiny charcoal colored body. Its skin was so thin that the bones could all be easily seen. Its extremities were long and thin. Hanging off the arms were hands with elongated fingers. Its neck was much longer then a man's and it had a joint half way up in which it jutted forward. The head hung in front of the body, its massive eyes which never blinked. They seemed to gaze off, just over my shoulder and miles behind me. They were empty and soulless. It had no nose, but below it was a small mouth full of serrated teeth. Occasionally a forked tongue slithered out.

"Forget what you see old man, move on and forget." The ghoul spoke in a male voice. The voice was of an educated man, yet one tossed in the perils of apathy. It was soft, but so empty.

"Forget what I see before me?" I asked, shocked that he would suggest anything so preposterous. "Why or how could I be expected to forget this?"

"Because you are a smart man and me being here demolishes everything you think you know. Please, stranger, be gone." The ghoul continued to look past me, and into oblivion with that hollow stare.

"What's your name?" I asked, trying hard to remain calm.

The ghoul chuckles, as he finally turns his head and looks me in the eye. Such terror I felt, emptiness as I gazed inside. There was no soul in this thing. "You are a stupid man. You are unaware of the dangers before you. You must go, unless you wish to die."

"Is someone going to kill you?" I asked the ghoul.

"No, I am safe. I am risking punishment by mingling with you, however." He snickers a little. "You should never ask questions. Any man who defies the spiritual being and tries to write off the mysteries of the universe in science will find it very hard to adjust to life after death. Ignorance is a gift you are taking for granted. Cherish it and forget what you saw this evening. If you insist to waiver this gift like a fool, then I shall grant you the knowledge you request. I must do so in haste, for the rest will be here soon. You do not want them to see you here."

I should have thought it over. Over eager to bring closure to this absurd discovery in the cemetery, I jumped on the offer. I didn't want, I needed to see more. With my words the ghoul stood up, towering at nine feet. He held out his right hand and told me to grip it. I did as he said, and felt a tingling throughout my body.

We took off like a rocket into the sky; whizzing and spinning. It was hard to comprehend what was happening to me, for that gauntly thing had torn me through the thin fabric which separates worlds, and I now I saw what the shadows saw. It was a world which is like our own, but dark, and empty. I saw the city of Providence from unbelievable heights as the gauntly ghoul jumped from cloud to cloud. Occasionally he would look back and tell me to make sure I did not let go of his hand, less I wish to drop. I held that rubbery skin tight.

Suddenly he nose-dived towards the earth, hurling himself like a kamikaze fighter at Pearl Harbor. My god, I cannot give justice when describing the terror of that descend. As we slowed down, exiting the clouds, I saw that we were no longer in my world.

I saw more of those rubbery, black gauntly beings. They lived here like we live in our world. All were around nine feet tall, moping around aimless. The streets were littered with human remains, those of which spilled maggots and vile viscera. I saw in the distance a gelatinous sort of creature, the size of a van and the color of vomit. It had no definite shape, and constantly shifted. It seemed to inflate and deflate. The thing spoke a strange tongue to one of those gauntly things. There were many other monsters as well. One such was a worm like creature with two legs. It stood erect, walking just like you and I. Some of the monsters looked like humans, however they had been drained of all emotion, empty and hollow shells. These apathetic husks seemed to wonder until the other monsters decided to feast upon them.

"Is this what you wanted to see? Have I fed your curiosity yet? How about I show you the Gallery?" and before I could respond, before I could beg him to bring me home, we shot up into the sky. I cried out in horror, and prayed for blindness as I saw what this monster called the Gallery in the distance. How such agony could exist? This was human suffering of unimaginable magnitudes. I never believed in god, but at this point I was certain that if he once existed, surely he was now dead. How could any god let such an abomination, such hatred and misery subsist?

We descended slowly; this tactic was to allow me plenty of time to fully comprehend the size of this place. It was a tower which stood miles high, and every inch of it had runes carved into the stone walls.

There were many open windows which vented both screams of the dying and the rotting stench of the dead. The whole scenario was something no painter could ever re-produce. These colors, they do not exist! How did my brain understand such alien colors?

Massive beasts flew past us, beast which looked as like a falcon but with a lizard head. They would drop from the sky, down into the town which surrounded the Gallery. The people in this town ran and hid as the monsters dove down and scooped newborn babies from the arms of mothers. I could only image what they did with them.

The gauntly ghoul landed on a windowsill. He lifted a long finger as it pointed inside. I did not want to look in, but could not help myself.

Never in all my years did I witness such perversions. Woman, men, and animals were all engaging in sexual acts. I saw one woman having intercourse with a wolf, as ran her tongue between the thighs of what looked to be a woman with a pig's head. This pig woman was cutting her own stomach open and letting her insides spill out onto the stone floor. As the steaming bloated snakes piled high, men flocked to her. Many of the men had animal heads such as jackals, hyenas, goats and ant eaters. Many feverishly tore into the entrails, devouring them as soon as they hit the ground while others desperately searched for an opening to insert their throbbing member.

There was a beast that entered the room. Its body was that of a man, one with well-defined muscle tone. Its head was similar to that of a goat. The only difference was that the fur was red. I remember wondering if this was his color, or from the blood.

Women, both young and old, ran over to him and fought each other for the right to give him oral sex. They tore each other's faces open. They clawed out eyes and ripped out throats as they desperately reached for the monster's genitalia.

Hulking men with massive muscular builds would walk the halls of the tower. They were naked except for an executioner's hood. They dragged long chains, and on the end of these chains were hooks. They would use these hooks to drag corpses to a crematorium to be tossed into the flames. The air stunk of death as the chimneys poured the rancid smoke into the sky.

"Is this hell?" I asked.

"Hell you ask? This is as close to heaven as you will get. The hell of this place is far worse. Let's visit, shall we?" And before I could answer we took off to the skies.

I was relieved to leave the Gallery, but my relief was short lived. Below us was an ocean. Instead of fish, it was inhabited with aborted fetuses which seemed to float. Swimming alongside were the ghosts of murdered children. I saw boats full of men actually fishing these dead children. Massive plesiosaur like monsters in the ocean were capsizing the ships as the occupants in the boats fought with the dinosaur beasts. They desperately threw spears and fired guns, screaming as the bloody waves carried off those who fell from the ships. The lizard like birds flew through the skies, swooping and diving into the ocean. When they surfaced they were carrying in their mouths the fetuses to feed their morbid appetite.

"Please, I cannot stand any more. Please return me to my world" I begged the ghoul as he carried me past the ocean, and through a wooden area. In this forest humans hung from every branch of every rotten tree. Such sadness was felt in the air, as the bodies looked up to the sky, a depression which was so thick it actually seemed to take the form of a fog. The gauntly ghoul jumped from cloud to cloud until we reached a clearing. It is here we stopped.

"This is the hell of this place. This is where every man and woman on earth comes when they first die. Gaze upon the sight ahead of you. O, curious man, rationalize this with science" What I saw was the most horrible thing imaginable. Nothing on earth can compare to the cruelty, the disgust, or the madness. I care not to share what I saw for it was so repulsive that I suddenly realized how much of a gift ignorance really was. We were born in shadow, because beyond that shadow is a world too ugly.

With inconceivable speeds, the ghoul tore me through the light. We traveled back into the shadows of our world. He jumped from cloud to cloud as we traveled faster than any airline jet. We tore through Berlin, past Tokyo, across Iraq, and through the United States. We traveled most of the fifty states, and when we returned to Swan Point, I saw thousands of those gauntly ghouls. They filled the cemetery and awaited our arrival.

I was overcome with fear as I began to realize what these things were. These monsters were all residence of this graveyard.

"You must go now." The ghoul said shortly after we landed on the ground. I did not question, for I wished to see no more. I started to walk off, leaving the dead behind me. Something made me stop. I turned to the ghoul asked him his name. He smiled, and responded "I am Providence".

I had not returned to Swan Point for some time after that. It was a few months later. Curiosity had gotten the best of me and I had to see if I could come across those ghouls again. Despite the revulsion I felt I still had questions.

I waited all night but there were no sign of them. When daylight hit, and I decided to return home, I happened to catch a gravestone in the corner of my eye. I could not help but smile. It was the grave marker of the horror writer Howard Phillip Lovecraft, a writer whom I spoke of at the beginning of my story. What made me smile was the inscription on his epitaph below his name, "I am Providence".

"Hello world and thank you for tuning in. I am Riley and I am seventeen years old and this is my beautiful girlfriend Maddison who is fifteen." Riley speaks into the camera. He then swings it around as Maddison poses in a cutesy way.

"Hello everybody." Riley positions the camera on his desk. In the background is a bed and on the walls are posters of Iron Maiden and Slayer.

"So you out there have waited all week for this and we are excited that today is the day."

"Yeah, I can't believe that it's finally happening."

"As you all know from following our video blogs you know how much in love we are and you know how special this night is for us."

"Seriously guys we totally have planned this right. We even bought new bed sheets."

"Yeah, what good is filming a masterpiece without nice sheets you know? So every avenue has been taken to make sure this life broadcast is perfect."

"I even sold my car to buy this HD camera you are all viewing this on."

"Well before we get started we would like to answer some of your questions. We have received a butt load of emails once we announced we were doing this and we are sorry to say we can't answer all questions, however we will try to answer a couple."

"First question comes from Jason in Kansas. Jason asks how we got this idea."

"Well Jason that is a very good question. Me and Maddie here were searching the internet one day when we came across some videos. We watched them and thought it would be really cool to film one ourselves."

"Ok Riley now this next question comes from Clair in California. Clair asks how you could do this to your girlfriend you claim to love and life with yourself after."

"Well love is a deep thing, deeper than anything physical. When this is done I will not love Maddie any less."

"And I want this. If you love someone enough you will do anything for them, including this. I think we have time for one more question. This one comes from Chris in Kentucky. Chris asks if we are brother and sister. Rumors have speculated that we are."

"Well Chris the answer is yes. This is my sister and we share a love most husbands and wives won't ever feel. This is why we are doing this."

"Ok, well that is all the questions now on with the show."

Maddison stands up and begins to undress. She removes her shirt and bra. Her tits are perfect size and perky with little pink nipples. She slides a finger down her flat belly and unbuttons her shorts. She turns and slides them off her round little ass. She is wearing only a thong now which she removes. Her pussy is shaven.

"I shaved for this today. I want it to be perfect." Suddenly a dick comes into the camera which is also shaven.

"Me to baby."

"I can't believe I'm doing this."

"We are writing history baby."

The two go over to the bed. Maddison bends over and shows her ass to the camera. Riley walks up and slaps it. She moans in pleasure as Riley turns her sideways so her side is facing the camera. He takes his hard dick and slides it in her from behind. He grabs her by the hips and pulls her in tight, each thrust makes her moan. He then grabs her by the hair and pulls tight. She cries out a little and then laughs.

"I can't believe we're actually doing this."

"Me to baby, in front of the whole world."

Finally Riley lets out a loud moan and pulls his dick out. He jerks it a few times as his sister turns around to take the load in her face. She gets it on her eyes, on her nose and in her mouth. Maddison gets up and rushes to the camera so the world can see her facial.

"That was the first time I had sex and it was great."

Riley rushes up and now their faces are next to each other. "Mine to. It was amazing."

"Now let the real fun begin."

Maddison rushes back to the bed and lies down. Riley grabs the camera and sets it up so it is looking down onto the bed. Maddison rubs the cum all over her face and she fingers herself with her other hand.

"You are so beautiful baby."

"Thank you."

Riley now enters the frame but this time he is wearing a leather mask. He looks at her.

"Now the real video begins."

"This is a snuff video and I want this. Remember no matter what I say police officers, this is something I want." Maddison says as Riley cracks her in the face with a fist. She cries out as her nose explodes with blood. A second fist collides and knocks out two of Maddison's front teeth.

Riley then retrieves something off camera. When he returns it is hedge clippers. He takes them and slides them over her body. Maddison cries out.

"Please, I have had enough."

"Shut the fuck up cunt." And with this he slides her perfect nipple in between the clipper blades and slams them shut.

The nipple pops off as Maddison cries out in agony. Riley drops into view of the camera and starts sucking the blood up into his mouth. He then takes the clippers and snip, off comes the second nipple. The crying continues as he slides the hedge clippers down. He positions them so her clit is resting in between the blades. He slams them shut and cuts her citreous off. She hollers in agony as she balls up, her hands rushing to comfort her pain in her private parts.

She is on the bed crying when Riley steps off camera again. For a few minutes he leaves his sister crying and then returns with a machete.

"Bend over."

Maddison rolls onto her tummy and bows up. She pushes her ass into the air.

"Do it Riley. Do it while I got the nerve."

Riley positions the machete and lines it up with her pussy. He then jams the large knife up her pussy. She pulls forward instantly and he jams it in all the way to the handle. Blood pours out of her pussy and sprays Riley's naked body. He then removes the machete and makes his way around the bed.

"Stay with me baby a little longer. Just one more thing to do."

"Do it!"

Riley positioned himself to the right of Maddison and raises the machete. He then brings it down in one chop and slices off her head. The head falls and rolls off camera. The headless body of Maddison collapses dead as blood pours from her neck and pussy.

The camera moves and now we see a naked, blood covered Riley. He raises his sister's head into camera view and kisses its dead lips. He then turns the head and jams his hard erection into her mouth. He moans as he masturbates himself with the severed head until he finally busts his nut. When it is done he picks up the severed head by the hair and puts it in front of the camera.

That is the moment when I blow my load onto my computer screen. I reach for a tissue as Riley stumbles around his room. I put my dick away and sign off the computer. I then stand up and walk out to the living room where my kid is watching television.

"Daddy!" My son yells as he runs up and hugs me. I hug him and sit down on the couch and watch cartoons.

"Stop hogging the blunt Jason!" Steve hollered. He reached out for the blunt. Jason handed it to him. The boys were in a graveyard, a place where they felt best, a place where they belonged. With their black painted finger nails and leather pants, the long hair goths thought it was the perfect place to get high at three in the morning.

Jason lifted his boot and kicked the grave stone. It fell over, smacking against the ground. Steve laughed and gave his friend a high five. Steve handed the blunt back to Jason when he saw something in the distance. It was a lantern glow.

"Dude what's that?"

"Grave robber maybe?"

"Let's check it out."

The two teens slowly approached the lantern and hid behind gravestones. The lantern sat at the end of a hole and inside they heard the sound of wood being smashed. A figure came out of the hole. He was carrying a woman on his should, a dead woman.

"Dude that man is massive." He had the physique of a body builder. His face was hidden behind a hood and he grabbed his lantern and walked off with the corpse.

"What the fuck?"

"Let's follow him."

The teens darted between gravestones as they tracked the man stealing the corpse. He carried it to a crypt where he stopped. He raised a boot and kicked open the door and went inside.

"Let's follow him."

"Fuck that." Steve whispered.

"Seriously dude, this guy is sick let's see what he's doing with that corpse."

"Fine but if he catches us it's your fault."

The two teens sprinted toward the crypt and slowly opened it. The inside was full of trash, old wrappers from food and beer bottles. This man was living here. Ahead of them there was a staircase that went underground. The boys descended the stone stairs deeper into the subterranean crypt.

It stunk of mold and wet earth. At the bottom of the stairs they could see the lantern glow. The boys stuck to the shadow as they watched. The man threw the corpse onto a stone slab. He ran a meaty hand to her face. He lowered it and in one motion tore open her dress. He pulled it off. Jason turned to Steve and mouthed "Damn she's hot." Steve shook his head.

The man reached up and grabbed at her tits. He squeezed them and ran his hand down her flat belly. When he got to her pussy he pried her legs apart and with his other hand he undid his pants. From within he pulled out a massive penis and pulled the spread eagle corpse closer. Jason and Steve watched in disgust as he slid deep inside of the dead woman.

He moaned in pleasure. He reached out and punched the corpse in the face. He then punched her tits and slapped her thigh. As he thrusted he moaned faster, breathing heavily until he finally came. He pulled out as his cum dripped from her pussy and onto the stone floor.

The hulking man turned and descended deeper into the darkness of the room. Steve looked at Jason and mouthed "let's go."

Jason smiled and walked to follow the man. Steve hesitated but chased after his friend. The boys found themselves walking down another hallway. At the end there was candle light. The shadows danced around the floor.

The room was massive. The ceiling was high and the other end was invisible in the darkness. The man was nowhere in sight. The boys clung to the shadows as they made their way into the room. Then they heard a noise. It was a low moan, followed by another one. From the shadows three figures emerged. They were naked women that moved slowly. Then the boys noticed the Y incision on their chests. These women were not just acting like zombies, they were zombies.

"Holy fuck dude." Steve whispered. Then there was a moan closer to them. So close it was right in the ears. Then Jason felt something brush him.

"Fuck move!" He screamed as the boys fell into the candle light. From the darkness more of the zombies emerged. There were now a dozen female corpses slowly walking toward the two teens. Then, from the shadows, came the roar of a chainsaw.

"Run!" Steve screamed as the boys sprinted down the hallway. In the original room the corpse was no longer on the slab. The boys stopped. "Where did she go?"

From the darkness the woman whom was torn from her grave jumped out and grabbed Jason. She sunk her teeth into his neck and ripped. Muscle and meat tore free as Jason cried out in pain. And the chainsaw noise got closer.

Steve looked at his friend and frowned. "Sorry Jason." He then bolted. He ran up the stairs with the chainsaw noise getting closer. He ran out of the crypt and into the night. He dodged gravestones as he ran from the chainsaw. He looked back and saw the hulking man with the dreaded machine.

The man stopped. The chainsaw noises ceased and suddenly all was quiet. Steve continued to run. He ran until he got to the cemetery gate and then he stopped and turned. There was no one chasing him. He got away.

A siren blared as a police car pulled up. Steve had never been happier to see a police officer.

"What are you doing trespassing?" The officer asked.

"Listen, my friend is dead in there." Steve got out between panting. He felt like at any second he would kill over.

"A lot of people are dead in there, but there are hours of operation."

"No, you don't understand. They got him; the man with a chainsaw. He chased me."

"Son calm down, you're not making any sense."

"I will show you."

The cop followed Steve as he led him through the graveyard. They stopped at the crypt and Steve pointed. "My friend is in there dead. They killed him."

"Who killed him?"

He couldn't say zombies. The cop would think he was nuts, hell he thought he was nuts. "People."

"So you're telling me that there are people in there, living people and they killed your friend."

"Yes."

"This better not be a prank punk." The cop drew his weapon. He looked at Steve and motioned for him to follow.

They made their way into the crypt and down the stairs. When they got to the room with the slab Steve whispered. "This is where it happened."

"Where's the body?"

"They must have moved it. I think you should get backup. There are a lot of them"

"Just shut up and follow me." The police officer descended down the hall with Steve by his side. The two made it to the room with the candle light when the officer put his gun away. He stood in the center and called out. "Lucas. Come out."

From the darkness came the hulking man still holding the chainsaw. He looked down at the officer like he was ashamed.

"Lucas, did you scare this boy here."

Lucas shook his head.

"Apologize to him."

"I'm sorry." He said in a deep voice.

"It's ok son."

"Son?" Steve suddenly felt terrified. He looked up at the cop. The cop looked back at him.

"He's sorry." The cop turned back to Lucas. "Now give him his friend back."

There was a moan in the shadows. Slowly from the darkness Jason emerged. He moved slowly. He had been turned into a zombie. Steve turned to run but the cop pulled out his gun and shot the boy in the leg.

"What the fuck?" Steve hollered. "You're a fucking cop!"

"But family comes first."

From the shadows came more zombies. Soon they filled the candle light. Lucas looked up and removed his hood. His face was a patchwork of rotting flesh which barely hid his skull.

"You see my Lucas was once a body builder. Took too much steroids and had a heart attack. I buried him in this crypt and you know what, he came to life. This crypt brings them back to life. These women, they are his now. They are all his wives."

"Please, let me go!"

"I am afraid it's far too late for that. Lucas, have at it."

Lucas pulled the string on the chainsaw and it roared to life. He dashed toward the screaming teenager and buried the chainsaw into his abdomen. The cop laughed as the blood sprayed the room. Then the zombies dropped down and moved in, all feeding on his remains.

Translucence: A disease in which the skin becomes semitransparent and takes on a cloudy appearance in which the organs and muscles are seen beneath the skin.

He watched them as they played outside. He always watched them. His glassy eyes darted wildly; desperate to capture every moment. He'd laugh and giggle as he watched the kids pretend to be pirates. He would bite his nails as he witnessed intense shootouts when they pulled out their plastic guns and played cops and robbers. When they played tag he imagined the exhilaration and adrenaline that one employed as they ran to avoid being it. He vicariously lived an ordinary childhood from this filthy cellar window. When the children would go home, and the day concluded, he would return to the shadows.

As they took off, and said their goodbyes, the boy peeled away exhausted. He felt like he had been among them, playing. His muscles had ghost aches which added a sense of reality.

"Damn, when Corey was running from Becky and turned that corner and almost collided with Bobby. I thought they would be bopping heads for sure. Earlier, when playing pirates, I could have sworn the evil pirate king, Peg Leg Bill, would have the last laugh. Boy do I feel stupid. I should have known Captain Peterson would crush him. He walked the plank and those sharks had one hell of a meal." He shook his head amused as he crossed the cold stone floor. He stopped at the mirror; the quicksilver glass was there to always remind him of what he was; a monster.

He looked into this mirror every day and hoped one of these time he'd see a normal boy; every day was another disappointment. His skin was still semi-transparent. It looked like a sick, hazy mix that served as a window to his insides. He looked like one of those pictures in a biology book, the one which showed where all the organs were located. His eyes were round and could be seen even when his lids were closed. He saw his heart beating against white ribs and the muscles that surrounded it. He saw his lungs swell and deflate…all evidence of life but was this life he was living?

His mother told him that the world wouldn't understand. Society was enslaved to ignorance and prejudice she had told him. She had told him that they would call him a monster, and try to hurt and even try to kill him. "They will bash you with sticks and burn you alive. I've seen them do it because some people have black skin, imagine what they'd do to a boy with no skin color." That is what she said, however he just didn't see it.

These kids outside, they seemed so nice. Their play was sincere and he couldn't see any sense of hatred in them. They weren't the malicious individuals his mother made them out to be; they were loving life and took full advantage of it. They were human, just like him.

He believed mother was wrong, but mother's law ruled. She was second only to god. She said that to him one night when he tried to challenge her. She was a strong woman and her strength became overbearing when his father died. She lived upstairs by herself now and cast him to the basement; two lonely people under the same roof.

Well he wasn't totally lonely; there was Rodney.

Rodney was a rat that shared this cellar. He was always close by, and often the nameless child would have long conversations with the rodent. Rodney never participated of course, but he did seem to listen quite well.

"Hey Rodney." The child called out as the rat trotted across the filthy cement floor. It stopped and looked up at the child. "Yeah I have been looking out that window again. What's it to you? You're still my pal."

The boy collapsed onto his dad's old army cot. His dad had died in Iraq. His mother had told him Iraq was full of treacherous, godless monsters who loved killing innocent Americans. What made them a monster was something mom called Islam. She once called it a religion of whores. For weeks the boy was confused, trying to figure out what a whore was. He held his ear to the vents to hear the television upstairs. After hearing the word a few more times he figured a whore is a woman no one likes.

How could a religion be a woman that no one likes?

"I know Rodney. It's torture. I just don't believe mom. I don't think she's right. The kids; they're all around the same age as me, eight years or so. They have fun and I don't think it's fair that mom won't let me outside."

Rodney just stared at him.

Upstairs he heard the cellar door knob turning. It was his mother. Was it feeding time already? Quickly he turned to Rodney and with his hands made a shooing motion.

"Get going Rodney, mom will try to kill you for sure."

The little rodent trotted off back into the darkness and just in time. Suddenly the dank and dark domain of this child was invaded with the artificial light from a normal world, a world alien to him. Cast in the doorway was the silhouette of his mother.

She made her way down the stairs. Each step she took made the old wooden steps moan and creak. When she reached the bottom she dropped a plastic bag on the ground. Although she was only thirty years old she looked ancient. Her short blond hair brushed behind her ears. Her thin frame was beginning to puff up; the years had been cruel to her.

"I left you a sandwich and an apple." Quickly her attention was stolen by the cellar window. The condensation had been recently wiped off. Her face began to squish up as the anger flushed her pale features red. "You little fucking bastard, I told you to leave this goddamn window alone."

"I'm not doing anything wrong, just looking out."

"I don't like it, no not at all. People could see you and they'd burn this house down. They wouldn't understand, no they wouldn't. You're jeopardizing both of our lives." She ran over to it and quickly covered the window with the sheet she hung from a nail. As she dressed it up to conceal it better she froze. Suddenly her anger was re-directed. "My god, these are rat droppings. Child, we got rats down here?"

"No, just one and he's not dirty; he's a friend."

"You truly are a curse boy. Satan put rats on this earth to disease god's people. Now know this, I will have this window boarded up tomorrow and I am baiting the place for rodents." The boy felt his world collapsing. His heart sped up at he felt ill.

"Mama, please don't do this. I didn't do anything wrong."

"You're birth was wrong." With this she stormed up the stairs and slammed the door behind her. The boy heard the locks engage. He scampered around looking for Rodney.

"Rodney, we need to get you out of here. My mother is going to kill you." The little rodent came running out from behind some old boxes and stopped at the boy's feet. The child began to tear up. "I don't want you to go but if you don't leave my mom will kill you."

The rat stared at the child.

"What?"

The rat turned its head slightly.

"Rodney, that…that's murder."

The rat continued its hard stare.

"But if I kill her I'll go to prison. I want to play with the other boys not go to jail."

The rat's tail dropped a little.

"I don't know."

The rat looked down.

"Ok then Rodney. I love you and want nothing to ever happen to you. I'll do anything for you."

They next day the child was impatient. He couldn't sleep the night before, dreaming of being in the world with the normal kids. He looked at himself in the mirror and tried to convince himself that they wouldn't be afraid. He saw his blood flowing throughout his body in a network of veins. He watched his muscles twitch and strain as he lift his arm. He closed his eyes, yet still he saw through the lids. He wasn't a monster like his mother had said; he was a human with an unfortunate disease.

The world would understand.

He replayed the plan of Rodney through his head. It was a good plan and he knew it would work well. Rodney told him to tell the police about the lifetime of abuse; of imprisonment. Rodney told him that no right minded person on this earth would put an abused child in prison.

The locks on the door began to disengage. The time was now. He needed to get his nerve up; needed to get himself ready to pounce. She came down the stairs holding some plywood and a hammer. She intended on totally destroying his only connection to the world. The miserable little bitch brushed past him, her long blue dress touching his arm briefly. The whore didn't even acknowledge him. Her dopey eyed glance proved this task she was set out to do was a burden, a wrinkle in her day. Wasn't he the wrinkle in her life? As she put the hammer and wood down he felt his hatred overwhelm him.

She was the reason he wasn't normal.

She was the reason he had no friends.

She was the reason for all this misery.

He wasn't her burden, she was his. He surely did something

wrong to deserve such a bitch for a mother. She really didn't think he was a monster; would you lay a hammer on the floor within arm's reach of a monster and then turn your back? Of course you wouldn't. She just hated him, and he hated her. That stupid cunt looking at the window trying to find the best possible way to block him from the outside world; why not just kill him? She took every possible joy from life and kept him away from it, why not just kill him and get it over with? She was a sadist and actually enjoyed his misery.

The bitch was now bent down trying to measure the little piece of plywood. The child reached down and grabbed the hammer. He held the steel tool in his hand. He raised it above and slammed it down with all his might.

The sound was hollow. It echoed throughout the cellar as the skull cracked from the impact. She let out a muttering attempt to yell but it was caught in her throat. She spun around on the ground as she spit blood out her mouth; the impact forced her to bite her tongue. Her eyes were wide open as she pushed herself into a corner, trying to get away from the child.

"What have you done?"

"I want to be free mama; I want to be with the other kids." He responded with a head full of confusion.

"They'll kill you. Don't you realize this? I have been among them; I know how they can be."

"I don't believe you. You hate me."

"Oh dear, I tried so hard to protect you that I made you despise me. I am not your enemy, they are. I'm your mother and you're my son."

Suddenly he felt bad as he watched the tears coming down her cheek. Was it true after all? Was she just trying to protect him? He had to admit, the situation was a little bizarre, but that didn't render it untrue. He felt his own eyes begin to tear as he looked into the eyes of his frightened mother.

Just then, Rodney came out from the shadows. He stopped and looked at the child.

"No Rodney, it was a misunderstanding."

The rat just stared.

"No she won't kill you, isn't that right mama?"

"No, I won't kill your friend." She played along as she tried desperately not to fall asleep. She knew if she was to fall asleep she would not be waking up.

"You see Rodney."

The rat looked up and its tail shifted left.

"She's just pretending?"

"No honey, I'm not pretending."

"She wants me to let my guard down so she can attack me?"

"Please don't do this, I love you."

"She plans on overpowering me and taking the hammer?"

"Please, oh god I'm sorry."

"She's planning to bash my head in, bury me and pretend I never existed?"

"Please I beg you son, don't do this."

"I guess it wouldn't be hard to hide the fact that she killed me, no one knows I exist."

"It's just a fucking rat, it's not talking. You just need help. You need help. That rat doesn't talk, your mind just isn't right. I can help you though, just put the hammer down."

"No, I think Rodney is right." And with this he raised the hammer and brought it down. He smashed it down four times with all his might directly in the center of her face. She screamed for the first two blows, but after that all one could hear was the child's grunts, the sound of shattering bone and the squishing of bloody meat and sinew. When the child pulled back he saw the face of a monster was now nothing more than hamburger meat.

The child dropped the hammer to his feet. He stumbled back a little, shocked. He turned and saw Rodney just staring at him. His little black beady eyes, his long nose, his pink tail; Rodney was pleased.

"I did it. I killed her." He suddenly felt an overwhelming joy, a sense of freedom. He laughed as he realized it was finally over. He could finally be a normal kid.

Outside he heard them; the voices of his soon to be best friends.

"I'm going."

The rat just stared.

"What do you mean? My mom was wrong. They will like me. I know it."

Rodney turned and quickly scurried off into the shadows.

"Don't be jealous Rodney. You're my best friend; you know that. I'll be back later. I'll tell you all about it."

The boy opened the front door cautiously. He wore a pair of shorts and a t shirt he found in his mother's closet. They were a little big but they would do. Clothes were not the biggest concern of his; his anxiety was. He was excited, yet frightened. He'd never been outside before. The whole experience made him nervous. The boy took a deep breath and stepped out into the sunshine.

He walked down the front steps and out into the yard. Fear and excitement overwhelmed him; his heart beating violently against his chest. Only a few feet away were the children he had been watching his whole life; the children he dreamed of playing with. He didn't care what mother said, nor did he care what Rodney said. He was going over to them.

As he approached they all stopped. They gawked at him in a state of awe. One of the girls, Rachel, had a look of fright in her eyes; however the rest look with curiosity. They looked at the boy's skin; saw his muscles and organs. They saw the bones and veins, the pumping blood. The whole thing was surreal to them, but for the boy it was even more so. Years in a basement and finally he was free.

"Why do you look like that?" Cory asked. The boy was prepared to answer these questions. It would be foolish to imagine that they wouldn't ask about his condition.

"It is a disorder. I was born this way."

"Are you a monster?" Becky asked. The boy from the basement frowned as he shook his head.

"No. I am a kid just like all of you. I was just born with different skin."

"What's your name?" Bobby asked. His name; he hadn't been given one. His mother would refer to him as the mistake, a monster and a product of her sins; none of these were his name however.

"I was never given one, but I do like the name Jared." As he spoke the name he felt suddenly a strong attachment to it.

A real name for a real boy.

"Ok then, we'll call you Jared." Bobby responded. "Give us one second Jared."

The group huddled. Jared heard hush arguing among the group. His head was full of games they were about to play. He was so excited he thought his heart would explode. Finally the group turned back to him and Cory stepped forward.

"Well you are welcome to play with us Jared. We are heading over to the gravel pits to play hide and seek; wanna join?"

Jared felt tears in his eyes. His smile was impossible to hide. He felt something he never truly felt before…joy.

"Definitely!"

With that the group moved out. They crossed through the woods and near the creek. They followed the stream a little while. Occasionally Becky or Rachel would look back at him with whispers. He saw they were still afraid. He didn't mind. He knew that by the end of the day they would all be best friends.

Once the trees broke he saw what the kids referred to as the gravel pits. This was a place where massive piles of stone lay. They stretched taller than a house. There must have been a dozen of these little mountains. The group stopped in front of one mountain and Cory turned to Jared.

"Ok do you know how to play hide and go seek?"

"Of course, I watched you play from the basement."

"What?" Becky asked alarmed. "Monsters live in a basement."

"Shut up Becky." Cory yelled. He turned to Jared and smiled. "She doesn't know what she's talking about. Well we will start with you being it since you are new to our group. We will hide. Give us until the count of ten before you come looking."

Jared eagerly nodded his head and quickly covered his eyes with his hands. He began to count as he heard the children scatter.

"Three, two, one; ready or not here I come!" He yelled. He quickly darted around a corner but saw nobody. He listened. He didn't hear anyone moving, nor talking. This was going to be difficult. He continued on and jumped out around another mountain of stone; nothing. "You guys are good."

He continued down the rows and searched. Finally he heard a hush whisper. He turned his head and zoned in. It was coming behind one of the piles. He slowly and quietly made his way around the bend and was shocked to find all six of them.

"Wow, this wasn't a very smart move. I found you all." He laughed. "You don't have to go easy on me because it's my first time you know."

"Shut up monster!" Cory yelled. Jared looked at him confused.

"What's going on?"

"We know what you are. You live in a basement and watch us. You plan on killing us and eating our skin." All the kids stared at Jared. They didn't look happy. These were not the faces he fell in love with.

"No, seriously I am a boy." He pleaded. "I'm not a monster. I promise."

"No boy I ever seen looks like a freak!" Rachel yelled. The others agreed as they began to hurl obscenities.

"Cory, Bobby; please believe me." Jared dropped to his knees as he begged.

"Dude, you didn't even have a damn name." Bobby responded. "You are totally a monster."

"And your terror ends here monster." The kids all bent down and each one picked up a big rock. Cory looked at his rock as a sadistic smile crossed his face. "I wonder if your blood will be green or black."

"Please, don't do this. I am a kid, a boy. I'm not a monster." Jared sobbed. His tears ran down his cheek as he fell to his knees. He shook his head in disbelief. "Please. Don't do this…"

A rock struck him on the face. His nose exploded in blood as the pain ripped through him. Cory stepped forward and looked down at the crying child. He laughed hysterically.

"This monster bleeds red." He pointed.

"Maybe he isn't a monster." Becky called out. "What if we're wrong?"

"I'm not a monster. Ask Rodney." He yelled as he cupped his nose, trying to stop the blood.

"Who's Rodney?" Cory asked.

"My friend, he's a rat in my house. I'll bring you to him."

"It's a trick. He wants us to go to his house so he can throw us in an oven. Die monster!" Bobby hollered as he threw his rock. It hit Jared in his arm and he hollered out in agony.

"Please…don't do this."

Each child raised their rock in their hands as they circled the child. They watched as the monster pleaded for his life. They imagined all the people he must have killed over the years. They wondered if the kids who they heard went missing wound up in his basement, their bones littering the stone floor. They knew they couldn't let this monster live.

They began throwing the ammunition with all their might. Jared wept and shrieked as each rock struck. The kids continued to hurl the stones until he was still. Cory raised his hand to stop the assault and listened. He heard no more cries, no more begging; he knew the thing from the basement was dead. He turned to his friends and grinned.

"He's dead. Let's go back to my place and play pirates now."

The atmosphere was drab. It seemed almost as if it had been plucked from an exceptional part of hell. The world seemed to be at the pinnacle of misery and depression as the dreariness fell down in sheets; the gloom swallowed up by the earth. The rain had slowed down but the clouds which starved the corn fields of sunlight were so thick that another round of storms was surely underway. The rain did nothing to wash away the stink of cow shit. It had been like this for the last few days, and because of this the residents of Clatonia were sinking into a deep hole of melancholy.

She pulled her old Bel-Air slowly up the dirt road toward her decrepit house. The home was a filthy color, a white which has been covered in filth so dense that no rain could wash it clean. It sat in the midst of a lifeless corn field.   She slid the gear shift into park but left the engine running. She knew she had to go home, but didn't want to. Margret strained her eyes and could see her two sisters; Kendra and Gretchen. They were in the old barn with shovels digging into the soggy earth. Margret let out a long winded sigh; she knew what they were doing.

"Another for the Potter's Field." And as she spoke to no one but herself, a thought had crossed her mind.

But do they know what I've been doing?

She feared this but knew that her two sisters had no idea. If they had even got a whiff of where Margret went every day, they would tell Papa immediately. Margret would watch her boyfriend join those who were planted in the dirt along with the three dozen others Papa carved up. Boyfriends were forbidden in this house, their bodies and beauty were intended for Papa only. He had told them this, only his seed was allowed to enter their bodies.

It's god's law, not mine girl. Do you dare defy the lord?

She believed Papa at one time. Her faith in her father died when her first child met its end at the hands of the evil man. She was only fourteen at the time and although she tried not to get too attached to the little fetus in her belly, she couldn't help it. It was maternal instinct to love your own child. Gretchen, god she had five kids with papa. Kendra had three. She knew what happened after each birth and for this reason she didn't want to get attached to the little baby in her.

But you did didn't you?

She did. She imagined taking off in the middle of the night and stealing her Papa's 1956 Skylark. She would slam her foot down on the pedal and the engine would roar. She would tear down the interstate toward…well did it matter? Anywhere is better than hell. Perhaps she would go visit family in Idaho, family from Mama's side of the family. They were normal people; they didn't know the dark torment that went on in the house. She could go there and hide, tell them everything. She could have her baby and live out the rest of her life.

She didn't go. She gave birth and Papa was particularly cruel to the newborn. She could only guess that he sensed her attachment. He used garden shears to cut off each limb. He them used a hack saw to remove the screaming babies head. Margret was naked, on her knees crying. This pissed Papa off. He told her she was ruining her passage into adulthood. He grabbed her and tossed her over the rotten wooden counter in the basement.

"You must pay for ruining this. How dare you defy the lord?" He unzipped his filthy jeans and reached his grimy hand over to her vagina. He scooped up some of the blood left over from the birth and she could hear him rubbing it on his penis. That night he gave her the worst punishment he'd ever given to any of the women in the house, he sodomized her. This made her unclean until her eighteenth birthday Papa explained. To die before then would reserve a place in hell. "You defied the lord; I treat you like a Sodomite. This is for your own good girl."

That was four years ago. She had met her boyfriend Teddy a year after that. He worked in town at a local general store. One evening, while she was in there buying a Coke, he asked her out. She was modest, skittish but he saw something in her. She agreed and they went to Briars Creek and drank beer. He was eccentric, beautiful and told her all about the Hippie movement. He sensed her sadness and he said in that cool tone "Listen girl, it's 1966 and your daddy is stuck in the forties. You need to feel love."

Of course Teddy didn't understand the extent of what happened at that old house in the corn field. If he did who knows what would happen. Teddy wasn't an idiot; he'd suspected that there was sexual abuse. Most of the daddies this far from the normal world diddled their daughters once in a while, some even played with sons. This was nothing new out here so Teddy had patience with her. When she finally gave him her body in the bed of his pick-up she'd felt something she never felt before, joy. She felt love. She felt hope.

As she sat in that car she saw Papa's old Skylark coming up

a side street. He didn't see her; he was driving with tunnel vision. He slowly headed down the driveway toward the house. She once saw Papa as the light of Jesus Christ brought to Earth, now she saw him as a boil upon this planet that needed to be excised.

As Papa pulled up her brainwashed sisters dropped their shovels and ditched the body they were burying. Like excited children on Christmas morning they skipped toward the house. Papa jumped from the car and ran to the trunk. It popped open and he reached in pulling out what appeared to be a burlap sack. His sisters were singing, that old Christian song that Papa made up. Papa claimed everything was for two things, the family and Jesus. If Jesus really wanted this, Margret wanted to take her chances with hell.

The three enthusiastically helped pull the sack into the house and closed the door. Margret knew it was time to go home. Papa and her siblings would be so thrilled that they'd overlook the fact that she had been gone all day.

***

"What's in the sack old man?" Sheriff Johnson whispered to himself as he watched Ken Baker bring the burlap sack into his house. His two oldest daughters pranced around their dad, singing and acting like a fool. The Sheriff continued to look through his binoculars.

He spit a wad of tobacco juice into a cup as he watched the youngest, Margret, drive up to the house. Once parked she stepped out of the vehicle and paused for a second, noticing that her father didn't even bother to close the rear trunk. She shook her head and made her way inside.

"You son of a bitches think you can bring Marijuana into my county and get away with it. You don't know I've been watching your daughter with that pot head Teddy. The lord doesn't approve of drugs Ken. Your entire drug dealing clan is going down."

The vigilante cop stroked the barrel of his shotgun and smiled as he watched the youngest girl enter the house. Would it be tonight? Is tonight the night he would bust the family; if the lord wills it.

***

"Good day, my sweet Margret." Mama turned to her daughter with her insane cheerfulness as she prepared to bake a cake. She was always cooking, never taking a moment to rest. The idle housewife will find reason to join the devil in hell. That's what she use to say after Jenny Hanson was caught sleeping with that trucker from Wyoming. Danny Hanson didn't take to kind to it all; he cut both their heads off and walked right into the Sheriff's department. He tossed the bloody messes onto the desk and said "Book me." Since them Mama decided to spend every waking minute working, to prevent herself from being persuaded by the pleasures of the flesh.

The kitchen was immaculate as always. Papa said that a house should be as clean as the Lord willed it. Mama had working limbs and energy. There was no excuse for filth or clutter inside this house. Although everything was sterile, every piece of furniture wrapped in plastic, the house had ugly secrets.

"Good morning Mama." Margret responded as she hung her car key on the hook by the door. Mama had an unnatural smile, she always did. One would imagine a woman living the life she had to be a miserable gloom, but the whole thing brought her closer to the lord. She welcomed everything; the incest, the abuse, and the murder.

"Go on, get yourself all dolled up. Tonight we are to have a special event. Tonight we will have a Moloch." The word made her cringe. She forced a smile and took off toward her room. As she turned the corner she was confronted by Gretchen.

"Good afternoon slut."

"Let me pass Gretchen, please I need to get ready."

"Shameful are we to hold secrets. I know what you've been doing little sister."

"I've got no inkling as to what you're talking about."

"Oh, I do believe you do. That little hippie boy; and Papa will find out soon enough."

"Again, I don't know what you're talking about."

"Go on; play the ignorant girl all you want. Tonight is the Moloch, wouldn't ruin that for Papa. Tomorrow however, let's say that Teddy will join the rest in the field and if you're lucky Papa will have mercy upon you."

Margret had heard enough. She pushed pass her sister and to her room. Once inside she slammed the door shut and stared at her reflection in the mirror. She knew tonight something would have to happen, because if not than her entire life would end as she knew it.

"If only the lord willed it."

***

"My loving family, we gather in this basement tonight to hold a sacred ritual to the lord almighty." Papa screamed with his hands up to the air. Gretchen, Kendra and Mama all had their hands in the air as they prayed. Margret didn't, she was lost in her mind desperately trying to find a way out of this mess. Papa noticed this but decided not to address it. "The crops have been dead for some time. The blood of sinners has spoiled this land. I have given the lord their bodies and hoped for the crops to return. We haven't given enough as of yet I reckon. My lord, today I offer you this body of a little girl. In return for this sacrifice I ask you to bless our crop once again."

Papa turned and pulled back a red curtain. Locked inside the furnace was a crying little girl no older than five. The Baker family seemed to be crying at the beauty of such an event; however Margret cried for the little girl. She wished she could go over there and open the furnace; release the girl and set her free into the world. She knew it wasn't possible. The little girl with her chubby cheeks and summer dress made her think of her child Papa killed.

"Lord Jesus Christ, king of the world, I offer this child." Papa hit the switch and the flames shot up. The little girl screamed as her flesh melted off her body. The child cried out and thrashed inside the furnace as the basement began to stink of burning flesh.

***

The scream of a child; he certainly heard this. There was no way he imagined it and this was proper justification to enter the dwelling of this family. He had positioned himself near the father' Skylark to investigate the contents of the trunk. He thought he saw blood but after that scream he was certain. He held his shotgun close to his body and approached the front porch. He opened the door just as smoke from the chimney began to spill into the sky above.

***

"So are you prepared for your punishment?" Gretchen whispered to Margret. Papa was in meditation, praying to the lord as he stood before the charred corpse of the little girl.

"Gretchen, I don't know what you're talking about."

"There's no way out of this. I saw you two having sex at the Briars."

"What were you doing at the Briars?" Gretchen choked back for a second. She raised a finger to talk but Margret cut her off. "If you saw me at the Briars you must've been there for a certain reason as well. I'm guessing it's that little bucktooth redneck who runs the service station. Sure would explain why you've been wearing a scarf lately. He leaving vampire marks?"

"Bitch." But before anything else could be said the basement door broke open and the room filled with a loud explosion. Mama, still smiling, flew back as her insides blasted out her back and hit the wall before she did. Standing from behind the smoking barrel of the shotgun stood Sheriff Johnson.

"Everyone put your goddamn hands in the air!" The Sheriff hollered as he pumped a fresh shell into the chamber. Everyone was silent, no one as silent as Mama. She had died within seconds of hitting the wall, that stupid smile still upon her face. Papa didn't seem to be too distraught over Mama's death. He seemed more concerned with the interruption of his ritual.

"Sheriff, we respect you as an authority of law but the law of god is almighty and I cannot have you using his name in vain." Papa said as he rose from his seated position. The Sheriff aimed the shotgun at Papa.

"Kenneth Baker, I wouldn't move another inch. If you move anything more than a frog's hair I will decorate your basement with the brains of each and every member of this fucked up family. I intend to take you in." The Sheriff now descended the stairs and made his way across the basement floor. He now stood before Papa.

"Take me in for serving the lord? My dear Sheriff, I do fear that Satan has-"

"Save me the bullshit Ken. This whole town knows you're fucked up but just not this much. You-"He was cut short as a knife ripped through his neck. The blade burst through the front as the blood sprayed across the room and into the face of Papa. Standing behind the Sheriff and jamming the knife deep inside was Margret. She leaned in and whispered into the dying man's ear.

"I'm sorry Sheriff, but this is my only way out of this hell." She immediately tossed the Sheriff down as Gretchen and Kendra stood in shock. Papa smiled at his youngest daughter but the smile quickly faded as she picked up the shotgun, pumped it and pointed it at the man she despised.

"My dear Margret, what's the meaning of this defiance?" He asked in a pleading voice. She shook her head.

"Papa, you're sick. Do you remember when Trevor broke his leg?"

"Hun that was a dog. Dogs are different."

"You said Trevor was in misery and the only proper way to give him relief was to end his life, do you remember?"

"I do, but child that was a dog. We are vessels of the lord and-"His speech was cut short as the buckshot unloaded into his chest. For a second the entire room froze. There was no movement. Papa spit up blood as he swayed like a drunk. Finally he fell backwards and slammed his head off the ground. From his body came a strange sucking sound as blood poured from his chest.

"Papa!" Gretchen yelled as Kendra dropped to the ground crying. Gretchen ran to the side of her dying father as she rubbed his forehead. "Papa, don't die."

"Join him bitch!" Margret pumped the gun and unloaded another shot. This one tore Gretchen's head off her shoulders. The headless body slumped over onto her father's body. Margret turned to Kendra. "You want to die next?"

"You know damn well that if you were to pump that gun one more time I would pounce on you like a rabid dog and bite your throat out before you had a chance to get a shot off." Kendra spoke with absolute confidence. Margret held the shotgun tight but was unsure of whether she should take the shot or not.

"Maybe so." The voice was that of Teddy. He descended the stairs with a pistol pointed at Kendra. "But I've got a clear shot and have been told I'm very good."

"Teddy, how on earth?"

"Not now sweetheart. Right now, my only concern is getting you out of here." He never once took his eyes off Kendra. "Kendra, do you hear me?"

"Fuck you."

"Sorry skank, not my type. Now this is how this little standoff is going to go down. Me and Margret are about to leave. Now, her car is a piece of shit and I don't think Ken has much use for the Skylark anymore. Do you Ken?" Teddy yelled over to Papa, but he didn't respond. "See, he doesn't mind. Now we're going to take it and leave. Do what you want here after we leave. The house and all the bullshit within it is yours."

Kendra nodded her head as she sat down on the floor in defeat. Margret turned and smiled as she watched her father's pupils dilate and his breathing stop. "Goodbye you murderous son of a bitch."

Outside the two young lovers jumped into Papa's Skylark. Teddy started it up just as Margret kissed him on the cheek.

"How did you know?"

"I went home and felt something was wrong. I decided to walk over and check on the house, see if anything was out of the ordinary. I saw the Sheriff's car and wondered if something happened."

"And the gun?"

"Call it redneck paranoia."

"Thanks god for that."

Teddy put the car in reverse and swerved around Margret's old Bel-Air. They pulled past the Sheriff's vehicle parked along the side of the road and peeled out toward the interstate.

"So where to?" Margret asked as her boyfriend guided the vehicle.

"San Francisco, of course." She smiled.

As they drove off she took a look back in the rear view mirror. She wanted to see her house one last time. She noticed in the distance the flames reaching the sky. She knew at that moment her sister had set fire to the house. She thought for a second about telling Teddy but refrained. As they drove on the clouds broke and the sun finally shined.

"I'm telling you, she's the type." Ted said as he placed a human brain on a scale. He wrote the weight down on a scratch pad. "I mean a woman like that has to suck cock."

"What do you mean?" Ted's partner, Steve, asked. Steve was using a tissue to clean his eye glasses. He frowned as he removed the blood which splattered in his face. No use in being upset so he forced a laughed. "What do you mean by a woman like that?"

"I mean let's go over the facts. She smokes."

"Right."

"She has thick lips."

"Ok."

"She bites her nails."

"And; this proves cock sucking how?"

"These all point to an oral fixation which can easily be satisfied by one thing; felatio. Man, do I need to spell it out to you? She's down to suck."

"I forgot, Ted, you are the almighty ladies man."

"I don't proclaim the fame, but the legends are all true. Many ladies have been brought to my house and broken open." Ted took the brain and tossed it into a plastic bag. The bag was then placed on a counter among saws and drills." Well it is clear what killed this young man. It is lack of blowjobs."

"Come on man." Steve leaned over to the computer and began typing a report. "Let's finish this up and get the fuck out of here."

"I know, however that will be your cause of death if you don't try anything tonight. No, this young man died of from a projectile entering the temporal and tearing through the diencephalons. It currently still is lodged. This said projectile is a .22 caliber bullet which was fired from execution range. By the markings on his arm this young man was a member of the exclusive after school club called The Crips."

"Gang violence, case closed. We can head out." Steve turned to write down some final notes as Ted covered the cadaver with a sheet. The corpse was pushed back into the freezer until morning where it will be picked up by whatever funeral home the victim's family had chosen.

"Not so fast." The front door swung open as a sarcastic and cocky Patrick walked in. Patrick was a white haired old pervert; he helped around the morgue with odd jobs, everything from changing light bulbs to fixing leaks, Patrick had done it all. Right now he was pushing in a gurney; and beneath that sheet was overtime.

"Come on man; don't tell me that's what I think it is." Ted complained as he locked the freezer. He shook his head. "It can't be."

"Sure is boys; I present you all with Jane Doe." Patrick pulled the sheet back. Laying on the metal gurney was a nude red haired woman in her twenties. She was about five foot four, slim build, and very striking…for a pregnant corpse.

"Holy fuck, leggo my preggo." Ted shouted as his annoyance turned suddenly into a morbid curiosity.

"Wow, never dealt with a pregnant corpse before. This is fucking creepy." Steve said as he made his way closer. He ran his eyes up and down her body trying to find any kind of cuts, gunshots, needle marks; anything that proved this woman was indeed dead. He found no apparent evidence during an initial glance over.

"What's more creepy is that no one knows who she is, but even more so is no one knows how she died. She was discovered in a hotel room."

"Drug overdose perhaps." Steve said. "I mean anyone can get pregnant. She could have been some junkie, the fetus a trick baby from whoring herself."

"Possible, but she was found among candles and pentagrams. Real creepy shit, ya know?"

"The fuck you mean?" Ted asked, feeling uneasy as he stared at the lifeless eyes.

"Satanic shit I guess. Don't know the details, cops tend to be vague; a mystery none the less."

"A mystery I elect to solve tomorrow." Ted shouted.

"I second that. Are you with us Patrick?"

"I want to get the fuck out of here as much as the rest of

you. You can go; I will lock her in the freezer."

"No, we'll do it. We don't mind." Steve answered as Ted shot a look of what the fuck did you just say.

"No might as well be me, I got some paperwork to fill out still and on top of all that I'm not so anxious to get home and see the old woman." The three of them laughed as Patrick made his way to the freezers. Ted and Steve quickly grabbed their coats, fearing Patrick will change his mind. .

"Alright then, we will see you in the morning Patrick."

As Ted headed out the front door he could have sworn he heard a baby crying.

***

That night Ted dreamed of the pregnant woman, however she was not the corpse which waited for them the next morning in the freezer, she was alive. The woman stood before him completely naked. Slowly she rubbed her hands over her belly, smiling at him.

"He's just like his father you know." Her voice was soft, insecure but sweet.

The light came in from an unknown source, a spot light of sorts, similar to those used in a low budget theater performance. The glow shined over her perfectly plump breast; over her light pink nipples. Ted felt a strong sexual draw to this woman, one he couldn't explain.

"Who's the father?" Ted asked the woman. Her timid cuteness immediately faded; replaced with a sense of confidence and arrogance.

"Oh, he goes by many names, but to pick just one, most call him Satan."

The light changed from a normal, neutral glow to a red tint. Her body so elegant and slender, except for the pregnant belly, moved closer as she wrapped her arm around his neck. Ted tried to resist, but found it impossible. He leaned in as their lips locked together. He felt her tongue slip into his mouth as he closed his eyes.

She ran her hand over his chest, down his stomach and beneath his belt. She continued until the flesh of her hand wrapped around his penis. He felt numb as stimulation shot throughout his body. He wanted her. There kissing intensified as he felt her fingers pulling his hair. He opened his eyes.

Her skin had turned a dark blue. Rotting chunks of meat were falling free, exposing the white bone underneath. The hair on her head was thin and her eyes were missing as maggots filled the sockets. Ted pulled back in revolting terror, trying in desperation to pull her hand out of his pants.

"Let go of me." He screamed.

"Oh come on, let's fuck. I can suck a mean cock." She opened her mouth as worms and cockroaches fell out... Her swollen blue tongue began to fall apart as it flickered like a snake's. "I'm the devil's little whore."

Ted shot wide awake. Drenched in sweat, he sighed as relief flowed through his body. He knew there would be no more sleeping that night.

"Then you fucked up man."

"I didn't fuck up, she just doesn't like to suck dick. Not all women do." Steve tried to defend his manhood. Ted shook his head and snickered.

"Man, I am telling you, all women do these days. It's like a requirement, a pre-programmed oral instinct. You just weren't hitting the right switches."

"You're so full of shit, just open the door."

As the door swung open Ted and Steve's smiles faded as their jaws hit the floor. There was blood was everywhere. The walls, the floor, even the ceiling dripped. Both of the men immediately ran to the corpse freezer and found one of the doors open. Resting upon the gurney was the corpse of Jane Doe, however her abdomen had been hollowed out and her internal organs scattered all around the gurney. It looked like some savage dogs ripped her apart. More disturbing, her baby was missing.

"What the fuck's going on?" Ted asked as he tried desperately to hold down his breakfast.

"The fetus was stolen." Steve responded as he shook his head in disbelief and made his way to the office.

"This is a fucking joke. I'm not cleaning this mess up. I'm going to fucking kill him." Ted was in total disbelief. He turned to his partner. "What are you doing?"

"I'm calling Patrick; that cocksucker is playing a sick

prank on us and I'm not in the mood."

"I don't know man, this whole thing…it just doesn't sit right."

"Well you ponder your little theory while I make the call." Steve pulled open the office door and immediately threw up. Quickly he slammed it shut and shook his head; his breaths coming out in nervous little bursts.

"Steve, what the fuck?" Ted called out as he ran to aid his friend. Steve just kept panting and pointing at the office door. Sitting in a chair was the corpse of Patrick. His eyes had been torn from their sockets, his nose ripped off; his entire face was gone. The only identifying factor that this hunk of meat was once Patrick was the clothing he wore. All around his body were hundreds of lit black candles. The flames danced wildly as they cast ominous shadows throughout the room. On the wall behind the corpse was a pentagram which had been drawn in blood.

"Listen man, I know this is fucked up but there's no time to figure this shit out. What we need to do is get out of here. The killers could still be here, you understand. Get your act together and let's go." Steve pulled himself out of it and turned away.

"Ted…I think I lost my mind." He said softly.

"I know man, this is crazy as hell."

"No, I'm not talking about Patrick. Jane Doe is standing behind you."

Ted saw absolute terror in the pale face of his friend. Steve raised his hand and pointed. As Ted turned he saw his nightmares standing before him. The corpse of Jane Doe was indeed standing there. She slowly began to walk toward the two men, dragging her left foot across the floor. Meat and blood continued to fall from the hole in her abdomen.

"My son needed to live." The corpse spoke. The two of them froze in horror. They couldn't move, instead they stood there and allowed the corpse to get an arm's length from them. She looked from Steve to Ted with foggy eyes. She raised a hand and put it on Ted's face. "Last night, we met."

"That was a dream." He managed to get out of his mouth.

"Ted, what the fuck is going on?"

"Go call the police Steve." Ted ordered. He tried to go himself but something held him in place. It was as if someone had cemented his feet to the ground. He struggled but it was to no avail. Some sort of spiritual shackle held him. "I can't move, you understand? I need you to go call for help."

"What's going on?"

"I don't fucking know but I need you to focus right now and call for help."

"You don't want Steve to know the truth?" The corpse asked as she ran her finger over his lips.

"Ted, what is she talking about?"

"I don't fucking know, just go call the goddamn police, Steve!"

"Ted was there the night I died."

"Bitch I have no idea what…" And like a flood gate giving way his suppressed memory came back to him. He had been there the night she died. "What the fuck is going on?"

"Those wild sexual escapades you tell everyone, those stories of kinky sex with nameless woman, they were created by you to fill in the gaps of time you couldn't account for. You often blacked out and your fear decided to create a lie. The truth is, during these gaps of time you were a participant."

"What is she talking about?"

"Tell him Ted. Tell him about the Coven. Tell him about the Temple of Luciferian Light. Tell him about the bloody orgies, the rituals, the animal sacrifices, the bestiality, the necrophilia; the corpses were provided by your morgue."

"Steve…don't listen to this. She is crazy."

Steve looked at Ted's face and didn't know who to believe. He could never imagine his friend and colleague engaging in such absurd conduct, but on the other hand there have been some rather extravagant stories. Was it true, was Ted a Satanist; and if so was he responsible for this woman's murder? This didn't matter, not now. Later he could sort this out, for now he needed to distance himself from this situation as much as possible, and save Ted if he could.

"I'm calling the police." Steve ran to the office as Ted stared long into the corpses eyes.

Like a projection he saw the events of that night unfold. After a ritual orgy they brought her into the room kicking and yelling. One of the followers put duct tape over her mouth. She wasn't pregnant at the time.

The robed followers took and tied her to an altar. She struggled to be let free; tears running down her pale cheeks. It was he who tied her right arm to the altar. The ritual continued on as the participants began reciting readings from some scripture.

"At the Sabbath, Lord Satan was said to take a woman to be had. He took this woman to one side of the great grove and made love to her, tasting her carnal nature. From this came a child, a child born of unholy blood. This child was a direct descendant of the throne of Hell. By fire and sulfur we invoke you, our dark Lord, to take this woman to your grove."

The group waited in fervent anticipation. There was a noise behind them, similar to a distant shattering of glass. This noise continued along with the grinding of stone. The sound of steam filled the room as the stink of rot invaded their nostrils.

The woman began to convulse violently as she jerked in unnatural contortions. Like a pretzel she twisted; she moaned in pleasure. This continued until finally she let out an ear piercing scream of agony.

The lights dimmed. They all muttered among the darkness, wondering if the ritual was complete. Suddenly the lights came back on and the woman's abdomen was massive. The ritual had worked. She was with child however she was dead.

"You see now, don't you?" She pulled herself so close that their eyes were no more than an inch from each other. Ted felt her still warm innards continue to spill at his feet as she ran her hand up his body. She leaned in and Ted met her halfway as they began to kiss.

"Ted?" Steve yelled. Despite his disgust, confusion and fear he knew he still needed to call the police. He ran to the office trying desperately not to look at Patrick's corpse. He reached for the phone and put the receiver to his ear.

Outside the room he heard Ted scream. Steve raced to the door, phones still in hand, and saw blood running down the woman's mouth. She laughed hysterically as Ted swung around. His lower jaw had been torn off. His tongue wildly flailed about in his mouth as he fell to the floor in convulsion.

"911 what's your emergency."

"I got a situation at the County Morgue in Carion."

"What is the situation sir?"

Murder, Zombie, Satanic Child?

"An attack and a murder; just send help now!" Steve hung up the phone. He shook his head as he tried to determine his next move. Ted pulled his bleeding body across the floor as he reached out for Steve. "I am so sorry buddy."

The woman continued to walk toward Ted, and behind them Steve saw a pair of glowing red eyes set back in the freezer. The eyes got bigger as they made their way forward, out of the darkness. It was a child, but not like any he had seen before. Its skin was blue and its massive mouth housed dozens of sharp teeth. On its head were small horns. Although this child stood no more than fourteen inches, its body was well toned with muscles, and from behind, a segmented tail.

It let out a deafening growl. The demonic child jumped

off the gurney, cracking the tile where it landed. It walked toward its mother and Ted. Ted continued to bleed from his mouth as the child walked.

"Go on, feed my child." The corpse spoke. The demon child pounced on top of Ted. It snapped his back, a sound similar to that of breaking sticks. The creature seemed happy with the pain it inflicted. It sunk its fangs deep into his neck and tore out tendons and muscle. Blood shot out like a broken water main, the bright red reached as high as the ceiling. The corpse mother smiled and stared lovingly down at her feeding child. "Go on, we need you to be strong just like your father."

Steve shook his head. There was no way this was all happening. He screamed out in terror as he watched his friend being torn apart. He backed himself into a corner as the child continued to tear chunks of meat from Ted's motionless body. Suddenly it looked up.

"Leave me alone!"

The child's attention was now re-directed to its next fresh meal. Steve flattened against the wall. He heard the police sirens. The demonic child screamed as its corpse mother laughed. The only hope he had left was for the police to arrive in time…

The water was tranquil. This is why Ken came here. He had been coming to the lake for a year now every day asking the Lord for help. His farm was failing, his family was lost and Ken knew only Jesus could set things right in their darkest hour. Finally, after nearly three hundred and sixty five days of coming to the lake, he appeared.

It wasn't a burning bush like in the Bible. No he came to him in his human form. He was majestic with long hair, white slacks and shirt. He crossed the lake, walking on the surface of the water gracefully. He stood before Ken who dropped to his knees and thanked the Lord.

"My Lord, Jesus almighty, I ask for your guidance on what to do."

"The answers you seek are simple. It is in the Old Testament, the book of Leviticus, in which people spilled blood for God. The blood sacrifice has stopped. Bring me blood, burn the fat on the altar and bury the bodies in your ground. Your crops will grow."

"Do you mean for me to sacrifice farm animals my Lord?"

"No, for too long this world hasn't shed blood. It will take human blood."

"Ok my Lord, I will do your will."

"And your daughters are to be touched by no man other than you. These children of yours will bear your children and you must sacrifice them to God almighty."

"Yes Lord, I will do your will."

When Ken came home he saw his oldest daughter Gretchen playing on the tire swing which hung from a tree in the dying fields. She was only twelve but who was he to question the Lord. Tonight it would happen. He would have sex with his daughter.

The next morning Gretchen was quiet. Lucille understood what happened; she said it had to be done if the Lord said it did. She was fixing coffee when she sat at the table with her husband.

"Ken, there is something I have been meaning to tell you."

"Go on dear." He responded with concern.

"Bobby; the farm hand."

"What about him."

"He's not the boy you think he is. He has come on to me; showed me his private parts."

"That son of a bitch." Ken slammed his fist onto the table. The coffee stirred a little in the mugs.

"Language Ken."

"I'm sorry."

"I was thinking, perhaps we can sacrifice him to the Lord."

"We do need bloodshed. If it be the will of the Lord we will do it."

That night Lucille invited Bobby to come to the house. She had told him that Ken was out in town and wouldn't be back for hours. Bobby, the naïve little hound dog of a young man he was, accepted the invitation gleefully.

"Why hello there." Bobby said with a smile as Gretchen opened the door. She was in the nude, her beautiful body cast in the glow of the lamps inside. She nodded at him.

"Come on in."

He didn't hesitate. As soon as he got through the front door he began unbuttoning his shirt. Soon his pants were down to his ankles.

"You don't understand Lucille; I have wanted this for as long as I worked here. That Ken is a chump to allow such a beauty be cooped up in those long dresses all day."

Struggling to get his jeans around his ankles he jerked and due to his focus on his pants he didn't see Ken emerge from the shadows with a hammer. Like the reaper of death Ken stepped out and struck with all his might, smacking the boy in the head. Bobby fell to the ground, unconscious but not dead.

"Did I do good Ken?"

"Yes my love, you did great. Like those actors in Hollywood."

"Thanks dear."

Ken dragged the man to the basement. Here he tossed the body on a table and immediately began tying him up, restraining him to the table without as much as an inch of slack. When it was proper and tight they waited, waited for the man to wake from his slumber.

Gretchen was wondering the kitchen. She tip toed as not to wake up her parents who she assumed were fast asleep. Her throat was parched. She quietly got a chair to boost her enough to reach for a glass in the cabinet. She filled it with water and drank it down.

Her parts hurt since Papa put his thing in her. She even bled a little. Papa said the Lord told him to do it and that Kendra as well as Margret would also have to do it when they got a little older. She didn't know why Jesus would demand such things but she was raised to never question the Lord, nor her Papa.

She heard a noise from the cellar door. It sounded almost like a muted scream. Gretchen walked toward the door and opened it. She descended the rickety stairs and in the shadows she watched as her Papa and Mama stood there with Bobby tied to a table. Ken looked up and saw his daughter.

"Don't worry Gretchen, come on down." Papa said. She nervously made her way down the stairs.

"It's fine Gretchen, it's the will of the Lord." Mama reassured with enthusiasm. Gretchen crossed the filthy basement floor to where her mother and father stood. Papa smiled at his oldest child. He rubbed her head and knelt down so he was eye level to her.

"What you did last night was a big girl thing. You are a big girl now. So I want you to do something for Papa, something only big girls do."

"Ok."

"Take this." He handed her a knife. It was large and sharp. Gretchen held it nervously in her hands. She smiled.

"It's cold." She laughed as the metal handle cooled her skin.

"Now I am going to place the step ladder here and when I do I want you to do exactly as I say."

"Ok Papa."

Ken moved, went to grab the step ladder. As he did he wondered if the Lord was watching. He could only hope. Lucille started singing.

"Amazing Grace, how sweet the sound, that saved a wretch like me."

Ken pushed the step ladder to the table where the gagged man flailed. He screamed but they were muffled by the rag in his mouth. Gretchen, with the knife in hand, climbed the stairs.

"I once was lost but now am found, was blind, but now I see"

"Honey, what you are about to do is something the Lord will love you for. This is your greatest moment. As you do this you will enter adulthood. Are you ready?"

"T'was Grace that taught my heart to fear. And Grace, my fears relieved. How precious did that Grace appear the hour I first believed."

"Yes Papa, I'm ready to do the Lord's work."

"Go on then my little sheep; bring down the wrath of god!"

"Through many dangers, toils and snares I have already come; 'Tis Grace that brought me safe thus far and Grace will lead me home."

"Glory be to the almighty God." Ken said as his daughter raised the knife. To him she looked angelic in the glow of the hook lamp. The face on Bobby was of terror as he screamed and kicked. He cried tears and then, with all her little strength, Gretchen brought the knife down and plunged it into his chest.

"Praise the Lord!" Lucille yelled.

"Praise the Lord!" Ken followed. Gretchen smiled at her parent's approval.

"Praise the Lord!" She said.

The bodies piled after that. Many drifters just passing bye were picked up. Lucille would seduce them and the Ken would kill them. Their bodies they buried in the fields and just like the Lord promised, their crops grew. It was a great harvest that year. And when Gretchen started to gain a little weight it was obvious the Lord was going to bless them with another sacrifice. Gretchen was pregnant.

Her dream had always to attend Brown University. While others were out partying it up in High School, she studied. While others had regular classes, she took advanced. She piled on the work so much that her sleep schedule consisted of only a few hours a night. Coffee became her best friend. Now she was here, the college of her dreams.

All her hard work was paying off and the time had come to let loose a little. Janice took up her friend Nadine's offer to go out for drinks at the Liquid Lounge off Thayer Street. As they sat there in the bar Nadine pointed out a guy.

"He's been eyeballing you all night." He was an athletic built man with short brown hair and beautiful eyes. As he shot pool and conversed with friends she noticed his charisma matched his looks.

"He's got a nice butt." Janice said as she sipped her drink.

"You want to go over there?"

"Why not, I don't get out often."

"Let's get you laid girl."

Janice was a very attractive woman. She had been born of Puerto Rican stock and was thick in all the right areas. Her long brown hair and beautiful brown eyes couldn't be ignored, that is if her slamming body didn't steal the attention first. She knew that she could have any guy she wanted and tonight she wanted the cute boy playing pool.

The girls strolled up with all the confidence that the alcohol in their blood allowed them. Nadine flocked to a blond haired man and smiled.

"You like black girls?"

"You like white boys?"

"I don't discriminate."

"Neither do I."

Janice sipped her drink as she swayed her hips to the music. She wasn't going to approach the man with the cute butt; no she would make him come to her. She smiled at him as she sipped the drink, the straw between her thick lips. The line was cast, the bait was taken and now she was reeling him in.

"Hey there."

"Hey."

"My name is Tommy. What's your name?"

"Janice."

"Well Janice, haven't seen you in here before. You live close by?"

"Yep, I stay at the dorms at Brown."

"Wow, pretty impressive."

"Are you in college?"

"Yes I am a student at RISD."

"Art student?"

"Art is life."

"So…want to play a game of pool?"

"Sure thing, what are the stakes?"

"Well art boy, if I win you need to buy me another drink but if you win you get to take me back to your place."

"I must warn you I'm pretty good."

"Me to, so play your heart out."

Tommy racked the balls. Janice grabbed a pool stick and stuck her ass out as far as she could. She looked up at Tommy and licked her lips. She struck and broke. The balls exploded all over the table as she sunk a nine ball.

"Looks like I'm stripes."

"That's good I play good with solids."

While the two continued their game Nadine and her boy toy were making out. At first Janice had the lead but soon Tommy took it. It was down to one ball each and it was Janice's turn. She smiled as she set up the shot. She took it and sunk her ball.

"Looks like I win." She said with a cocky attitude. "You owe me a drink."

"So what will you have to drink?"

"Well let's get a sex on the beach, hold the beach and bring it back to your apartment."

Tommy lived close by. The two made it up the stairs stumbling and laughing. Tommy fumbled in his pockets for the keys as Janice cupped his crotch. She felt a big bulge and got excited. The two piled into the apartment and Tommy hit the lights.

"My roommate is staying at his girlfriend's house tonight, so we have the place to ourselves."

"Great."

"Come on let me show you something."

Janice followed him down a short hallway to a bedroom. The walls were covered in a blue cloth panel. She smiled.

"Interesting wall design."

"You don't understand. These are soundproof panels. Once I close this door no one will hear us. Trust me; we will wake up the neighborhood without this room."

"Why did you soundproof your room?"

"Im a guitar player and love to practice late at night."

"And they really work?"

"No one will hear a sound."

Janice slammed the door and unbuttoned her blouse. She removed the shirt to reveal her red bra. Tommy followed by removing his shirt. He had a perfect body with a nice chest and abs. Janice unhinged her bra and slid off her pants and underwear. Tommy followed and Janice was nearly thrown back at the size of his dick.

"Come here." She whispered. Tommy approached the beautiful brown skinned girl as she dropped to her knees. She positioned herself as she took the hard cock into her mouth. Her head bobbed as she sucked on it. Tommy moaned as she ran her tongue from the base of his balls all the way down the nine inch shaft. She ran her tongue around the head and then stood up.

She made her way to the bed and bent over. She propped her ass up in the air and seductively smiled at him.

"I want your big dick up my tight Puerto Rican ass."

Tommy fished for the lubricant in his drawer and quickly lubed his cock. He put some on her asshole and a second later he fed it in inch by inch. Janice screamed out in pleasure as the cock slid deep inside her ass.

The sex was great. Janice laid there in the bed out of breath and sweaty. She leaned over and kissed Tommy on the lips. He ran his hand down her brown body.

"Thank you for the wonderful night, I needed that."

"Thank you."

"I should get going; Nadine is probably worried about me."

Tommy climbed out of the bed and walked over to the dresser. He opened his drawer and pulled out a pair of handcuffs. He tossed them on the bed.

"Put them on."

"No, really I got to go."

"I'm not asking." Tommy reached back in his drawer and pulled out a gun. He pointed it at Janice. "I said put the fucking cuffs on. Cuff yourself to the bed now or I will make that pussy hole a hell of a lot bigger."

"Tommy this isn't funny."

Tommy nodded his head as he approached the bed. He looked at her and she smiled at him taking it all in as a joke. He raised a hand and balled up a fist. He smashed it forward as her nose burst with blood. She fell back in the bed, banging her head on the headboard.

"Now you know I ain't fucking around. Put the goddamn cuffs on. This is the last time I tell you."

"Ok." Janice put the cuff on a wrist and then cuffed herself to the headboard. "Are you going to rape me?"

"Baby, what I am going to do will be a work of art. This room is soundproof for a reason. I like to pick up stupid bitches like you at bars and here I can do whatever I want. Go ahead and scream, no one will hear you."

"I won't give you the satisfaction."

"Oh trust me, you will scream. They all do."

There was a knock at the bedroom door. Tommy opened it and in walked a drunken Nadine and the blond guy from the bar. Nadine laughed when she saw Janice.

"Goddamn Billy, we came back to early it looks like."

"Shut the fuck up and get in the room." Billy demanded.

"Don't talk to me like that or I won't suck your cock."

Billy and Nadine entered the room as Tommy closed the door and locked it. Nadine saw the blood on Janice's face and rushed to her with concern.

"Oh my god did he do this to you?"

"Nadine, we are in trouble."

"Damn right you're in trouble." Billy laughed. "Now take your clothes off."

"Fuck you."

"My boy said to take your fucking clothes off." Tommy raised the gun. Nadine's eyes shrunk to pinholes.

"Now the party can really begin!" Billy shouted.

Nadine removed her clothes. She cried during it. Billy grabbed a video camera and began filming.

"Yeah nigger bitch, get naked for us."

"Why are you doing this?" Nadine asked.

"Because we are sick fucks who love to torture women." Billy responded as he chucked a bottle of beer at Nadine's leg. She was now naked and Billy stood with the camera. "Now I want you to get to the end of the bed and lick Janice's pussy."

"Please, let us go." Janice begged.

"Begging, I like it. Our audiences will love it to."

"Audiences?" Nadine asked.

"Yeah, we run a website of torture videos. We got millions of subscribers. Sick fucks who jack their dicks to shit like what we are about to film. We aren't college students, we are pornographers." Tommy laughed as he sipped a beer.

"We specialize in real sick stuff, as you both will soon see. Now Nadine are we going to have to put a bullet in your head or are you going to lick that pussy?"

Nadine crawled onto the bed and buried her face between Janice's legs. She licked her pussy. As she did Tommy squatted down. There was a plate under him. He strained and let out a couple of stools onto the plate. He picked up the plate and brought it over to Janice. Billy continued filming as Tommy reached for a fork on the dresser.

"Have you ever eaten human shit before?"

"Fuck you."

"Well open wide." He scooped a chunk of the steaming pile and with his free hand he pried Janice's mouth open. He jammed the turd in her mouth and he worked her jaw to make her chew it. "Swallow it."

Janice gagged and then vomited. The shit and vomit mixture flew out and onto her tits. Nadine looked up crying.

"Please Tommy, we won't tell anyone."

"Shut up and eat her pussy!"

Billy rested the camera on the dresser and he fumbled around in the room. When he returned to the bed he held a wooden paddle. With one whack he slapped Nadine's ass. She screamed out in pain.

"Come on, you black bitches are supposed to be tough. Take another." He swung again. She cried out as he grabbed her by the back of her head and smashed her face into the pussy. Tommy picked up a chunk of the shit. Billy pulled Nadine's hair and as she gasped for air Tommy smeared the feces on her face. She gagged and puked all over Janice's pussy.

"Yeah, now lick it up!" Nadine lowered her head and began licking up the vomit. Billy then took off to the back of the room again and this time he returned with a cattle prod. He aimed and jammed it into Nadine's unlubed asshole. She cried out and then screamed as he hit the switch. He then removed the prod and smacked her with it. When she moved he jammed it forward and shocked Janice's pussy.

The girls cried and begged as Tommy went to his drawer to remove a staple gun. He then began stapling Janice's big tits. While this happened Billy urinated on Nadine. The girls spent the next hour being beaten and humiliated. When they were done filming the men left the girl locked in the room and went back to the living room of the apartment.

"Nadine baby." Janice called out. Nadine was in the corner covered in welts crying in a fetus position. "Nadine please I need you to be strong."

"They are going to kill us."

"No they aren't if you will pull yourself together." Janice reached with her free hand and pulled a staple from her tit. She straightened it out. "I need you to come here and get this cuff off me."

Nadine got up and made her way to the bed. She took the staple in her hand and put it in the hole. She fumbled with it but had no luck.

"Try sticking it in the area with the teeth, maybe we can slide the cuff off like that."

Nadine jammed the staple into the area with the teeth and pushed hard. After a couple seconds came a click and the cuff came free. Janice was free. She stood up, covered in puke, blood and excrement and looked at Nadine.

"Now listen. We are getting out of here and these fuckers will die. So get on your game girl. We are getting out of here."

Tommy and Billy were smoking a blunt in the living room when Tommy asked Billy to check on the girls. He got up reluctantly and made his way down the hallway. He unlocked the door and entered. He immediately saw that

Janice was no longer tied to the bed and before he could say a word a wooden paddle came up and smacked him in the face. He fell like a ton of bricks on the floor. Janice and Nadine made their way out of the room. They were careful not to let the floorboards creak under their bare feet. Nadine held the paddle tight as they snuck up behind Tommy.

"What the fuck is taking you so long." And as he turned the paddle came down and knocked him out.

"Wake up boys." Janice whispered as the two naked men opened their eyes. "Rise and shine."

"What the fuck!" Tommy yelled as he struggled to get up. They were both tied to the bed.

"You fucking bitches!" Billy yelled. Nadine picked up the video camera.

"We are rolling." She laughed.

"You bitches are dead; you spic cunt and you nigger twat!"

"Oh no white boy, you had your chance to kill us. Now it is our turn." Janice then reached for a pair of scissors. She laughed as she grabbed hold of Tommy's dick.

"No, please."

"I love it when you beg." She then placed his penis in between the two blade and snapped them shut, cutting off this cock. She took the cock as Tommy cried and bled and wiggled it in Billy's face. "Open wide cock sucker."

Billy clenched his mouth shut. Nadine put the camera on the dresser and picked up the cattle prod. She positioned it and jammed it up Billy's ass. As he screamed Janice jammed the severed dick in his mouth.

He spit it out. "Fucking bitch!" Janice then put Billy's cock in the scissors and cut it off. He cried out in agony as blood poured from his stump. The girls took a seat and watched.

"It takes about seven agonizing minutes to bleed out boys. And while you slowly die I want you to think about one thing. I want you to ask yourselves how you got so comfortable that you let two bitches get the upper hand."

As they bled and screamed Nadine filmed. A few minutes later both men were dead. The girls went to the computer in the living room and removed the SD card from the camera. They found that their website was up and logged in. They uploaded the video and named it "Revenge of the Women". The girls got dressed and walked out of the apartment.

"Well that was one hell of a night." Nadine said.

"Yeah, next time I think I will just stay in and study."

The story I tell is of utmost importance and it must be told now. You must understand that my ability to recollect has been eroding from my brain these last years. It is an ailment which has been turning me into a forgetful and confused shell. Nevertheless this story is one which needs to be heard for I am alive by no stroke of luck but by the will of the Alabama gods.

1854 was the year my tale begins. My name is Fantine Bellamy and I am a descendent of a wealthy French family that migrated to the Americas in 1803. My father, Jacques Bellamy, turned quite a profit from selling garments he had sewn together. They were beautiful things; gowns which one swore cost fortunes but were mere pennies.

My mother was Isabella Bellamy. She was a nurse; however she had passed during my birth. Father never did re-marry. This isn't to say he didn't bring home an occasional lady friend, for he did, but he never settled. When I asked why he shrugged and said that my mother was irreplaceable.

We lived on the shore of a lake. My, this lake was beautiful I say. Sure we would be confronted from time to time with the horrid face of a scaly alligator, but for the most part the atmosphere was an intoxicating blend of exotic birds and frogs. Ever enchanting was this that I often found myself by the water and lost in it. Tranquility is something I once took for granted.

Anyhow, my tale begins one summer's eve. I had trotted along a well-worn path used by locals headed to the lake to fish. I cannot stress enough that these were leisure times full of relaxation. A great many days I spent snoozing away the hours beneath an old tree. How I long for those carefree days again.

It was down this trail I heard a woman crying. I was struck with curiosity at first but my curiosity turned to grave concern when I turned a bend to find a battered woman in the nude. She lay on the dirt with her arms shielding her head from invisible assailants. I rushed down to her aid.

"Miss, are you ok? Can I help?" I asked her. She looked up at me and my heart began to swell. It was obvious what had happened to her. Some of the local men had their way with her and beaten her nearly to death. The savage monsters even scratched her skin and bit into her. Like a wounded animal she reached out a hand which I took into mine. I helped her to her feet and assisted her back to the house.

My father saw us outside and rushed to aid. We carried her inside and laid her down on a bed in a room we used for visitors. No sooner had her head hit the pillow had she passed out from exhaustion.

That night I stayed up with her, keeping watch over her to ensure she was fine. I looked down at her slow breathing, her breasts as they rose and dropped. I felt a magnetic draw to her. I mistook this for sympathy but soon realized it was a strange sexual attraction I had felt to her. Being the era it was I shut the thought out of my mind and lay down next to the nude girl. That night we slept together for the first time, but not the last.

***

A few days went by and her scratches began to heal

remarkably. The first day she didn't talk much but began to eat. The second day she told us her name, Isabella. How queer it was to hear my mother's name spoken in this house in reference to a living woman, especially one around the same age as myself. Father seemed just as odd about it. My father had clothed her in some of his dresses he had made. By the third day she seemed to resemble a normal person.

"Where do you live?" My father finally asked. To this question her eyes dropped into her lap and she let out a heavy sigh.

"I do not have a home. I have been on my own for many years."

"Well I helped nurse you back and thus by the Alabama gods I have sworn a new pact to protect you. We have plenty of room here and you may sleep in the guest room as long as you will."

"Thank you Mr. Bellamy."

"Call me Jacques."

***

Isabella and I had grown quite close over the next few weeks. We had discussed a great many things and often swam in the lake. I felt my attraction to her growing which was strange for lesbianism was nothing I had felt until this moment. I had always been attracted to men but this woman had something that drew me in. I desired her more than I had ever desired a man.

I think she sensed this as well and often she held my hand

in hers when we walked. My heart would flutter as I felt her cool soft hand in mine. I would flirt with a slight rubbing of my thumb against hers and she returned the gesture. One day by the river we had stripped down to our under garments as usual but she didn't stop there. Within seconds her garments were on the dirt and she was as naked as the day I met her.

She stood there in the hot Alabama sun with her perky breasts and soft elegant curves. I couldn't resist as her full lips pulled back in smile and revealed her pure whites. I took my undergarments off as well and now we both stood naked on the shore.

Isabella came in close to me and raised her hand. She placed it behind my neck and pulled my body in close to hers. Our breasts touched and I felt a warm sensation between my legs as her erect nipples teased my own. She leaned in and we kissed. She took my hand and led it to her breast. I cupped one of them and our kissing intensified. Soon we were on the ground with her on top. She looked me in the eyes and told me she wanted me. I told her I wanted her too. We made love all afternoon under a tree among the intoxicating soundtrack of the Alabama wilderness.

***

Our lust began to blossom into love and father began to sense this. He watched with awkward eyes as we held each other no different than lovers did. He even made a comment about how he never sees me with boys anymore. I knew what he was hinting at and told him I didn't need a boy, not as long as I had Isabella.

***

It was one night, three months later, when my whole life began to change. Fall was creeping and it began to grow cold. Isabella had moved into my room at this point and we shared a bed, sleeping in the nude entangled in each other's arms. That night I had a wild dream.

Isabella was in the woods. She was naked and on all fours. She howled to the moon like a wolf and within seconds three wolves arrived. They were drooling, terrifying beasts and much bigger than any wolf I had ever seen in real life. Their fur was a dense black and their eyes a burning red. They approached her slowly. She didn't seem scared at all. She was calling them.

My mind was shaken when the wolves began to engage in sexual acts with Isabella. She threw her head back and moaned as the beasts penetrated her mouth, vagina and anus. They bit her and scratched her with their claws. She moaned out in pleasure as she climaxed. I turned away in disgust and when I turned back I gasped.

The wolves had transformed into demons. They stood six feet tall with massive horns. They were black and looked to be silhouettes with red eyes. They looked down at her and spoke in a different language, one so foreign I couldn't compare it to anything earthly. This made Isabella cry as the demons began to spill smoke from their bodies. Within seconds they were gone and what was left was a crying Isabella exactly as she was the moment I first laid eyes upon her.

A scream had awoken me. When I opened my eyes I saw that father stood before our bed with an axe in his hand. He had had a menacing look on his face, a twisted contortion of insanity. He didn't speak but his intentions I could read in his eyes. He was going to kill Isabella.

She rolled out of bed just as the axe came down. It split the mattress as the blade buried into the wooden floor. I panicked and jumped up. He struggled with the axe for a second and this gave Isabella enough time to scamper into a corner. She screamed as my father retrieved his weapon from the floor and raised it above his head. He turned to her.

"You must die demon. I have spoken to the Alabama gods and they told me about your intentions. Leave us alone."

Isabella cried out and begged him to stop. What madness had possessed him? I didn't know what to do and before I could think my body began to react, as if someone else was controlling it. I reached over and grabbed a pair of garment shears off the dresser and dove toward my deranged father. I buried the scissors into his neck.

He screamed out in agony, dropping the axe. The weapon fell to the the floor and seconds later my father joined. His eyes began to roll back in his head and I watched my father's existence fade from this life and into the next. When I was sure he was dead I approached my distraught lover.

She dove into my arms and began kissing me. She thanked me for saving her life and cried onto my breasts. Her tears were warm as they ran down my naked body. She looked up at me with a quivering lip and spoke three beautiful words.

"I love you."

"I love you too."

We didn't contact the authorities. Our unorthodox relationship would surely be used against us so we decided to instead put my father's body into the lake. We had tied heavy rocks to his corpse and took the boat out. When we reached the center of the lake we pushed him over. When it was done I felt a sensation of freedom I never felt before. My lover climbed upon me and we made love in the boat under the fall sun.

When winter came our chores began to intensify. We had to cut wood and ration the food we gathered all summer. Father was the hunter but Isabella was a good replacement. She was even better than he was for she had a real skill at it. She would enter the woods and within an hour or two return with enough meat for a week.

Things seemed wonderful until one night while eating dinner by candle light. When we were done we listened to the howling winter wind as we sat by the fire wrapped tight in each other's arms. Then we heard the howl of a wolf.

Isabella jumped up and screamed. Panic took over as she ran on all fours to the far corner of the room. She dove beneath the table and curled up in a ball. She looked like a frightened dog.

"Isabella, what is it?" She wouldn't talk or move. I reached beneath the table to tend to her and she lashed out and scratched my arm. Her nails even drew blood. I jumped to my feet and stared at her in shock.

The next day she apologized for the previous night's behavior. She explained that she had a fear of wolves from when she was homeless in the woods. I wanted to tell her about the dream but found it inappropriate. I took her into my arms but felt that something had changed.

Isabella had changed.

***

I was lost in a dream, a beautiful dream in which I was by the lake on a lazy summer's afternoon. I was allowing the sun to shine down upon me and stared up at it. Then I heard the howl of a wolf.

I jumped up and saw the three wolves from the earlier dream. They approached me in a column. I quickly got to my feet and took a defensive stance.

"Please, if we meant to hurt you I assure that you would already be dead; we are here for Isabella."

"What do you want with her?"

"The Overseer misses her. He wants her back."

"Who's the overseer?"

"He rules the Gloom. Don't worry mortal, just return the girl."

"Never."

"She isn't human, she isn't in love; she can't feel love. She's using you. Be careful. We warned you."

Outside a wolf's howl had awoken me. I felt an intense cool breeze. The window was open, and I saw that Isabella was gone.

I walked all night looking for her. I pulled my coat tight around me as the wind tore through my soul and froze my bones. All around me seemed to be the howling of wolves. I ignored them and continued on.

I walked along one of her hunting trails that she often took. I continued on for a while and then I saw in my lantern's glow blood upon the dirt. As I looked ahead I saw more and knew something was wrong. My walk turned into a jog and quickly into a sprint. I dashed through the woods and continued to follow the trail until I came to a large rock.

On top of the rock was Isabella. She was naked and covered from head to toe in blood. Beneath her was the torn open carcass of a wolf, and not just any wolf but one of the demonic ones from my dream. She stood there with the innards of the wolf handing from her mouth as she chewed on them. She hadn't noticed me.

"Isabella!" I hollered up to her but the wind stole my voice and sent it in another direction. I called out to her again and this time she heard me. Her were a blazing red and she opened her mouth to reveal sharp fangs. She hissed and spit like a wolf.

I turned and ran. I dodged the branches and roots as I ran back to my house. I heard Isabella running after me. I glanced back to see her running on all fours like a wolf. I was no match for her and within seconds she pounced on top of me.

"Hello lover." She spoke in a demonic and twisted voice.

She followed this up with insane laughter as she drooled blood upon me.

"Isabella, what's going on?"

"I have a gift for you. You will join me and we will live in the Gloom."

"Isabella, what are you saying?"

Before I could mutter another word she sank her teeth into me and I felt pain at first but that soon diminished. I felt a sexual awakening within me, an orgasm which ran through my veins. I was drunk on the sensation as I felt everything go numb. Then I passed out.

When I opened my eyes Isabella was gone. I climbed to my feet and reached a hand to my throbbing neck. It itched and my body felt different.

From the woods came a small wolf. It walked up to me. I was scared at first but the fear quickly was replaced with a love as I realized I was looking at my Isabella. I dropped to my knees and opened my arms. The wolf came to me and began to lick my face. I turned my head and caught our reflection in a puddle. I too was a wolf.

The gift of lycanthropy given to me by my lover has lengthened my existence. The year of my writing this is 2011 and much has changed in the world. Isabella has since passed away, taken back to the Overseer after six hundred years upon this earth. Me, I continue to live my life all over the world. My name changes every couple decades, however I like Fantine the best.

He'd spent the entire afternoon pursuing road kill. Sure there were healthier things for a nineteen year old man to be doing, like working or dating, but he wasn't an ordinary man. He had one desire in life, and that was corpses. This is not to assume that Simon wasn't a sexually active male, he got more than most his age; he just had unusual tastes. He was a necrosexual, and he loved to have sex with road kill.

The first time was the best. He was only thirteen years old and had a head full of confused thoughts. He loved gory movies and had a strong sex drive…but he realized early on that his sexual attraction wasn't to anything alive. He was turned on by the dead.

He fantasized every night. He masturbated while thinking of that cold flesh deprived of oxygen, the skin in various states of decomposition. Men, women or animals…it didn't matter to him. The only requirement that would satisfy his morbid fetish was that the subject was a cadaver. He'd never murder anybody; in fact he'd never even had sex with a human. His lovers were those killed on the side of the road and to him Highway 44 was an orgy of dead meat.

His first sexual experience was with a dog. He saw the maggot infested hunk of meat baking in the sun. The pungent odor aroused him, and he felt like his erection would break off in his pants at any moment. He looked at the decaying animal and eagerly unzipped his jeans. From this point on it became an addiction.

Of course no one knew of this. Necrosexuals are not ones who live out loud. He lived with his mother and father in the good old suburban town of Seekonk, yet the community had no idea how sick he was.

But he didn't see himself as mentally ill now did he? Who was he really harming? Necrophilia is essentially a victimless crime and it's not like he desecrated loved ones. No, he only took those who were tossed away like trash to begin with. He satisfied his strange sexual urges by recycling the dead animals he discovered.

He had been hunting all afternoon but route 44 was vacant. He took his explorations all around town and still came up empty. A neighbor's dog got his attention and he thought how easy it would be to kill it. He could crush its head with a rock but no, that would be sick. He had standards.

It was behind a grocery store on Route 6 where he caught a scent. It stunk of death, and his nostrils picked up the stink like a bloodhound. As he got closer to the pungent odor his erection grew. He wondered what he'd find. As he opened the dumpster he was surprised to put it mildly.

There, sitting on a pile of rotting vegetables and expired beef it sat. Tossed away and left to be taken away to the local dumping grounds. What he found was the severed head of a blond woman.

He almost collapsed to the ground and even ejaculated in his underwear as he stared at the head. Her face had been frozen in the final moments before her death. Her cloudy colored eyes were open, staring blankly at him begging to be fucked. With a shaking hand he scooped it up and stuffed it into his back pack.

He'd take her home. This would be a special night. Tonight he'd have a human. He'd finally have his first sexual experience with his own specie and a female at that.

Twice on the way home he had to stop and masturbate in the woods. He was so overcome with excitement. It took all his will to not pull the head out and make love to it in the secrecy of the woods. No, this was to be a special day. He felt something new…was it love?

When he got home he ran to his bedroom and tossed the backpack onto the bed. He closed the door and hit play on his iPod. The loud death metal music filled the bedroom as he quickly undressed. He pulled his lover from the backpack and placed it onto the center of the bed.

She looked up at him. He named her Lauren, what a lovely name for such a beautiful woman. He bent down and placed his warm lips on her cold ones and slipped his tongue inside.

He felt something enter his mouth. He was a little crazy but not crazy enough to actually believe this severed head was sending her tongue his way. When he pulled back he felt it still in his mouth. He spit out a cockroach. This was it; he was so turned on right now that the romance was over. He gripped the head in his hands and jammed his erect penis into the open mouth.

With each violent thrust he felt closer to god. He felt a sensation no dog or squirrel or even goose had ever given him. As he came in the back of that head he felt bliss that couldn't be matched.

When he was done he watched his semen drip out from the severed neck. This turned him on again and this time he decided to try something else, something he had learned from fucking a dead deer. He took his penis and jammed it into the eye socket. The squishing sound as the eye ball liquefied around his dick caused him to last no more than a couple seconds. He had sex with the head six more times before he was done.

He lay there on his bed with the head on his chest. He looked at it and felt something in his heart. A flutter, he felt what all those high school boys and girls felt; love.

He loved Lauren. He never wanted to leave her…except he knew that their time together was short. This was the problem with necrophilia. She would decay, like all the others and she would leave him. He couldn't handle this thought. He needed to do something.

The stink was bad, worse than any animal. When his parents came home they would smell it for sure. He knew he needed to do something and that's when the idea hit him. He could boil the meat off. He could put it in a pot and boil it until it was nothing more than a skull. The smell would be gone and he could keep Lauren forever.

He imagined staying up late and watching Texas Chainsaw Massacre with Lauren, kissing her skeletal lips as he masturbated himself onto her cranium. His parents wouldn't be home for hours. If he started now he could pull it off.

He got dressed and ran to the kitchen with the head. He grabbed a pan and filled it with water. When the water was boiling he took the head and looked her in her one remaining eye.

He smiled at her.

"I love you Lauren. We're going to be together forever now." He then tossed the head inside the pot. As it boiled he killed time by watching one of his favorite movies, Halloween.

Hours had gone by and he had fallen asleep, dreaming of his new life with Lauren. He dreamed of all the hot nights they'd have. He dreamed of carrying her around in his backpack and bringing her to the movies. He imagined sitting on a hill with her and watching the sun set. He was pulled from his slumber when he heard the front door open.

He looked down at his watch. It was eight thirty. He overslept and now his parents were home. He nervously got up as they entered the kitchen.

"Hey honey, what are you cooking?" His mother asked. He nervously glanced around the room as his father smelled the air.

"Damn, that smells good kid. What is it?"

"Stew." He muttered. He thought for a second. "Lamb stew."

"Lamb stew, I never had it before." His father responded looking pleased.

"That is a weird smell, but it don't smell bad." His mother added. "Is it done?"

"No, it is just a little longer; I need to add veggies."

"Ok there champ, we'll go shower and get settled in while you cook." His father took off to the bedroom as his mother kissed him on the head.

"You are such a good boy" She took off leaving him in the kitchen with the boiling head.

He went through the refrigerator as he pulled out more ingredients to add. A little carrot, some potatoes, an onion, a little garlic…some salt and a season blend. He added all this and let it cook a little more.

He nervously dropped a ladle into the pot as he scooped the contents into three bowls. His parents eagerly waited at the dining room table, discussing their work day. As he brought the bowls in he wondered how it would taste.

Moments after placing down the bowl his parents sipped it and smiled. His father leaned back with a satisfying grin.

"Goddamn Simon, I think you discovered your trade."

"You're one hell of a cook honey. Seriously this is amazing."

Simon looked down at his bowl and scooped the contents into his mouth. He let the stew swish around a little bit and smiled. It was good; no it was amazing.

They ate their soup. When they were done Simon even insisted on doing the dishes. When he said his goodnights he went back to the kitchen.

He saw the bedroom light turn off. He was alone. He fished the skull out of the pot and looked at it. He smiled as he kissed its forehead.

"Thank you Lauren. I never knew I was a cook until tonight."

That night he slept with Lauren in his arms as he dreamed of his future with her sand his future as a chef.

When I make a mistake I try to ignore it. I move on as if it never happened. I don't remember things as they happened, but rather as I want to remember them. This is the only way I have complete control of my life. I know it's a lie, but I would rather live a happy lie than a miserable truth.

The city is full of garbage. Even the best poets cannot beautify the city of Brockton. It's a festering asshole just south of Boston. It's the vile epicenter of disgusting filth. I fucking hate this city.

It's three in the goddamn morning. I have a killer hang over and sitting across the table is this miserable sub human garbage. He's some mid-twenties douchebag with baby blue eyes. His shoulder length hair is greased back to allow one to take in his handsome facial features. His scruffy beard, that one which is common among the outlaw only added to his mystique and charm. He was the bad boy women fantasized about. He was the complete opposite of me.

I'm forty six, balding, slightly overweight and have tired bloodshot eyes. I have a raspy cough due to excessive smoking. My voice is broken from whiskey, as broken as my soul. I'm the ugly, old, bald asshole whose slut bag wife left him…and who did she leave me for? It was a man just like this good looking little fuck, this still in diapers cunt head.

I'm a detective for the city of Brockton, and this young punk before me is accused of murder; yet I'm the shit-bag. I'm the vile and disgusting aging old bastard.

He smiles at me. I want to take my hand, curl it up and smash his cheek. I want nothing more than to shatter his perfect fucking nose. I bet so many women spread their legs for this little bastard, this insignificant human compost. He possibly fucked my wife. He's her type. She likes them young, attractive and with a bad boy streak. Yeah, my bitch whore of a wife wants the complete opposite of me. She can fuck men half her age and do it behind my back, yet I'm the scumbag.

What was the text she sent me? I believe it said I want a divorce Danny. After this she sent a sad face and the words I'm sorry. According to the time stamp on the texts it took exactly forty seven minutes for her to send the second part. I think the guilt hit her after that young lothario fucked her brains out.

But enough of me and my shitty life…I got a job to do.

"So who's the crispy woman in your apartment?" I ask. He continues with that stupid smile, that shit eating grin which makes me want to take my ball point pen and gouge out his goddamn blue eyes. I want to use my car keys and cut massive gashes across his handsome face. I want to make him hideous, a freak at a circus side show. "Hey, are you a friggin mute or something?"

"I'm sorry detective, but I'm just trying to get to understand who you are." He responds in a cocky way, it nauseates me.

"Oh really, well is it clear now?"

"Crystal." The confidence of this guy makes me insane. I want nothing more than to yank his perfect teeth out and jam them down his throat.

"Well I'm just so fucking honored. May I continue with my interrogation?" He motions for me to continue. I feel my stomach heaving as the old whiskey burned an ulcer in my gut. I have to get a grip on myself.

This room is small, an old interrogation room with a one way mirror. The room was empty except for the table and this cocksucker handcuffed to it. There's our chairs, of course, and a video camera mounted on the ceiling. This room seems empty; however it was bursting with animosity. I'm not in the mood for games, yet this little twat wanted to play.

"What was it you asked me?"

"Who is the burnt woman we discovered in your apartment? Does she have a name?" He looks at me inquisitively. I knew I wasn't going to get a straight answer, why would I? "An ID?"

"Do you have an ID?"

"Just answer the question."

"Let me ask you a question. Your wife, what happened to her?" I knew what he was trying to insinuate. It didn't piss me off; actually I kind of wished it was true.

"Good try, but this woman in your place has been dead for nearly a week. I saw my wife just the other night."

"What I meant was that the skin on your finger where a wedding ring once was is pale. You recently stopped wearing it…what happened?"

"Is this really how you want to spend your time? I have you in here facing a murder charge. You go before a judge in the morning and you want to chit chat about my soon to be ex-wife?"

"I think it's important. We need to build trust amongst us. I also think that you need to get it off your chest, and once you do you'll think more clearly…you'll understand more of what I'm about to tell you."

"Goddamn, you are a character. If I tell you do I have your word that you will tell me who the woman is?" He leans in as he raises his eye brows.

"More than that detective; I'll tell you every detail of her torture, of her pain. After I explain how she died the name I shall reveal."

"The name I shall reveal, listen to yourself; so cheesy. I also want a confession."

"Why of course, although I doubt you can handle the truth."

"Listen kid, I promise to take it like a big boy." I cracked my neck as I watch the little bastard stare up at me; stare like some little pissy pants baby eager to hear a bedtime story. This little shit didn't deserve to know about my wife, but if it was going to get him to confess I can hurry home before sunlight broke. I could take some aspirin and fall asleep. I had enough of the real world for one day. "She was getting bored with me. She said I had gotten too old. She said all I did was drink and work. Perhaps she's right, but I choose to think otherwise."

"Oh, this is understandable. Nobody wants to be known as a monster." I searched for what this man intended to do. He was up to something, but what? I watched as he seemed deeply devoted to my story; his glassy stare as he envisions it all. "And did she cheat on you?"

"She did."

"How did you find out?"

"She had a video she recorded with the man. She had it on her laptop. She didn't think I would see it. Her computer had been running slow due to spyware. I was trying to help it run faster by cleaning it out."

`"Was it a sex video?"

`"Yes it was. It was-"

`"Exciting wasn't it?"

`"What the fuck is wrong with you? It was devastating." He

was trying to break me down, but why?

"Did she cum?"

"Do you want to keep your teeth?" It was working.

"What did we agree on detective? You tell me your story and I will tell you mine." My eyes began burning with the fires of hell, my nostrils flared and at this moment I want nothing more than to pull my service weapon out and unload into his forehead. This is what he wants. I can't let him win.

"Yeah she came like a goddamn banshee."

"Did he cum?"

"Yes, all over her face. Is that what you want to hear? I didn't realize what a whore I married."

"She doesn't sound like a whore to me, just adventurous. If you tried some of those things…do you think it would be different?"

"I don't know, maybe. She's my wife…you know how hard it is to…"

"Blow a load in her face?"

"It's different." It was true. The mother of your children, the woman you stood before the altar and vowed to always protect; it seems wrong treat her like a porn star.

"But she married a man who did these things didn't she? She married a man who treated her like a woman in public, but a whore in the bedroom. She married a young, hard bodied, strong, sexually driven man. Now she's left with this pathetic limp dick prude who will occasionally slam her from behind if she begs enough times. The passion is gone, and now so is she."

"I guess." Why did he want to know this? Keep your head together because he is up to something. He's trying to confuse me...but what if it's true? What if I were to leave here and march back over to the house they shared in Stoughton? What if I kick open the door and throw that snotty nosed brat onto the front grass? What if I were to take my wife and show her what kind of fuck machine I really am? I could treat her like the little slut she wants to be. Maybe then all would return to normal. "I told you so let me hear your story."

"I still haven't seen your ID detective..."

"I'm going to bash your head in if you don't start cooperating."

"I want a name at the very least detective."

"Detective Bradshaw."

"Danny?"

"Tanner." At this he looked a little confused. I smile. "Oh, did I just shit in your cereal?"

"No, but I think you don't know your own name."

"Just tell me about the woman."

"She was beautiful; a woman of loyalty. She worshipped the ground I walked on. She made me feel like a man. She was gorgeous and everything was perfect."

"So you killed her?"

"Oh, we'll get to that. Now first let me tell you what I did. I decided I needed to get her to come to this abandoned warehouse. It's right off of Chandler Street in Worcester. I told her there would be a party there, a rave. Well we drove down and she sucked down some Mr. Boston Vodka. She had no idea that I drugged it. When we arrived she was passed out. I dragged her inside, stripped her nude and tied her to an old table. When she had woken she thought we would make love. Do you know why?"

"She trusted you. She could not imagine what you intended to do to her."

"Yeah, that adventurous sex life your wife left you for was common for us. This woman was a real kinky bitch and it turned her on to think that this was a new game. I reached down with my fingers and felt her pussy. It was soaked."

My head began to hurt. I raised my chubby index finger to my temple and squeezed my eyes shut. It felt like someone was ripping at my brain.

"Pay attention, I don't want you to miss the good parts Danny."

"The name's Tanner. I'm listening. Go on." I yell as I struggle to get through the pain.

"Well first I decided to change her face around. I pulled out a pair of needle-nose pliers. She made a joking comment about how hard her nipples were, and begged me not to use it on them. She was shocked when I jammed it into her mouth and wrapped the steel around her front tooth. I squeezed until I felt it crack and then yanked with all my might.

"Next I decided to remove an eye. I used an old spoon and scooped it out. Do you know how funny a bitch looks with one eye, it's hilarious. Well after this I used a knife..."

My head was throbbing, and my vision began to shift. I felt feverish and started to see doubles. My heart slammed against my chest. The little prick handcuffed to the chair looked at me laughing.

"My god, don't freak out now Danny, there is so much more. I took a hammer to her chin and sliced off her clitoris with a fillet knife. I used old fish hooks to peel back her pussy lips and tried to see how many dead rats I could stuff in her cunt. Do you know how many I could fit?"

My arms were going numb. There's a heavy weight on my

chest as my mind turns into chaos; a flood of random thoughts and images. I see the rats laughing from inside that woman's vagina. They laugh at me for being such a stupid fucking old man. I see my wife. She's young, no older than eighteen. She keeps telling me that I should have never gotten old. She tells me I should have burned out long ago. She tells me that I'm a pathetic old bastard who didn't know how to fuck her. I feel like I'm having a heart attack.

"I got four in there. I'm sure I could get more but I ran out of rats. God, you should have seen what I did with her tits. I took this fork and knife…" His words were turning into gibberish. He continues on but I only hear every other word. "Fucking…torn…tit sack, whatever it's called…anal…intestines hanging out…wife."

And then I suddenly feel normal. The images, the numbness, the pain, the panic; it's all gone. Sweating I look up at him and asked "What did you say? She was your wife?"

"No…she was your wife Danny."

"My name is Tanner."

"Let me see some ID" Sick of his games I reach into my back pocket and pulled out my wallet. I opened the front where the ID was kept next to my badge and froze. There it was, but not the name I expect. It said Detective Danny Bradshaw.

"What the fuck is going on."

"You just don't get it do you?" And then for the first time in my drunken life I felt clear. I began to remember. The hammer smashing in her face, the gasoline all over her body, the match lit, the flames as she burned and it's me standing in the light, the light her burning body gave off. All this time and it was me. The burned woman was my wife and I killed her.

Clarity washes over me, and the feeling is awesome. I shake my head as I began to laugh. He follows my lead and begins to laugh too and this made me laugh even harder.

"You are truly fucked you know that?"

"I know. Wow, I really killed her." I look up at the young man confused but amused at the same time. "Who the fuck are you?"

"I'm in your mind; you made me up. You're not a detective, you're an inmate. You killed your loving, devoted wife one night and turned yourself in. Don't you remember?"

"Not really, kind of I guess." I look around the room and nothing changed. Everything remained except the man in front of me was no longer handcuffed. He reaches into his pocket and pulls out a deck of playing cards. As he cuts the deck he laughs.

"Sorry but you are truly fucked in the head man." He places the cards down and reaches under the table. He pulls up two shot glasses and a bottle of whiskey. I nod in approval.

"Just shut the hell up and deal the cards." And the two of us smoked cigars, drank whiskey and played poker into the late night hours. I knew none of this was real, I knew what really happened. I don't remember things as they happened, but rather as I want to remember them. This is the only way I have complete control of my life. I know it's a lie, but I would rather live a happy lie than a miserable truth.

The wind carried the cold November air throughout the bare tree limbs; limbs which hung low to the ground giving them the appearance that they were skeletons in mourning. The rain was light but the clouds were quickly taking over the skies as the darkness blocked out the sun. It could only be assumed that the velocity of the rain would surely pick up. Laura, pulling the hood over her head to block the raindrops, carried on towards the house.

It stood two stories, every window boarded up with plywood. It looked as if every inch of this house had been spray-painted with graffiti; the artists being the local teens whom stood defiant against the "No Trespassing" sign posted at the front.

The iron fence was rusted, each post bent in a different direction and many posts were missing. Overgrowth quickly covered the fence, which imprisoned the house.

(Laura you don't have to do this)

She stepped across the broken concrete walkway; memories of her childhood streamed through her brain like an old reel to reel movie. She was in awe at the state of this house; a living nightmare. It was something from a horror movie, a place which breeds dread and bleeds misery. This house went to hell, and it's hell where this house shall remain.

She pulled open the front door and stepped inside.

She almost collapsed, for although she expected the inside to take a likeness to the rotting exterior it had not. To her surprise the house was beautiful inside. The carpet was nice, rich and vibrant with colors. The walls were clean and free of graffiti. Instead they were plastered with family portraits, portraits of her and the many others which made up her family. There were smiles, sometimes genuine, other times forced.

A giant chandelier illuminated the room; the warm glow creating a comforting atmosphere of low light ambience. This light complimented the fine furniture all around her. The house, it was precisely as she recalled, but how on earth was this possible? How could such life be preserved within this carcass of a house?

"Laura? Come here sweetie" A woman's voice called from upstairs. That beautiful, low and wonderful voice was so familiar; could that really the voice of her mother?

"Mom?" Laura called out. Her voice got caught on the way out but somehow she managed to get it out.

"Coming mommy!" an excited young girl's voice replied. Laura made her way over to the stairs as a little girl with a purple dress and pigtails trailing dashed out of a room and across the hall. She ran to the far left room laughing. "I'm coming."

Laura felt her chest constrict, her breath shorten and a sense of fear travel from her abdomen to her bowels. What was this she was witnessing? Was she hallucinating? Were her memories so vivid they manifested before her eyes; if so how is it possible

(Laura, turn back you fool. This isn't meant to be seen. The fact that you are seeing it is devastating in itself. You stupid bitch, don't you understand the term paradox?)

She carried herself on fragile legs that moved like iron weights but wobbled like old chair legs. She used the hand rail for support as she practically pulled herself up the steps, fearing her legs would give out along with her bladder. When she reached the top and turned towards the room she finally collapsed like a sack of flour.

It was her mother. She was so young and stunning. Her red hair was tied up with a few curly locks falling in her face. Her makeup was applied with perfection and helped emphasis the natural beauty that was already there. She wore a sundress, with graphics of flowers all across a white fabric. Her lips, her cheeks, her eyes…it all was so real.

(Look at her Laura. There she is. Didn't you miss her?)

"Mom?" Laura called out, but she was either ignored or not heard. Her voice seemed different than the ones of her mom and this little girl. Her voice seemed more watery, atmospheric and ethereal; in their voices she could hear a hint of static. It was like they were being played on an old tape.

The room walls were blue with little balloons. A banner hung in the room proudly proclaiming "It's a boy". Her mother was standing beside a crib, her hand inside as she played with a little baby. It was her little brother Danny.

"How was school today?" She asked the little girl.

"A boy kept…"

Laura opened her mouth and spoke along with the child, their voices in synch. She remembered this conversation. "…pulling my hair. It made me real mad."

"Oh honey, that means he likes you; he wants to be your boyfriend." She said to the little girl.

Both Laura and the little girl responded. "Yuck, boys are gross." She couldn't help but smile. Warmth overcame her as she felt like she was inside the body of this little girl. Her mind felt free like a child's, a freedom which one loses as they become an adult.

There was a sound outside of a car door slamming. Laura's mom and the little girl jumped; Danny began to cry. Her mom's face quickly changed; her smile dropping off her face along with her skin tone. She was petrified. Her lips trembled; she swallowed and cleared her throat. Nervously she threw on a fake smile.

"Honey, I want you to go and get ready for bed, I'll be in there in a few minutes. Daddies home and mommy has to talk to him." She tried hard to sound calm, and she could easily fool a child into believing her, but Laura was grown now. That gullible world was no more and now she could see the panic and fear; she could see that which she was blind to all those years prior.

"Ok mommy, I love you."

"I love you too Laura." And the little girl turned and ran towards Laura. The little girl ran right past her; her pigtails brushing Laura's side. She felt the butterflies in her stomach rise. She turned to watch the little apparition of herself skip down the hall and turn a corner into a room. She wished she could escape this adult body; abandon it like a hermit crab vacates its shell.

A scream tore her attention back to the room, however everything had changed.

The walls were grimy, and covered in graffiti.

(Joey jacked off here-1998…Tif and Patrick forever…Tif is a whore…Fuck you pussy…If you want good head call Tif…Joey jacked off again-1999…Tif is a slut with HIV, call her 1-434-875-5565)

The floors were a terrain of filth. Garbage, needles, condoms, porn mags, dead bugs; it all littered the floor of Danny's room. The beautiful, surreal ghost world was gone. She was left in the decomposing innards of a rotting house.

Her mother was in the far corner, back to her and crying into her hands. She stood before a filthy crib. Her dress was all torn. Her hair a mess, full of twigs and mud and as the ghost cried she heard the door downstairs opening. It was her father.

Laura ran over to her mom. She knew this situation was insane, her mom had been dead for so long. There was no way this was real, however her rational sense of things was buried now. She was living within the instant, and at this moment her mother was in trouble. "Mom, don't cry! I won't let him hurt you."

The woman turned around. Her face was sunken in, her skin decomposing. Her face was full of exposed bone and sinew. Her eyes were bloodshot; her skin pale as paper. "You are too late Laura; you are far to fucking late. Look what he made me do!"

And the woman thrust her arms forward, wrists pouring blood onto the floor. The blood flow was absurd, flowing like a busted pipe. If this kept up she feared the room would surely flood. She imagined drowning in this room, sucking in mouthfuls of blood while floating here for eternity.

Laura turned and ran out of the room; leaving behind the screaming, bleeding corpse.

(That's right Laura, run away, that's what you always do isn't it? Run away. You spent your entire fucking life running, why stop now.)

"Shut the fuck up and get out of my head!" She screamed as she dashed down the stairs. The living room was the same as the upstairs, a shit hole of trash and filth. It was a perfect reflection of this house and a superb metaphor for her life since she left this miserable place. She rushed across the floor and pulled on the door handle, but it would not budge. "Open you fucking cocksucker!"

(Laura you're fucked, I told you not to come here!)

"Please, let me be!" She screamed into the air as she frantically smashed her fists against the plywood which covered the broken windows. She beat her little fists until blood began to fall down her hands, screaming on the top of her lungs.

"Laura."

The voice came from behind her, and when she spun around she nearly fell to the ground. Standing in the door frame was her father. He was tall and a little fat from drinking. He was wearing a muscle shirt which advertised "Bush" beer. His short, greasy hair hung just above his brow.

"Daddy?"

"What's the matter Laura?"

"You… you're dead. Mom is dead. Danny is fucking dead!

Why is this happening?" She cried out as she collapsed to the ground. Her father smiled, took a sip from a bottle of Jim Beam, and shook his head.

"Laura, you are one fucked up bitch. But haven't you always been?"

"Fuck you!"

"I play with your pussy a little and you run and tell mommy. Of course I killed her, Danny to. But the truth is that you don't understand. I'm not dead. Your mom's not dead. Danny's not dead either…"

"Fucking liar!" She screamed as she got up and pushed past him. He laughed.

"Laura, it's not as it seems, we all create the world we live in!"

She ran down the hallway which seemed to grow, stretching forever in front of her. She couldn't even see the end. The walls were covered in what looked like blood. Trash littered the ground at first but soon this was replaced with bones; bones of dogs and cats. After a few more feet these bones began to resemble those of people.

She continued to cry out and scream as her father's laugh throbbed through her feverish head. She clawed at her eyes, wanting to rip them out and forget everything she saw. She now wished she never came here.

(I told you…)

"You say one more goddamn thing I swear to god."

(What? What are you going to do?)

She stopped in her tracks and reached into her waist band of her pants. She pulled a small revolver from her waist and placed it hard against her head. She screamed out. "I will blow my fucking brains out and kill us both; miserable fucking whore!"

"Why would you want to do that?" A man asked as he stepped forward from the shadows. He was well dressed in a red suit and tie. His hair was well groomed, a handsome man. With his manicured hand he motioned for her to lower the gun. "Why spoil such a pretty face?"

"Who the fuck are you" She screamed out as she swung the gun forward; pointing it at the man. Her heart beat increased, her breathing was rapid and chaotic. She ground her teeth as she spoke. "You got about three fucking seconds to explain yourself before I rip a hole through your pretty boy fucking head."

"Big sister, this is how you treat family?" as asked laughing.

"I don't understand? My brother died."

"No, I didn't die; in fact I couldn't be more alive. I'm a very successful business man, a real estate king of sorts. Mom and dad are quite proud of me."

"What's going on?"

"I see and understand your confusion. I can't say any more. Just know this one thing big sis; we all create the lives we live and we all decide where they go. This house has a million doors, all which lead to a million lives. You have been given a chance to open a new door; onto a new life…don't fuck it up again?"

"What are you saying? I'm lost."

"You always seem to get lost. Honestly I don't understand why you call this a vacation. Keep going and maybe we'll see each other again; if you pick the right door that is."

"Which door?" But before she could ask anything else the man collapsed onto the ground. Within seconds the body disintegrated to bones.

(How many times will you walk this hallway?)

"What do you mean? I never have been here…" And before she could finish she knew it was a lie. She had been here many times. She has come to this house every night, and traveled down this hallway each time. She began to realize and allowed herself to understand. Suddenly she was no longer afraid and no longer was she confused.

(Ah, you see again now don't you.)

"I am sorry. I always choose to forget."

(I am glad you see now. Your vacation choices suck. Welcome back to Hell.)

"Home sweet home; I just can't seem to find the right door."

(Ha, you got to keep trying sweetie. There is a life out there that is just waiting for us; that is if you would stop coming back to this goddamn house.)

"I know I got to; the nightmares are so strong. The dreams kill me in that world."

(Hold on to your vacation as long as possible will ya?)

"Yeah, this time I will try hard to not be some socially retarded, emotional roller coaster."

(And stay the fuck away from the house.)

"I will." She quickly began removing her clothes until she was naked. She continued down the hallway, skipping now past the old bones and rotting limbs. She skipped past the blood drenched walls, past the agonizing screams of the tortured, past the windows which looked out onto a world of pain and misery.

When she came to the end of the hallway she found herself in a giant spherical room. The room seemed to stretch miles in all directions, and every inch of the room was covered with a door; every door was labeled with a different name.

Her skin began to fall free from her bones like liquid. It collected in a pool beneath her hooves and revealed not bones, but the red scales of a beast. Her head was that of a massive hawk. Her body was the shape of a woman but skin like a red snake; behind her was a massive tail made of flames. She raised her arms as bat like wings expanded a mile out on each side of her, and like a bullet she shot into the air.

She flew as she read out loud the names. "Bethany Smith, Chad Rogers, Danny Glover, Richard Philips, Ricky Lawrence, Rachel Gothier, Becca Downs"

She flew for weeks as she read out loud the names. She was looking for her next victim, the next woman or man she would possess; her vacation.

The Corpse Whore

"Valdese Accounting, how may I assist you?" He answered the phone in his bogus, pitiful work voice. He detested the voice. This was the voice of an ass kisser. There was no better way to acknowledge defeat and at the same time totally empower those listening on the other end. It was bubbly and pleasing to hear…not to him though. To speak like this made him want to run to the nearest window and swan dive out onto the pavement below; splatter his stupid fucking head all over the street below.

"Yeah, I got this bill in the mail from the Caldwell Community Hospital. The bill here states I owe one thousand and twenty three dollars. My question is, are you out of your fucking mind?"

This is what his life had boiled down to. All honors in high school, no criminal record and a college degree to top it off; and now this was his life. He woke up from a restless sleep, drank cheap instant coffee and swallowed empty calories. He drove from Hickory, a place which kind of resembled modern existence (at least there was a Starbucks) and made his way to the little shit hole called Valdese. This town was the spunk from a redneck's cock that dripped down when he pulled it out of his sheep's ass. This was a hick haven and he constantly had to deal with their verbal, unintelligent, assaults.

"Let me look into this sir." He typed into the computer data base. "It looks here that you were treated for a laceration of the left thumb."

"You guys gave me a shot and a Band-Aid. How the fuck does that cost one thousand and twenty three dollars? How about I lacerate your throat?"

And this would go on back and forth. This was his lot in life, he was a whipping post. He was a bitch boy. Scott Blakey wasn't a collector of debts; he was an outlet for the community.

Your life sucks and you need someone to yell at? Than call none other than Scott Blakey. Call now and for a limited time you can unleash a verbal assault. The smaller you make him feel, the bigger you feel. Call today before this limited time offer expires and Mr. Blakey takes his 9mm pistol and blows his fucking brains out!

It was all a waiting game until five o'clock. Once five came he would punch out and make his way to his 1993 piece of shit Honda Accord. He would sit inside and grip the steering wheel. The plastic smiles would prance past him to continue on with their soulless existence in plastic American society. He would act the part and wave. He fucking hated his coworkers but it was ok he would tell himself...he was off to see Kappy.

Kappy was a smut peddler. He wasn't just a smut peddler; he was the fucking messiah of it. He operated right next to a Baptist church. The whole arrangement was poetic and beautiful. Redemption was sold right next to the wildest pornography in the world. Come pray to Jesus and on your way home pick up this month's issue of "Teen Twats".

Looking for tranny midgets with giant cocks...Kappy has it!

Fat woman femdom and face sitters…Kappy has it!

Crack whores sucking off for a rock…Kappy has it!

He has it all; from bestiality to pedophilia, to necrophilia mags, scat reels and genital torture flicks. If Kappy don't sell it, than it isn't worth a shit.

Have you ever seen a woman's labia nailed to a wood board? How about shit covered midgets blowing loads in the face of an eighty year old woman? Ever see a crack whore swallow a gallon of Donkey cum. No? Well go see Kappy, because he has it.

He had seen it all. Scott has exposed himself to every depraved sexual fetish on earth. Some did it for him, others didn't, but recently he was running into a problem. It was actually more of a crisis. The thing was, the very fabric which held this perverted little world together was about to tear. The old glory days of excitement were fading. He didn't feel the spark from looking at the forbidden worlds anymore. He was losing the thrill. It was beginning to resemble his job…routine.

The thrill is all he had. Without the thrill he would lose his mind in the world of the mundane. He would collapse in the boring person he was, realize how much his life truly sucked and take a bullet to the skull.

He…needed more. If Kappy couldn't help he knew he was done for.

The store was hidden, accessed by a side entrance beneath an old antique store. Within the low light atmosphere there were rows of the stuff that would make the average Joe vomit. Sketchy people of all kinds browsed here. He saw sex offenders, construction workers, doctors, dentists and even priests. There was an unwritten rule at these kinds of places; no one talks. To tell non porn addicts of another man's addiction would ban you from the porn underground. This was punishment enough, because your average porn addict can only find so many places to get his DVD copies of corpse porn.

Kappy was a fat, greasy old Jew stereotype. Years ago, when the cocaine got him in trouble, he found his way from Yonkers to North Carolina. He decided to set up shop and found that there was so much demand in the south that he had no need to return to New York.

"Scotty my brother, how have you been?" He asked with a fake attitude. Kappy was the Santa Clause of the porn underground

"Got off work…could use something new."

"Well I got a nice 8mm reel of a local girl getting gang raped by farm boys."

"Eh…looking for something new."

"I get it; the rape porn is no longer fresh. What you need is a new avenue to explore. Are you interested in kids? I got a couple magazines of little girls and boys. Soul kissing and, eh, you know what else. If that's too young I got the tween thing too. Not quite kids but no quite teens."

"Na, I never got into pedophilia. It makes me sick to be honest." This obviously offended Kappy who shot a warning look to Scott. To Kappy it seemed Scott was forgetting the first rule of the porn underground, don't judge another's fetish.

"Says the man who watches rape fantasy; to each their own I suppose. Well I got a fresh new necrophilia reel, but it is in 16mm." He looks down as he thinks. Suddenly he shoots up with excitement. "Oh I got a great VHS tape of a woman getting fucked by a monkey of some sort. You got to see the dick on this thing, real sick shit. I bet he tore that bitch all up."

"Na…I think I exhausted all my options Kappy. I think I explored all the porn I can. I think the time has come to move on; find the next big thing." Kappy looked disappointingly at his loyal customer, but he understood his pain. It happened to him once or twice.

"No, don't say that. I'm sure good old Kappy can dig something up. Wait a minute." His eyes widened as he rushed to a box in the rear of the swap. Scott followed him, feeling his curiosity grow, but he didn't have much hope. "It's in here. I know it; here!"

Scott pulled a leather book from the box. It was red; ancient and filthy looking. Scott couldn't even understand how this book hadn't disintegrated in Kappy's hand. He held it up to his mouth and blew off the thin layer of grime. On the front cover was a weird symbol made up of lines and arrows.

"What the fuck is this? I'm not into erotica; sex novels don't do it for me."

"This isn't erotica, its rotting erotica. This is a foul work of art dating back to 1430's…or some shit. Some magician wrote it. It is a grimoire for sexual gratification."

"Sex magic? You got to be kidding me. You don't even know who wrote it."

"Listen man, I'm a porn dealer not an occultists." Kappy leaned in as his eyes wandered to ensure no one was eavesdropping. "This is some serious shit. I'm not lying to you."

"What the fuck is it?"

"Have you ever heard of Popo Bawa?"

"No, what the fuck is that? Sounds like a cartoon character."

"Hardly; it is a Swahili demon known for his sexual assault. He was known for sodomizing both men and woman. Popo Bawa is a sex demon and this book speaks of another sex demon; a female known simply as Oza. She is the beautiful rotting whore. She comes to you and will fuck you, reinvent what you define as sex. This, my longtime friend, is the pinnacle. Do not give up on porn without trying this first."

"Are you serious? Listen man I don't believe in that shit. If you don't have some good fuck films or spank mags to offer I guess I'll just get going."

"I am telling you from experience Scott." Kappy reached out his chubby little hand and grasped Scott by the arm. His eyes were wild as he looked at him hard. "I have done the ritual."

"You have done it?" He asked, trying desperately not to roll his eyes.

"I'm inviting you to join me during the ritual. If nothing happens you can write me off as insane…but if I'm right?"

"If you're right I'll fuck a demon?"

"Man I know it's some crazy shit to swallow; seeing is believing." He had to admit, Kappy was a salesman and he talked him up. He didn't really believe, but thought there must be something if he was willing to go through all this.

"Ok, let's fuck a demon. What do I need to bring? Lubricant, lingerie, dildos; help me out here man I never fucked fire pussy."

"Listen to you, ya fuck. Here I am trying to help and all you can do is be a smart ass. What we need is a woman. Anyone will do." A woman; he sensed a scam.

"I'm telling you man, this better not be some cheap role playing bullshit."

"It's not man. Just be here tomorrow at six; and bring a bitch!"

***

That night Scott's head was full of confusion. Was Kappy insane? How sane do you have to be to get into the smut business in the first place, but this was just out of this world. Still…he couldn't deny the excitement he was beginning to feel.

That night he didn't sleep a wink, instead he just stayed up all night wondering what sex with a demon would be like.

***

"Valdese Accounting, how may I help you?" The man on the other end was yelling about money and bills and a free county. He called him a fagot, a fuck head, an asshole; but Scott didn't hear him.

"Ok sir, call again anytime." He was distracted. He thought about his meeting tonight.

"Scott are you ok?" It was Brenda. She was the office rat, some little nympho bitch every swinging dick in the building has broken open at least once. She was attractive in a weird way; a thin and pale little sex twig. Who was he kidding, not a soul would look at her if she wasn't so good in bed. Just then he remembered Kappy. He needed a woman.

"I'm fine now that you're here." He said. She smiled at him flirtatiously. This was going to be easy. "Listen I got this party I'm going to after work. I'll be meeting at a friend's house beforehand; would you be interested?"

"Yeah, I got nothing to do tonight, why not?" This was too easy.

"Great, pick you up at five thirty."

***

Scott pulled into the Kappy's driveway. He was already outside waiting for them. He helped Brenda out of the car. She was wearing a long, flowing red dress and her hair was done up.

"Holy shit, get a load of you gorgeous, where you two headed?"

"I thought we were going to a party." Brenda stated as she quickly shot a look back at Scott.

"Oh, I'm just fucking with you, of course. I need to get

dressed up still. You two feel free to come in and wait." Kappy quickly recovered. He led the two of them to the basement level where all the pornography rows are. They continued on to a door that led to a second level of the basement he didn't know existed. It was dark and no sooner did Kappy turn on the light did he see it was a ritual bedroom of sorts.

The floor was hardwood. In the center of the room was a bed with chains fastened to the bed posts. To the far corner of the room was an altar with the book Kappy had showed him earlier. Immediately Brenda shook her head.

"Listen Scott, I wish you were just straight up with me. I normally wouldn't mind fucking you and your friend but I'm on my goddamn period. I thought we were going to a party."

"Calm down Brenda. It's ok, trust me." Scott said as Kappy locked a deadbolt. Scott looked up at him alarmed. "What the fuck are you doing Kap?"

"It is about to begin. Miss, please lay down on the bed."

"I just said that…"Kappy slapped her hard across the face. She stumbled back and was lost in a mix of pain and excitement. She took a second to catch her breath and closed her eyes. "Ok, you woke me up. Tell your friend I like it rough but take it down a notch, almost chipped a goddamn tooth."

"Shut the fuck up bitch and take your goddamn clothes off." Kappy demanded. Again the jolt of excitement ran through her body and she felt per panties getting moist. Scott looked on with confusion and terror. Was Kappy really this insane?

"Yes master." With a seductive smile she made her way to

the bed. Once at the edge she slid the red dress down her body. She was now wearing nothing but a black bra and panties. She slid the panties down her long legs before unhinging her bra. She turned toward the men and smiled. "Are you going to chain me up master?"

"Yes. Lay down."

"Kappy, what the fuck's going on?" Scott was getting impatient.

"Scott, don't break character. If you're going to have this attitude you can meet us upstairs and wait for us to get done playing."

Kappy made his way over to the woman and began securing the restraints. Scott shook his head in disappointment. This seemed to all be a ploy so Kappy could get off to some weird fetish. There was nothing here for him. He wanted to go.

"The ritual begins." Kappy said as he walked toward the table with the book. Brenda put up a little struggle as she played along.

"Please, don't hurt me. I promise to do anything you want master."

"By Samigina, by Vassago and to the endless chaos of SitraAchra shall I venture? Let my voice transcend the barrier; let my desires no longer be denied. Dark lord, oh he who dwells in the Gallery. By the anti-cosmic gods I call thee forth, oh beautiful demon. I call you Oza, and offer this sacrifice."

"Sacrifice, Oh come on Kappy this is getting a little ridiculous now." Brenda said as she rolled her eyes.

"By fire, by blood, I offer this woman to you oh great demon. Oza, materialize in the flesh from the realm of spirits. I demand you stand before me and take this sacrifice!" Kappy let this last word ring out. For a second nothing happened. Scott shook his head and Brenda laughed.

"So where the fuck is this demon?" No sooner had she finished her sentence had the lights began to flicker. Brenda laughed even harder. "Nice theatrics Kappy."

In the far corner of the chamber the candles suddenly lit all at once. The flames were normal at first but quickly turned to a deep blue color. The temperature of the room dropped so rapidly Scott could now see his breath.

"Seriously guys, occult fetishism is so 1970's." She teased. Scott couldn't talk. He watched as a thin layer of frost suddenly crystallized over the ceiling and walls. This obviously got Brenda's attention as well. "Ok Kappy. How the fuck did you do that?"

"What's happening?" Scot finally managed to get out.

"She's here." He replied with a smile.

"Fuck this shit, let me go!" Brenda shrieked as terror began to set in. She desperately struggled to pull herself free. This was no longer the playful tugging of the chains, but a desperate attempt toward self-preservation. Scott watched as her face twisted and she cried out; then he saw why she was acting like this.

The demon's face was a patchwork of blue, rotting flesh. Her eyes sat in their sockets like mounds of jelly surrounded by maggots. Her lower jaw was missing so much meat that all one could see was a jaw bone. Her teeth glistened through the holes in her cheeks. Her hair hung in long black strands and ran down her nude, decaying body. Her breasts were ample, veiny and blue. A massive hole in her abdomen revealed her decomposed organs which were blackened and oozing a viscous green fluid. Like a wild animal she snapped at the air with her teeth as her thin, skeletal corpse body drunkenly walked closer to Brenda.

"What the fuck is that? Get that thing away from me. Scott please let me free." Brenda cried out as she screamed on the top of her lungs. "Oh Lord Jesus Christ; please save me."

"My whore." The beast screamed in a voice which sounded dreadful; full of distortion. Oza jumped up onto the bed and now straddled the screaming nude girl. She cried out and begged to be let free. "Don't cry little slut. This won't take me long."

The demon bent down at a squat as if attempting to urinate. She screamed as she struggled to push. She looked like a rotting corpse trying to give birth. Suddenly a fang slid out of her vagina. The nail continued to slide out of the rotting slit. Six inches and then what followed was the pink colored earthworm looking tentacle it was connected to. It fell out and rose above her head as a sort of vaginal tail. Suddenly the nail split in half revealing a mouth full of teeth. The vaginal tentacle screamed as it suddenly darted forward and into Brenda's vagina.

Brenda immediately ceased all movement and became stiff. The tentacle slid deeper into her body as Brenda began to moan. To Scott it sounded as if she was actually reaching an orgasm.

"That's right my little whore." The monster hissed. Blood began to spill from Brenda's mouth. Oza salivated as she continued to jam the tentacle deeper into her sacrifice. There was a sucking sound, like a vacuum cleaner. Brenda's body began to convulse as blood gushed from her mouth like a busted water pipe.

Brenda's body began to deteriorate. Her face began to rot away. Sinew and bone were clearly visible as she continued to convulse. Every vein in her body blackened with death as her organs burst within her, almost like a bag of popcorn in a microwave. Oza laughed as the vaginal feeding tube sucked the life from Brenda's body until all that was left was a lifeless skeleton.

The lights cut out.

Scott began to panic. He heard quick movement within the blackness, like a wild animal running free within the chamber. He heard the contents of the altar fall over. He heard heavy breathing and a heartbeat. Suddenly he heard Kappy screaming.

"No! Please don't do this, please don't…" His voice was cut short and all Scott could hear was gargling. He slowly walked backwards as he tried to feel for the door. He needed to get out of here. Then he felt the breathing on his neck.

It was warm and with it came an enchanting fragrance. He felt two hands run up and down his chest as they rubbed his abs. He felt a tongue running down his neck. He was terrified, but turned on.

Again he heard the sound of an animal smashing through the room and then there was a light. All around him was empty night.

He was no longer on earth. There was no ceiling, no walls, and no floor. He was suspended in darkness completely naked. Standing before him was the most gorgeous sight he had ever laid his eyes upon.

Her face was human although her eyes were significantly larger than normal humans; resembling those of cartoon aliens from the fifties. Her small nose and thick lips sat on a perfect complexion of tanned skin. Her hair flowed like a black river down her body. From the sides of her head grew two massive red horns.

Her breasts were large and had the same flawless complexion as he face. Her thin, well-toned athletic body continued on until the hips. Here in her pelvic region was her trimmed vagina which throbbed with moisture. Behind hung a segmented tail the color of her flesh. Her legs were similar to that of a goat with a thin layer of white fur. The meaty thighs carried on to the hock. Below this was a bony shin that ended in a hoof.

She was flawless.

She leaned in and let a forked tongue run along his earlobe. Her hands ran up his naked body and across his pectoral muscles and over his shoulders. She draped her arms around his neck as she pulled her face in close to his. She whispered in his ear. "You bring me a life and I redefine what you call pleasure."

Suddenly Scott was lying down as Oza jumped up on top of him.

***

After what seemed like days Scott was back in the basement.

The demon was gone. On the bed was the skeleton of Brenda and across the room, by the altar, was the skeleton of Kappy. Scott walked over to him and smiled.

"Well old friend, you were right. You made a believer out of me." Scott leaned down and took the red book from Kappy's skeletal hand. He looked down at his watch. It was 6:01. He had only been gone for one minute.

He got dressed and made his way back to his car. As he pulled onto the main street he felt a new confidence he never felt before. It was a happiness that he thought was impossible to achieve. He found a new addiction. Now he was off to satisfy his craving.

He needed another woman.

"Listen man, I'm not calling you a loser, seriously." Ted was eating a beef bean burrito as he sat at a stainless steel table. He took a bite and chewed it slowly, tossing out all manners and talking regardless. "I mean it's pretty pathetic that you haven't had a chick in over a year, but that isn't me calling you a loser."

Steve was draining a corpse on an embalming table. He watched as the machine kicked on and began removing the blood from the body. Her name was Mary Lynn and Steve knew her. She was a beauty in her time. When Steve went to Dorchester High School he dreamed of fucking her. That was nearly twelve years ago and now she was dead from a heroin overdose. Welcome to Boston, home of the lethally pure heroin.

All over the city people were dying from this shit. It wasn't anything to be alarmed about, so the Boston PD wanted us to think, but the hoods from Roxbury certainly didn't seem to have much care for their clientele.

"You are calling me a loser. It's not like I haven't tried." Steve lied. He knew he didn't try. He considered himself to career oriented.

"Bullshit. I tried to hook you up recently." Ted shouted back at him. "She wanted to fuck like something wicked."

"Sarah; are you fucking serious. She's a goddamn whale man."

"Fat girls put out." Ted said as he wiped the burrito mess off his face with his hand. He was disgusting.

"No, I need a woman like good old Mary Lynn here."

"Dude, you sound sick right now." Ted shot a horrified look at him.

"I don't me dead you fucking moron. I'm talking about equal in beauty. You remember?"

"Of course man, I fucked her in like tenth grade."

"Now that's bullshit."

"Whatever man, the thing is you are putting the pussy on a pedestal. You have it to high with standards that don't match a man like you."

"Fuck you man, I'm not some hideous ghoul."

"I didn't say you were, I am sayiny, however, she is way out of your league."

"Back then?" Steve asked as he adjusted the tubes.

"Back then and now. Her corpse is even too beautiful for you man. Don't you realize, you need to pump a nut in a few nasty bitches to boost your confidence? After a few months of mediocre you'll be drowning in drop dead gorgeous pussy man. "

"Why the fuck do I talk to you?"

"Because you're a creepy mortician and no one likes talking to morticians." As much as Steve hated to admit it, Ted was right. Since he joined this profession he lost friends every day. Ted was the only one that stuck around. He was a medical examiner. Now women find that interesting. They think they are some CSI dork with cool stories…when Steve was just a mortician and everyone thinks all morticians are necrophiliac.

"Well listen man; I'll be at The Tam tonight."

"Why the fuck you like that place so much, it's a dive bar."

"Yeah,and? The women in their got shattered egos which makes it easy hunting. Even a loser like you can find some ass." Ted got up and made his way to the door. Steve was relived.

"You said I wasn't a loser."

"I was lying, now get done with that corpse and meet me for drinks. Tonight we're going to get you laid."

The door slammed behind him and Steve shook his head

"Mary Lynn;Not even dead he said." Steve leaned over her and touched Mary Lynn on the arm. She was cool to the touch but still not as cold as she could be. No, this wouldn't set in yet. She hadn't died too long ago. "I wonder."

Steve took his right hand and pulled off his glove. He looked around to ensure no one was watching and placed his hand over her right breast. He cupped it and closed his eyes imaging her alive. They would be in a back of a car somewhere and she would have her shirt up. She wanted him and he wanted her. The thought got him aroused and although it disturbed him he was overcome with the fact that he was actually holding the tit he dreamed of for over a decade.

"To kiss those lips." He smiled at himself as he opened his eyes and leaned down. He was an inch from her lips and smiled at her. "Tell me you want me."

Of course she didn't reply but in Steve's lonely mind he made her reply;her voice as beautiful and elegant as he remembered it.

"I want you Steven. I always had a crush on you. Kiss me." He leaned down and placed his lips on her dead mouth. He slid his tongue inside, not surprised that it was a little dry. He ran his right hand down her waste, past her public line and slid his index finger deep inside her pussy. It was still wet enough.

He imagined her moaning. He imagined her gasping. He used his free hand to take her left arm and slid it down the front of his pants.

"What a nice, thick dick." She responded in his mind.

"I know."

"I want you to fuck me Steven."

He wasted no time. He tore his shirt off and pulled down his pants. Within seconds he was on top of the embalming table, naked and staring into her dead eyes. She wasn't dead though, not to him. He imagined her lively and moving, talking and wrapping her legs around him. He slowly slid deep inside her.

Good thing she was dead, because it only lasted four seconds. But in Steve's mind they had been going at it for hours. He collapsed onto her and kissed her neck. "I love you Mary Lynn."

"I love you to."

"What the fuck?" The voice shouted from across the room. He turned to see the frail seventy year old janitor, Patrick. He had a disgusted face as he watched the man he worked with violating a cadaver.

"Patrick, it's not."

"You're going to jail you sick son of a bitch!" He yelled as dug into his jacket for his cell phone. In panic Steve reached for the closest object and threw it at him, hoping to knock him to the ground and prevent him from making that phone call. He hit, but unfortunately what he threw was a large bone saw. It landed right in the middle of Patrick's head, between his eyes. He dropped to the floor dead.

"Holy fuck!" Steve yelled as he jumped off Mary Lynn. He quickly got dressed and began pacing the room. He just killed a man. He didn't want to go to prison, no he heard about what they do to men who were weak in prison and Steve was as soft as baby shit. He needed to think.

Hide him.

He could hide him for tonight. He could toss him inside one of the meat freezers and sleep on a plan tonight. That was the only idea he could think of. It had to work. He dragged the corpse of Patrick to the freezer, slammed the door shut and locked it. He put a tag on it that said Do not use, out of service.

Steve then cleaned up the blood and returned Mary Lynn back to the freezer. Before he did he kissed her lips one last time. "I love you."

***

"Bro, you are such a faggot. You flaked on me again and there was mad slampigs there. Little Irish sluts all ready with their tramp stamps showing. Fuck man, its ten degrees outside and these sluts wore skirts. You know they wanted to fuck."

Steve couldn't listen to his shit today. Last night he didn't sleep at all. He stayed up and wondered what he could do with the corpse. He was clueless. He had no idea at all and now he had to listen to Ted's macho bullshit.

"I'm sorry, I had the shits."

"Bullshit, your pussy was sore and you were scared as always."

"No man I'm serious, I don't feel like myself." And it was true. Since he had sex with Mary Lynn he felt strange. He didn't know what to do. Who the fuck was he now? Was he really some sick pervert? Was he the pervert everyone already assumed he was?

"Whatever man, you done with that broad from last night."

"Her name is Mary Lynn." Ted sensed he hit a nerve.

"Jesus man, sorry." Ted trotted over to Steve. "Tell me the truth, you fucked her last night. Is that why you didn't come to meet me?"

"Get the fuck out of here."

"Why not, I would."

"You would?" Steve asked, curious if he wasn't the only one.

"Fuck no you sicko. What am I some depraved pervert. Sorry I like my pussy alive and well." Ted looked at his watch. "Well let's get her done we need to have her ready in a couple hours."

Steve opened the stainless steel door to her meat freezer and pulled it out. Both men gasped in horror. The body was still there however her stomach was round and big…like she was-

"Holy fuck she looks pregnant."

"That's ridiculous" suddenly Steve wondered about not wearing a condom. "Must be gas trapped inside of her abdomen."

"Well we need to deflate this bitch. She is being fitted for a funeral."

They rolled her out and Steve grabbed a scalpel. He positioned it above her. He knew this was strange but he felt bad putting the knife to her belly. He didn't want to-

"Holy fuck something moved in there!" Ted shouted. He wasn't lying, Steve saw it to. It looked like a snake or something was trapped inside. They stared at it, hoping it was their imagination but then it happened again.

What the fuck is going on?

There was a thrashing from one of the meat freezers. It was loud and deafening as it echoed throughout the morgue. It sounded like someone was kicking the door from the inside, the one marked out of service. The one Steve hid the corpse in.

"What the fuck is in there?" Ted shouted as he turned toward it.

He wasn't dead? I'm so fucked!

Ted approached the door and reached out for the latch.

"Ted, don't open that please." The door continued to be kick and was almost busting off the hinges. From inside was a growl, almost like a dog. Ted reached out and pulled the latch open.

Patrick dove out on top of Ted. He still had the bone saw embedded in his head. He was clearly alive but not the same person he was the day before. Patrick wrapped his hands around Ted's throat. Patrick opened his mouth and bit down. When he came up half of Ted's throat was handing from the old man's mouth.

Ted screamed in agony as Patrick jumped up. He was far too strong to be the seventy year old feeble man. It was almost as if he was possessed. Patrick let out an ungodly demonic scream and rushed toward Steve. All Steve could do was close his eyes and wait for his death.

But there was no death. There was no impact. Before Patrick could reach him something had pounced on top of him. Steve opened his eyes and watched as the small creature excavated the old man's innards. Long strands of intestine and bloated organs covered the floor as this small demonic creature feverishly tore open the man.

Steve needed a weapon and fast.

He turned back to Mary Lynn and reached for the knife he was going to use to deflate her. It was only a stupid fucking scalpel but it was better than nothing. As he reached for it he saw that Mary Lynn's bump on her belly was now a torn open hole full of blood and viscera. The creature, it came from her. Quickly he turned to defend himself from the thing.

There it stood staring at him. It was no taller than a toddler. Its skin was the color of black stone and its eyes were deep red. Upon its hairless head grew two horns. Its feet were hooves and attached to his wrists were dreadful looking claws. It stood there breathing for a second and looking curiously up at Steve.

"Daddy." It spoke to him in a child's voice. Steve collapsed to the ground and watched the ugly little demon as it approached him with its arms out. It embraced him and laid its horned head onto Steve's chest. Then he felt a hand drop down on his shoulder, a soft hand.

He turned and saw it was Mary Lynn. She was now standing next to him, the blood and guts still leaking from her abdomen. She smiled at him, her eyes also glowing red.

"I love you Steve." She said in that voice he remembered so well. She knelt down and wrapped her arms around Steve and their new child. She kissed Steve's forehead. "We're going to be a happy family."

Steve cried however his tears were not out of sadness, not out of fear. His tears were that of joy. He turned to his new wife and kissed her lips. Then he kissed his new baby on the forehead.

And they lived happily ever after…

She moaned and with each moan it sounded like symbols crashing from within her toothless mouth. Then came a sickening sound which reminded Mitch of a wheezing beast. Her fat, disgusting body road his dick as he thrusted into her diseased twat. He didn't wear a condom, he never did. Half the thrill of fucking meth whores is not knowing what disease you'd get next. Chlamydia, gonorrhea, herpes…maybe he'd finally get the bug.

Her tits sagged where they were skinny up top and fat on the bottom. They were stretched out down her fat pimply belly. Her gigantic ass continued to ride as she moaned and came. And at that moment of absolute disgusting torture…Mitch blew his load.

The bitch rolled over, her Titanic body nearly breaking the bed in half, and snorted a line of meth. Mitch laid there in heaven wondering what the clinic would say he had next.

Sex had always been a torturous struggle for Mitch. At thirty four years of age the construction worker had done it all. He had sex with old woman, fat women, teens, kids-he was even known to take in a man once in a while just for the strange of it. Sex had been a curse of his. That's why he fucked fat disgusting Providence meth heads. The thrill of catching a disease is all he had left. It was kind of like sexual Russian roulette.

"Ok sweetie, I'll see you later." And the whore left. She left him alone with the book. The book he had found at one of the houses he was working on. He ran his hands over its cover. The book captivated him, drew him in. He saw it tucked away in the bookshelf during his break and he knew at that moment that it was something he had to own. It was an occult book called Rotting Erotica.

This was not some ordinary grimoire of incense and chanting. No, this book went beyond that and drove head first into human sacrifice. If it worked, IF it worked, the book promised him that he would have sex with a demon; a fucking sex demon.

Now he wasn't some Satanist or witch or anything like that. He hated movies like the Exorcist and had a hard time enough believing Jesus rose from the dead. But this book, it seemed to call out to him. He tried to ignore it, to continue installing the new hardwood floors of Mr. McGomery's house but he couldn't stop. He stole it and took it home and now that he read it, studied it, it was all he could think about.

He went to sleep and dreamed of fucking demons. When he woke up his sheets were wet. He would work on houses with a hard on, thinking of what demon pussy felt like. He began watching movies like the Exorcist to understand, to help his imagination. He was obsessed.

The only problem was that it involved a sacrifice. He wasn't a murderer, but was sacrifice really murder. He didn't have to hold the blade, nor did he have to make the slice. All he had to do was present it and then reap the reward. It still was a morally conflicting inner argument but it was leaning in one direction. He was tired of jacking off to demonic movies like Alucarda. He was tired of cleaning his sheets. He was tired of fucking meth broads and barely catching a nut. No, he needed some fire pussy, he needed the demon.

As he rode down to the Warehouse District in Central Falls he thought about who he would pick. She had to be young, a new face and one that wouldn't be missed. White was out of the subject. Cops look too hard for missing white girls. Mexican or Black would do him fine. Then he saw her.

She was a thick black girl not a day over thirteen years old. She strolled down the street in booty cut off shorts and those fuck me boots she probably stole from her mother. Her massive breasts were spilling out of her halter top. Mitch had never seen her before and since he frequented the prostitute game quite a bit this meant one thing. She was new and there was no way anyone would miss her; a young new black girl ready for the kill.

He pulled up his truck to the curb and leaned over to the passenger window.

"You on the clock?"

"You a cop?"

"Do I look like a cop?"

"A lot of them don't look like cops these days, especially in prostitution stings."

"Never seen you here before."

"New around these parts; so what you looking for?"

"Come back to my place for a little perk and then a little fun. How much would that cost?"

"With the party favors I can do you for fifty."

"Great, then climb on in."

She climbed into his truck and they were off. This was going to be easier than he thought. Back at the house Mitch prepared a stem with a crack rock. He lit it and inhaled the smoke. He turned to the girl and smiled.

"So what's your name beautiful?"

"Ebony."

"What a beautiful name for a beautiful girl; you from around here Ebony?"

"No, ran away a couple years ago. Folks from Virginia; just got into Rhode Island couple days ago." This was perfect. It almost felt like fate had dropped her into his lap. She took the stem and loaded a rock. She hit it and exhaled. "So we going to fuck now or what?"

"Sure, come into the bedroom."

She made her way down the hallway as Mitch led her. The bedroom was typical of a single man full of mess and old beer bottles. She smiled as she saw the bondage set on the bed.

"You're kinky…I like kinky."

"Yes I am. Go ahead. Get undressed and lay on the bed and I will strap you in."

"Ok daddy." She slid out of her clothes, which weren't much to begin with. She quickly climbed her fat body into the bed and laid down in position. "Like this daddy?"

"Yes…you look like an angel." Mitch secured the restraints he bought at the local sex shop. When they were tight he walked over to the dresser and retrieved the book. He opened up to a page and spoke. "By Samigina, by Vassago and to the endless chaos of SitraAchra shall I venture? Let my voice transcend the barrier; let my desires no longer be denied. Dark lord, oh he who dwells in the Gallery. By the anti-cosmic gods I call thee forth, oh beautiful demon. I call you Oza, and offer this sacrifice."

"Is this some sort of role play?"

"Exactly." He turned the page. "By fire, by blood, I offer this woman to you oh great demon. Oza, materialize in the flesh from the realm of spirits. I demand you stand before me and take this sacrifice!"

"Oh I like it daddy. Come over here and fuck me."

The lights began to dim. A cool chill ran through the room and the sudden darkness and drop in temperature scared Ebony. She began to struggle.

"Ok, I'm scared. What's happening?"

"Honestly girl...I don't know yet."

Then there was a scream from the darkness. It sounded like a monster from hell itself. From the hallway came a corpse like woman. She was a foul creation dripping with rotting skin and maggots. She turned toward Mitch and approached him, leaving behind a trail of old skin and bloody footprints.

"You summoned me?" She groaned.

"I did Oza."

"Where's my sacrifice?"

"Over there." Mitch held his arm up and pointed to the terrified girl on the bed.

"Oh hell no; somebody help me!"

From Oza's pussy spilled a large phallic feeding tube just like the book explained. The rotting animated cadaver descended upon the bed like a wolf stalking prey. Ebony screamed in horror as Oza climbed onto the bed. The feeding tube rose up and brushed Ebony's face and then it ran down her body. It stopped at her vagina. Suddenly it darted inside the girl and she bolted in her restraints. She screamed in agony as the life was sucked from her body. Ebony began to decompose. Her skin, her organs, they all disappeared within the demon until all that was left of the child prostitute was a skeleton.

Where the corpse of Oza once stood now stood a sexy exotic woman. Two red horns parted her hair as she looked at Mitch with big black eyes. The phallic tube retracted inside her as she approached him. She was within an inch from his body when he felt her segmented tail run over his hard erection.

"Thank you for feeding me."

"Do you do anal?" She laughed. He was now naked and the two of them were suspended in empty space. They embraced and kissed. Mitch ran his hands down her body as he slid inside her. The pleasure was beyond human comprehension. It was like no joy on Earth and before he blew his first of many loads he knew he found a new love. The world could keep their meth whores, he had Oza.

Chapter One

The rain had fallen for three days. It ripped through the state in sheets and had been responsible for a few flash floods in the area. Mr. Bilkton, if he was still alive would say that he had only once before seen the Teller's Creek so high. He would tell a drawn out tale of fighting Nazis and returning home to see this creek pouring water into the street. Being a religious man, Mr. Bilkton would try to present this as evidence of the coming apocalypse.

The bar was usually packed during this time of the summer, and even more so when it rained. The people of Estill Springs had very little to do when it involved the nightlife, since the town was so small. The natural hang out for these country boys and girls seemed almost like a throwback to the old western days of saloons. It sat on the outskirts of town with that big neon light that always seemed to have a letter out. The blue letters shined through the rain as it read The Snake Pit.

The parking lot was a mud hell which was full of pickup trucks. Among all the Tennessee license plates, one car turned and pulled into the lot. His tag wasn't from Tennessee, but California. It was attached to a Mercedes Benz. Those beneath the front canopy, sucking in the smoke from Marlboros, naturally stared at the German engineered automobile.

Some gawked; others laughed. "Looks like another liberal fag got lost." One stated as he spit a wad of dip into an empty

Budweiser bottle. "Maybe he's just turning around, needs to reverse his direction and pulled in here to turn." Another suggested, but this theory quickly died when the engine ceased. The door opened and when they saw Tanner step out, they nearly died with laughter.

His suit must have cost more than every person at the bar's entire wardrobe combined that night. They all would call the color gray, except for Terrance. He was a secret homosexual and loved fashion. He would call it a three piece charcoal suit which looked like a design by Alexander Price. Of course he couldn't allow the rest to see how astonished he was so see such a lovely suit so he joined in by calling the man a fag. As he clicked his fancy little alarm and made his way toward the front door he stopped for a second to frown at his muddy Italian shoes.

"Aw, such a shame to mess them der nice shoes up." One teased. His girlfriend, obviously impressed with the car, hit him on the chest.

"Nice ride you go there." One of the toothless wonders snickered. Tanner smiled at him.

"Yes it is. Thank you very much."

"Would be a damn shame if a scratch were to happen upon it." The toothless wonder continued as he stood up from the barrel he leaned on. He smiled as he shook his head. "Be a damn shame. You see all these here pickup; well they all got dings and shit because us country boys like to get twisted before we hit the road and we tear shit up once in a while. Be a damn shame if someone accidently hit that nice set of wheels there, I reckon."

"Since I could buy every one of you a trailer with the

money I paid for it, I'm sure it would hit a nerve." A couple chuckles emerged from the crowd. The toothless wonder looked aggravated by this.

Terrance watched the man. His face showed hatred but the truth was that he was lost in admiration. Years of sucking off the few farm boys who knew he was gay made him forget what existed outside of small town America. He wanted to move to California.

"Well why then are you parking it here?"

"That's my business."

"I reckon you mean another tone city boy."

The man climbed the short steps under the canopy. He approached the man and stood a mere six inches from his face. The toothless wonder continued his ridiculous attempt at a smile.

"Listen, I'm here for my own reasons that do not concern you."

"Just let this be clear; this is our place. The only men here like pussy, not cock."

"Well than we got something in common after all."

"Well that may be so, as it seems, but our ladies in Estill Springs are for the men in Estill Springs. Do you understand?"

"I do, I doubt I'll find one worth my time anyway." He looked around. "Wouldn't want them to get pig shit on my Armani sheets."

"Is that so?"

"Yeah, I tend not to like women without teeth and smelling like cow shit."

One of the bigger guys stood up and cracked his neck. He raised a meaty hand on the city boy's shoulder and grunted at him.

"I don't like you."

"Good for you, I will be tormented that we'll never play a game of horseshoes together."

"You're a sarcastic little prick."

"Well I see you are the more educated one of the lot so I assume you are the diplomat. You see, although it may not be visible to the naked eye, I carry a nice gun on me. It is a .40 caliber Sig 226. Now I can pull it out, aim, and blow the remainder of your teeth out of your redneck heads before even one of you can spit a wad of dip. I may not take you all out, but while you are stunned I will be reloading to take out the rest. Now I'm not trying to start any shit but I will gladly finish whatever is started."

The meaty man smiled at him and chuckled. He turned to the others who nervously laughed as well.

"You are a cocky little fuck, but you're alright for a Californian."

"I am glad to be accepted."

"Just don't get out of line, ok?"

The inside of this establishment was something right out

of a movie. It was a hot, sticky place full of tables made from old barrels, a dance floor full of locals trying to get laid and a bar with an impressive showcase of alcohol. The walls were plastered with pictures of outlaws, snakes, and various types of guns. From the rafters, suspended by wire, was ancient looking farm equipment. For a second he imagined what kind of damage the scythe could inflict on one of the women in here.

Eyes followed this man to the bar, where he took a seat next to a massive man with a full beard and a shirt covered in sweat stains. He smelled like a mixture of motor oil and shit. When he noticed the new guy sitting next to him he turned to the man with a look of surprise. "A fag?"

"I just got clearance from the welcome committee outside."

"Jud let you in here?" The fat bastard asked, astonished by this little bit of information. It seemed to take him a second or two to properly process it and it wasn't because he was drunk, it was because he was stupid.

"If you are referring to the massive man outside; than yes."

"He must be drunk or something. Ok then." The fat man returned to his beer as he stared at the television set, lost in the empty space between him ears.

The man that ran the bar saw him and immediately headed into his direction. He had long blond hair which hung past his shoulders. He wore a T-Shirt for a band called Hayseed Dixie and seemed to have most of his white skin covered in tattoos. This man he recognized. He approached and smiled.

"Tanner?" the bartender asked.

"Yes, I presume you are Chad?" The city boy responded.

"Chad, you know this clown?" The fat bastard then asked.

"More than one might imagine. What will you have, it's on the house." Tanner relaxed with this man's generous hospitality. He glanced at the beer display and squinted.

"I think it is safe to assume you don't carry Braufactum." Tanner asked, still scanning.

"No, never even heard of it."

"I'll take a Heineken then."

"German piss." The fat man hissed at him as if Tanner's words were blasphemy.

"You don't say Mr…"

"The name's Bubba."

"I would have never guessed."

Chad smiled at his new friend and handed him a beer. Tanner sipped it and tried to enjoy the setting as he waited for one more to arrive.

***

As if Jud and his crew didn't get a laugh enough at Tanner and his Mercedes, here came a Mazda Miata. The red car pulled in and parked next to the Mercedes and the jester crew couldn't help but laugh.

Pat was a gauntly man. He wore black leather pants with straps hanging off. He proudly wore a tight Joy Division band t-shirt which hugged his skinny frame and his long black hair fell over his pale face, a face with piercings in his septum, lip and eyebrow. He smoked a clove cigarette which he tossed from his black nail polished hand.

When he approached the bar the crew burst out laughing. Pat shot a menacing look at the bunch.

"Look its Columbine High's unknown gunman." A woman cried out.

"Damn, you are way out of our dress code, bro." One of the rednecks managed to get out between sobs of laughter.

"Don't fuck with me." Pat replied with confidence. This made them laugh even more as Jud approached the little man.

"Why not?" The colossal redneck asked. Pat reached into his pocket and pulled out a badge. It was a Tennessee Metro Homicide Forensic badge. Of course the rednecks didn't read it; the shape alone was intimidation enough. They grew quiet and went back to ignoring him. That is except for Jud. He gave him a long, drawn out look of hatred as the little fool entered the establishment.

A few chuckles and awkward looks later Pat saw the well-dressed man at the bar. He strolled up and sat down next to him. Tanner ran his eyes up and down his body and smiled.

"Pat?"

"Yeah, you must be Tanner." He responded in a soft

voice, nervously looking around. Chad approached the new comer.

"And I'm Chad."

"Great we're all here now. Let's talk." He nervously blurted out. Chad shot a look at him which warned him that is wasn't safe to talk here.

"No, not now; we must wait until I close up, then we can discuss things."

"What do I do until then?" Pat asked, confused and irritated.

"Drink." Chad laughed. Pat managed a smile.

"I don't typically drink but fuck it. I'll have a Coors Light."

***

The rest of the night was rather low key. A few new comers ragged Tanner, but word spread quickly about the badge the freak held onto. This was the kind of place where there were more arrest warrants than clean people at any given time. They did not want to bring heat down upon them, so naturally they left Pat alone. Once the last of the drunks were pushed out to drive their massive pickup trucks down the muddy back roads of Estill Springs, the outside lights were cut out and the three were now alone.

Chad led them over to a table near the dance floor. He took a seat.

"Well my plan has worked thus far so now we will

proceed."

"I'm curious as to what this will be." Tanner eagerly listened.

"Well let us start with introductions. I'm Chad Browning. I own this bar, The Snake Pit, and also live here. I'm a hunter, having grown up in Morganton North Carolina. My nickname is "The Woman Hunter" because I kidnap prostitutes from the major cities, set them free in the woods, and hunt them. After I kill them I field dress them, stuff them, and hang them from trees. My body count is right now at thirty six."

Pat nodded with approval as he nervously drummed the wooden table with his fingers. Already his queer behavior was bothering Tanner, but Chad didn't care.

"I'll go next." Pat eagerly jumped in. "I'm Pat Heath. I'm a forensic tech who works at a body farm."

"What the fuck is a body farm?" Chad asked with intrigue in his voice.

"It's a place where we leave cadavers out in various natural settings and study decay. This helps us with timing death."

"Wow." Chad nodded with approval. "This I need to see."

"Yeah I saw a documentary on this." Tanner added, trying to find a common ground with the little gothic freak.

"Anyway, I grew up in Illinois and moved here to Tennessee and work at the body farm. It's only like an hour from here."

"No way." Chad's jaw dropped. All his time living here and not once did he know there was a body farm so close?

"Yep. I'm an artist. I kidnap women and put on a show. Usually this is done with lights and music as well as cosplay."

"And that is?" Tanner asked.

"Costume play; I dress up. I torture the women mentally and physically all while documenting my work before, during, and after. I do this with photos. When I am done I bring the bodies in the body farm so they're never found."

"Never?"

"Fuck no, we got pigs and worms and shit there to eat the bodies when we are done. I then leave the pictures in random bathrooms for someone to find. I have been called the Deadly Photographer and my body count is thirteen."

Chad nodded toward Tanner to tell his story.

"Tanner Rothstein. I live in Long Beach California, attended Brown University in Rhode Island, and own a business called Rothstein Enterprises. I'm a seducer of women. The woman must be attracted to me for this to work. I win them over, usually poor girls, and then strangle them. I then dress them in expensive dresses they could only dream of wearing in life; Versace, Prada, and Gucci. I make their dreams of being glamorous come true in death. I then dump them in Hollywood with a fresh bouquet of flowers. I'm called The Good Taste Strangler, a reference to my clothing choice for my victims. My body count is at nineteen."

"How we got into this lifestyle is irrelevant. We all have our reasons and no one here is judging; quite the opposite actually. I reached out to you both with the goal of performing the ultimate kill." Tanner and Pat's ears perked up.

"Ultimate kill?" Tanner asked with a hint of mistrust. "Excuse me if I sound coarse but what the fuck is an ultimate kill?"

"This shall be a victim which will be a worthy adversary. She is a woman who embodies characteristics which will satisfy a seducer, an artist and a hunter all the same. We will all get our chance to play with her, and when it is done we all will kill her…together."

"Sounds beautiful." Pat replied with a genuine tear in his eye. "How poetic. I mean it's-"

"You must forgive me now if I sound suspicious, but I have been schooled to think a certain way and to re-wire my brain otherwise takes far too much effort. My question is then, why?"

"Because the thrill for the kill gets sour; we've all been there. This is a new experiment which will live up to all our needs."

"How do we kill her in the end?" Pat asked. "I mean Tanner strangles, I mutilate and you shoot. How do we decide?"

"I thought this one through as well. Are you familiar with the story The Lottery by Shirley Jackson?"

"Of course." Tanner responded.

"Good. The ending of that story is how I picture this ending. We will all stone her to death, none of us have done that before." This interested Pat immensely.

"It's perfect, but who would the woman be?" Pat asked eager to hear.

"I've been watching her for a while now. She has a little something for everyone. She's a gorgeous woman, sensual as well as sexy. She is strong willed and will certainly need to be wooed. Tanner this is perfect for you. She is a sculpture and I have seen some art work in her apartment that demands a darker taste. Her mind seems strong. I think that Pat can find something there."

"Yes, I can." He responded with a smile.

"And as for me, she is an ex-soldier, served in Afghanistan. She was kidnapped in 2006 and remained a prisoner of the Taliban for over two years. She survived by escaping. This is my worthy adversary, perfect for a hunter."

"This woman, she certainly does sound like the perfect victim."

"Her name is Debbie Lingle."

Chapter Two

The music vibrated throughout her apartment as she danced, or at least engaged in an activity which she referred to as dancing. She swayed her way between her furniture as the chorus of the punk song sped up. As she felt her heart race with the beat and her worries and fears evaporate like rain fall in a desert she flung her hair in every direction as she just let go. When she caught her reflection in the mirror she paused for a second to scruff up her hair, giving herself a more punk look as she scrunched up her lip and sang along with the song lyrics, trying to impersonate a meaner person than she really was.

"Butcher baby you're dressed to kill. Butcher baby I know you will. Butcher baby today is the day. Butcher baby they're gonna put you away" As she continued to shake her head to the tune she began to unbutton her shirt. Halfway down she tore it open and flung it across the room, revealing a black bra. This didn't stay on long either and within a millisecond she was topless and dancing toward the leather couch.

She jumped up onto the couch and watched herself in the mirror. She ran her hands down her perfect body as she slid her thumbs into her tight jeans. She slid them around to the front and undid the button. Within seconds she wiggled out of those until all that was left was thong underwear, which didn't last. Now, completely naked, she jumped off the couch and started head banging to the music.

The whole time she was ignorant of the eyes observing her. The three men were in a parking garage adjacent to her apartment and watched her through a set of binoculars. The only thing she was aware of was the sound of the congested traffic in Memphis, background ambience drowned out by the punk song. It was so loud that it took a few seconds before she noticed the heavy knocking on the door. It wasn't until the door was almost off the hinges did she reach over and turn down the volume. She ran to the door and cracked it open, sticking her head out to shield her naked body.

It was her neighbor from down the hall. He peered at her through his Dolce and Gabbana eye glasses as he shot her an inquisitive look. "Hello Debbie, I hate to be a bother."

"George, sweetheart, you're never a bother. I apologize; I get a little carried away." He understood. He couldn't imagine how she could go through life with a smile after what she had been through. Sure, being a homosexual in backwoods Tennessee had its share of torture but it was nothing compared to what this girl went through. He honestly felt bad even asking her to turn down the music, if anyone had a right to blare music it was her.

"Well nice to meet see you Debbie's head, but where's the rest of her?"

"Well Georgie I am naked and I know how you are oh, so grossed out by the female form."

"Well, naked and listening to The Plasmatics in the middle of the day on high volume…do I sense a little lesbian dissidence here? My gaydar is going off."

"No George, I still like dick."

"See we got something in common." He responded with wide eyes and a limp wrist raised to his mouth in a how dare I say that manner. She smiled and shook her head.

"You mean to tell me that you don't like this?" She swung the door open. George played along and pretended to act like a vampire reacting negatively to sunlight. He hissed and moaned as he dropped to the floor. He held his fingers out in the sign of a cross.

"My eyes, my poor fagot eyes." He cried out as Debbie stood there laughing.

"Holy shit!" There was the sound of a boy, a boy she knew all too well. His name was Toby. He was a fat little twelve year old who also lived in this apartment building. He now stood in the hallway with three other dice throwing Dungeon and Dragon friends. All four boys stood there with their jaws hung open.

George jumped up and acted like a shield for her. "Don't look, it's evil and will corrupt you!" He joked.

"Sorry kids! George I'll turn the music down."

"No problem, just hide your dirty pillows before they corrupt a mind of another pre-teen boy. Before you know it they will be jacking their little pecker in the bathroom. It will be chaos."

The door slammed and Debbie pressed against the door laughing hysterically. George was a great friend of hers, they both worked at a barista downtown called The Bean Room. They shared a love for trashy horror movies, dancing and even had the same taste in guys. Since she returned home she made an instant connection with him.

He'd recognized her from the News. Many did in fact, but he

didn't approach her for this reason. He claimed it was because he sensed a soul that was broken, detached from society and in desperate need of a friend. The truth was, however, he saw her flirting with Jaime Champs, a local boy he wanted. He decided it would be a challenge to steal the straight boy from a beautiful but emotional basket case.

Jaime Champs turned out to be total straight after all with no chance of hopping the fence. It was a waste of time for them both. To Debbie he was just like the thirty or so other men she dated since returning home to find out her husband had re-married. No one even told her this, not a warning. She found out when she returned to the house they shared to find a new woman living there. Son of a bitch, how long did he really wait? There was a four month old infant in the house. She had been gone for nearly three years in total.

She couldn't blame him; she couldn't blame anybody except for herself. She was a young soldier with a head full of patriotic horseshit and dreams of becoming something bigger. Who was she thinking she was, fucking Rambo? She left the FOB that morning and it was during a rest point where she wandered too far out. She saw a rifle in the sand. What a cool trophy she thought. It wasn't until the buttstock of another AK-47 smacked the back of her head did she realize she was a fucking idiot.

How long did he wait?

Long enough she supposed.

***

"She is very beautiful, I must say. Her breasts are exquisite, her tone well maintained. She must have hit the gym hard after returning to America." Tanner felt the erection in his pants growing. This was not because he was sexually turned on by her amazing body; no this would be the emotions of a normal person. He was aroused as he pictured her screaming with him on top of her choking the life from her.

No, you are to use stones this time.

He had to admit that he thought the stone thing was a little lame, but the rest of the plan was coming along pretty good. Pat even decided to lend his location of the body farm to stage this night. He had come out here with low expectations, but now he was ready.

"Let me see her, does she shave?" Pat hollered as he pulled the binoculars. His jaw dropped as he slowly placed his hand down the front of his pants. "My god, she is hot!"

"Motherfuck!" Chad yelled as he slapped Pat on the back of the head. He dropped the binoculars and turned to him.

"What the fuck was that for?"

"Stop jacking your dick; don't do that shit around us."

"It's a disorder, I can't control it. It stems from sexual abuse."

"Does that explain why you're so fucked up?"

"Not at all, I kill because it's fun." Chad burst out laughing and Tanner followed. He had to admit, although these two were far different breeds than himself, he was enjoying their company. He even was looking forward to the kill.

***

"No mom, I'm not going to do it?" Debbie spoke into the phone. She was still naked and now lying down on her bed. The television played softly in the background as she stretched out. She looked at the scars on her legs, and thought of the ones on her back, the ones from when those animals whipped her. It didn't bother her anymore, beauty marks. "I'm not going to sell my story to some shit bag journalist so he can exploit it."

"Honey, see reason. You went through hell, a hell no one can imagine. Don't you think others can learn from it?"

"How does one learn from a story of some slimy towel head jamming a glass coke bottle up your anus and shouting How's that Cola taste now infidel slut?." Debbie swore she heard her mother shutter over the phone. She heard her voice cracking as the sound of pill bottles opened. She knew the routine. Her mother had taken anti-depressants and anxiety meds since she went missing. The way she acted, you'd think she was kidnapped.

"I'm…I'm so sorry honey. I cannot imagine…"

"You're right you can't so don't even try. Just forget this conversation completely."

"Are you doing ok?"

"I'm fine-"

There was a knock at the front door. She shot up in bed. She wasn't expecting anyone. It couldn't be George again, the music was off.

"Mrs. Lingle, this is Tom with Maintenance." The voice seemed friendly enough but she was suspicious of everyone.

"Who?"

"My name is Tom; I'm here to spray your apartment for bugs."

"Can you come back?" She sounded a little irritated.

"Who's there honey?" Her mom asked, concerned for her daughter as she pictured the Coke bottle sodomy.

"It's the bug man." She replied.

"I can't I'll be on another floor tomorrow." She hesitated and sighed.

"Ok, give me a second." She got up from the bed and threw on a pair of yoga pants and fumbled with a tight shirt with an image of Buddha on the front. "Mom, I got to let you go."

"I love you sweetie."

"I love you to."

Chapter Three

"So what will it be sweethearts?" Gretchen, a bubbly teen asked. She stood there with her pen in her lips and trying desperately to make her cleavage distract customers from the baby bump beneath her apron.

"I'll have a coffee and two waffles." Tanner answered. Gretchen couldn't help but stare at him. He was like a movie star, handsome. She imagined being swept into his arms and carried to a bed where he would lie her down and please her like a woman was meant to be pleased.

Tanner, being the predator he was, naturally sensed this. He would lie if he didn't admit that the thought of strangling a pregnant teen didn't appeal to him, but he had to stick with the plan. Besides, he couldn't be leaving strangled well dressed women this far outside of California. If they were to see this it will open up more doors which may lead to him being caught.

"No problem sweet heart, and for you sir?" She turned to Pat who had creeped her out. He looked older than he was, sickly almost. He hid behind his long hair and refused to even make eye contact.

"Coffee, black; that is all." He mumbled, staring at his black painted finger nails. Tanner shook his head at this display.

"And I'll have a ham and egg biscuit with a glass of orange juice if you will miss." Chad chimed in; trying to pull her attention away from the basket case Pat was proving to be.

"Ok then, I'll be right back." Tanner smiled at her. She smiled flirtatiously back. He imagined wrapping his hands around her neck and squeezing the last of her breath out. He would finish it with a quick snap and then it would be done; another well-dressed corpse to add to his collection.

She could have the life she dreamed of, but only in death.

"What the fuck is wrong with you today?" Chad shot at Pat who turned up at him and smiled. Chad shook his head as he saw the glassy look in his eyes. This pissed Chad off immensely as he pushed his silverware away from him. "Jesus Christ, that dumb son of a bitch is fucking high."

"It's wearing off. I didn't know we would meet up so early." He confessed, continuing his desperate fight to distinguish between reality and fiction.

"What are you on?" Tannner asked, a little concerned.

"Ecstasy. I'm coming down so don't worry."

"This is just fucking great." Chad looked at him with aggression in his eyes. He wanted nothing more than to beat this little pansy's head off the table. "Don't you do it again."

"I was nervous; you need to understand that I am not a very social person."

"As if that much isn't obvious; for now on you stay clean during this." Chad demanded, almost like a father figure. This seemed to be insulting to the young Pat who looked up defensively.

"Excuse me; explain to me why I need to listen to you?"

"Because if you do it again we both will gut you alive."

Tanner joined in. He himself was known to take a pre-work out drink before a kill, just to give him the little kick, but to use drugs during something of this magnitude was just irresponsible. He agreed with Chad, and wanted nothing to do with it.

"Fine, fuck I'll stop."

"Good." Tanner turned to Chad. "So how did the bug spraying stunt work?"

"Pretty amazing actually. I've got some pictures while she was in her room trying to ignore me. We'll go over them together. Now we discuss the plan."

"Tell us wondrous leader, what's the fucking plan." Pat asked sarcastically.

"Tanner is going to seduce the girl and win her heart with his good looks and from the knowledge we acquired from the pictures I took last night."

"Fucking genius with the pictures, real good plan. The only real question I think is when are we starting today?"

"Right after breakfast."

**

"Hello can I help you?" Debbie asked. She stood at the cash register as the man rambled off his order. All morning she had been distracted by the handsome man at one of the tables. He kept looking at her between his reading of the newspaper. She thought it was all in her head at first but when George noticed it to there was no denying it.

"Go talk to him." George said with a playful push. She was hesitant as always. Ever since she had returned from Afghanistan her track record for men sucked and she had decided that she was doomed to be disappointed, to be alone forever "If you don't I will and trust me sweetie, I've turned men gay who were far straighter than this hot little number."

"Listen to you. How do you know-" and George cut her off as he shushed her with his index finger pressed against his lip.

"Here he comes."

"Hello." The man spoke. Debbie turned to him with her face lit up. She was lost in his statuesque features, his chiseled face and gym toned body.

"Hello can I help you?"

"My name's Tanner. I was wondering if you wouldn't mind joining me at my table. I'd like to talk to you."

"I wish I could but my shift doesn't end for a few hours." From earshot George heard this and rushed over, nearly dropping the Ice Caramel Macchiato all over the floor.

"Sweetie she would be delighted. She was just about to take her break." With forceful eyes Geroge shoved her on. She knew that if she didn't then George would never let her live this down.

If nothing else what harm is a good fuck?

"Ok." She turned and leaned down to the register as she typed in her ID number on the time clock. "You got half an hour."

Chapter Four

Her half hour break wasn't enough to get to know the man, but enough for him to ask her out on a date. Debbie looked through her wardrobe as her mind went wild with possibilities. She held dresses against her naked body as she repeated his name. "Tanner."

She told her mother who was ecstatic to say the least; she was already planning a wedding. Her mother had blamed herself for Debbie's torture at the hands of Afghani terrorists. If she just supported the marriage and helped pay for it Debbie wouldn't have joined the army to pay for the wedding with her sign on bonus money.

Of course Debbie could hear them still; the conversation in Arabic as they beat her and raped her. They were always there. Out the corner of her eye every shadow was one of them. She saw their bearded faces and wild eyes as they brandished more utensils to inflict agony upon her body.

She shut that out of her head. She vowed to have a good time tonight. As she held the perfect dress up to her body she smiled and nodded. "Tonight you're going to get yourself laid."

***

Their date had begun with a trip to the movies and then went to enjoy dinner at "La Senorita". While eating steaks and nacho chips the two began to discuss Tanner's job.

"I work at a corpse farm." He said in a matter of fact tone. The combination of words obviously stopped Debbie in her tracks as she let out a low, nervous laughter.

"A corpse farm?" She squinted as if somehow this would help her to understand what he meant.

"Yeah, it's a place where forensic teams study the decay of bodies." He noticed her look of disgust but also noticed her curiosity was caught. She paused for a second as if processing the information. He saw her record collection in those pictures. She loved punk and Death Metal. She certainly had a morbid side, perhaps was a goth girl in high school even.

"How do you get bodies?"

"People donate them."

"You're kidding me."

"Nope; you'd be surprised how many we get. They all want to help after death, altruists even post mortem. We study the process. Some we put in direct sunlight, others we submerge in water, others we bury a foot deep while others we experiment with known disposal techniques killers often use."

"It's hard to believe such a place exists."

"I can take you there." His smile seemed off, artificial. She began to hear the men arguing in Arabic again. They pulled out their dicks and urinated on her head. They ran garden shears over her tits and jammed a toilet plunger into her ass. She began to feel sick and when she looked up at Tanner she saw him with a long beard. He was speaking Arabic.

Debbie, this isn't true. Not every guy you meet is trying to kill you. This one actually likes you.

"Yeah, I'd like to see it." She forced out of her mouth. She wasn't sure if she meant it or if she was just being nice. Regardless she knew they would be heading over there before the night was through.

"Fantastic. We'll go after we finish our meal."

***

The drive up was long. The whole time Tanner filled the car with friendly chatter but still Debbie heard the men who tortured her in the back of her mind. They called her names. Dumb cunt, you're heading into a trap. She knew she was paranoid but as the car drove through the night and into a desolate dirt road she did begin to feel the tension grow.

You need to start trusting people.

"So tell me about your time in the service."

Service? She never told him about being in the military. There it was; the red flag! This wasn't what it appeared to be. This man had studied her and now here she was in the middle of the woods with him all *alone*.

Ok, so you might be right. He may be a creep after all. You need to keep the conversation going so he doesn't suspect that you are on to him.

"Nothing too major; I did a tour in Afghanistan. I don't talk about it often."

"I can't imagine the horrors you must have been subjected to." As he spoke Debbie pulled her cell phone out of her pocket and glanced. No signal. "What are you doing there?"

"I was going to check my email." She put on a fake pouty face as she held the phone up to him. "No signal."

That's right, you're doing well.

"I hate it when there's no signal. There never is out this way."

Think. Think.

She turned her eyes to the door and examined the lock. It was engaged. She would need to be fast to pull the mechanism up, open the door and dive out before he could react. She needed to go now! She pulls the plastic piece. The locking mechanism wouldn't budge.

"Child safety locks silly." His smile was sinister as he nodded his head. "Nifty little invention."

"You have kids?" She asked as her breathing got shallow. Her panic was not obvious.

"No, in fact I do not."

"Then why are these locks engaged."

"You're a smart girl. I see you figured it all out so let's cut the-" Debbie slammed her purse in his face. He jerked to the left and pulled the car into that direction. The Mercedes hit a tree and came to a stop. Debbie quickly reached into her purse and pulled out her little compact 9mm pistol. She kept it close to her body so not to have it taken from her but kept it on Tanner the entire time. "You stupid fucking bitch!"

"Shut the fuck up! What did you think you were going to

do with me? Rape me?"

"That isn't my style." Tanner reached up and touched his nose. He frowned. "Bitch you broke it."

"So then what?"

"What's with all this past tense? I was and still am going to kill you."

"Looks like you're at my mercy now."

"Think again." He pointed to the window. She turned to see two other men holding AR-15 assault rifles pointed in her direction. Tanner smiled at her.

"We're ready to play now."

***

She had been out for quite a while. The man with the long hair had administered a drug. It took effect immediately and she was gone. Her eyes were still closed but she heard what sounded like millions of pigs being slaughtered. The squeals were terrifying. When she opened her eyes she was happy to see speakers in place of actual slaughtered pig.

To her surprise she wasn't restrained. She stood up quickly and assessed herself. She was fine. The room was small and covered with strange paintings on the walls. Some were depicting women being sodomized by wolves; others had children disemboweling their own parents. The strobe light certainly wasn't helping her pounding headache. She searched around until she found the exit.

Outside the rain poured and once she cleared the door she slid down a muddy hill. She fell several feet until she did a face plant into something squishy. Raising her head she was horrified to see that her face caved in the rotting remains of a cadaver's abdomen. The blackened organs and maggots spilled out.

Debbie screamed in horror as she desperately clawed at the wet soil. She dragged herself up the hill. She was greeted by several more corpses in various starts of decomposition. They were tied to trees and hung from branches.

"Welcome to the corpse farm. You didn't think it was just a clever name now did you?" The voice spoke over a P.A. system. Debbie turned her head as she stood at the top of the embankment. The rain was coming down in sheets and the moon cast eerie shadows.

"WHAT THE FUCK DO YOU WANT WITH ME?" She hollered in every direction. There was laughter on the P.A.

"I want you to run! Run along little rabbit! Run!" The memories of Afghanistan returned to her. She remembered how they treated her and now it was about to happen all over again. She looked around for a weapon. There she saw a massive branch. She reached down and as she picked it up an arrow shot into her left arm. She screamed out in agony. "I said run!"

So she ran blindly, deep into the corpse farm.

***

Chad watched his prey. She looked so goddamn beautiful as she quickly recovered from the scares Pat had set up. He knew she was stronger than that, too strong to be taken in by some psycho mumble jumble. Sure he thought Pat could be a little eccentric but the fact remained that the mental torment added to the thrill he supposed. For Chad though, it was all about the hunt.

She turned around corners with elegance, just to collapse as she hit a slick patch of mud. Chad raised the bow, pulled the arrow back and aimed. He followed her and as he took in a breath. He held it and let go as the arrow was sent whizzing through the air.

**

She felt the arrow tear through her leg. She screamed in agony and tried to ignore it, but it was excruciating. She collapsed onto the dirt as she rolled over onto her back. Now, staring up at the moon, she saw those Arab men all around her kicking her and yelling at her in a foreign language. They would soon rape her.

Debbie snap out of it, you're not in Afghanistan you are here in America and these guys brought you here for one thing.

The voice was right. She needed to pull herself together if she wanted to get out of this. She got out of that POW camp all those years ago, had she not? Surely she could handle a couple hillbillies with a bloodlust. She just needed to get her head on straight.

From the woods came a metallic object. It pierced just below her shoulder and ripped out her back. It was a massive hook and before she could further examine it she was being pulled through the woods.

Get your head together, this night is about to get a lot

worse.

Chapter Five

"So tell me about yourself." The skinny man with the longish hair smiled at her. The room was small and the lighting was low. It was completely bare with the exception of her, him, the chair she was on and a table with an assortment of sharp and blunt objects. Their original design and intent was less sinister however it was this special mind that perverted them, using them to remove flesh from the human body.

"Fuck you." She managed to get out, barely able to function. The throbbing in her arm and leg from the arrow were bad, but the hole from the meat hook was a whole other problem. It was so excruciating that she felt faint and knew that at any given moment she could pass out.

Don't do it, don't give them the satisfaction.

"Ok, well looks like we need a nice ice breaker, something to tear down the walls that are locking you out." The skinny man turned to the table and reached down for a hammer. He wrapped his fingers around the handle and raised it high. With one quick whack half of Debbie's front teeth shot out and skipped across the blood stained wooden floor. Blood poured from her mouth as she screamed in agony. "Did that do it? Did it?"

Again Debbie ignored the man as she tried to get herself focused. With blurry vision she looked up at her captor. Was that a turban on his head? She didn't understand him well, was he speaking Arabic?

Come on Debbie get your shit together girl.

"No huh? Well I guess-"

"What do you want to know?" Debbie mumbled as more teeth dislodged themselves and fell in her lap. This brought a smile to the skinny man's face. He knew she was tough, but to be this unbreakable so early in the game made him realize it would be a challenge to have her begging for death. He loved a good challenge. For now he kneeled down at the girl's feet and smiled.

"I want to know what such a beautiful girl like you is doing getting caught up with a bunch of serial killers."

"I guess bad luck. Sucks sometimes ya know." Her casualness infuriated the man. His smile dropped off his face and he quickly rose to his feet.

"You know who I am, don't you?"

"Some loser who women refuse to fuck so you resort to mutilating them?"

"Exactly." The man turned to the table and reached down for a mask. It was a ceramic mask, a demonic looking thing colored red. It looked Japanese. With quivering hands the small man pulled the mask closer and onto his face. Once it was on he snapped up and Debbie knew she was now looking at a different person. The masked man turned back to the table and reached down. He picked up a stainless steel instrument. It looked almost like a long needle. He held it up.

"What's that?"

"Trocar." And without giving her a second further to

contemplate what this tool was it was jammed into her right eye. She screamed out in pain as she jerked on the chair. She watched out her good eye and saw the man place the other end into the mouth of the mask, and then into his own mouth. He seemed to be using the device like a straw. With a menacing smile the blood spilled down his mouth and dripped off his chin.

The Trocar was pulled free and before she could recover his bony finger jammed forward and reached deep into her skull. She felt the digit wrap around something elastic inside her head and pull. At that moment, like a television turning off during a power outage, the eye stopped working as the man pulled the gooey mass from her socket.

The man looked down and shook his head. He saw the floor was now covered with urine and feces. "My god, you shit yourself."

"Sorry sweetie…" *That's right Debbie, stay strong.* "…but you are…" *Don't give him what he wants.* "…going to have to do a lot better if you want to get me to beg."

The masked man dropped the eye. He turned his head sideways as he studied her. A low laugh came from within the mask, a laugh similar to that of a demon.

"Challenge accepted."

***

Tanner and Chad were watching the television while Pat was in the back with the girl. Tanner had his first part fulfilled by seducing her, Chad got to hunt her and now Pat would break her. When all three got their fill they would kill her together. They patiently waited as they watched the whole show on the television from a live feed.

"He really is sick, ya know?" Tanner laughed. "I mean, Jesus. He just jammed a solder iron up her ass."

"That's bad but not as bad I think as when he cut off her pussy lips and then jammed the nail covered dildo up her cunt."

"Really, you think that is worse." Tanner asked, almost like the two were discussing musical tastes.

"Oh hell yeah I do. Listen, a little burning in yer cornhole is prolly like extreme hemorrhoids. The pussy torture, shit man there isn't nothing like it."

"I supposed I can see your logic."

"Looks like it's coming to an end. Get ready Tanner."

***

Pat used garden sheers to cut her lips off. He used a blow torch on her tits and with a lock cutter removed every toe on her right foot. He cut her loose, tossed her to the floor and beat her with a barbed wire covered baseball bat. She screamed in pain, hollered but never begged. She never gave her torturer the satisfaction. When her screaming fit was complete and she regained her composure she began laughing manically.

This goddamn bitch has lost her mind.

He was done, there was no more playing around. He would break her, even if it killed her. He turned to the table and picked up a hammer and a hook like bladed weapon used for filleting. He stood over the woman as she lay in her own piss, shit and blood. She laughed hysterically as the blood from her toothless and lipless mouth spilled on the ground. She looked up at Pat and even gave him the middle finger before busting out laughing. The laughter stopped as the hammer came across her face, shattering her jaw.

"No more playing around." Pat pulled the mask from his face and tossed it across the room. It shattered when it hit the wall. He took a knee and with the hammer in his hand he smashed down onto her right arm, right above the wrist. He pounded until the spot on the arm looked like a thin fabric of flesh. He then took the blade and cut her hand off. "Oh we aren't done yet sweetheart."

He then took the knife and started at the elbow. He skinned her arm, right down to the white bone. After a few moments the broken and splintered bone was exposed. Pat laughed as the door bust open.

"What the fuck guys?" He hollered. "I'm not done."

"You goddamn idiot, you're going to kill her." Tanner yelled.

"I'm not."

"Look at her, she's nearly dead." And they were right. The woman was no longer laughing, too weak to do much else other than breath and exist, and even that was expiring. Like a disappointed child Pat slumped down and shook his head. "It's not fair. She's so damn stubborn."

"Get your pictures and let's do this." Chad demanded. Pat

looked up at the two but knew this wasn't open for debate.

"Fine." Pat dropped the blade on the floor next to the hammer and stood up. This next part was usually his favorite, taking the picture, but something felt wrong. He didn't get her to beg, didn't get her to break. He felt like he had met his match. And then he felt the crack.

The hammer smashed down on his foot. He felt every time bone in his extremity break into a million pieces as the pain shot up his body. Pat dropped to his knees and before he could react to the assault the hook blade entered his throat, tearing his esophagus out. It hung from the hole like a dead snake spilling blood. Pat reached up and as the world around him grew dark he saw the woman staring him in his eyes with a smile. The dried blood, the mutilated face, the eyeless socket; he was looking right at death as he slowly made his exit from this world and into the next.

***

Chad nearly pissed himself when he saw the woman smash Pat's foot with the hammer. When she took the blade to him he nearly shit himself. How on earth could such a woman as this exist? How on earth could she have this much strength, this much fight left in her? She was a prodigy, something Chad had never seen before.

Debbie dropped the blade and retrieved the hammer as she slowly rose to her feet and for the first time in Chad's life he felt fear. He didn't even know what the feeling was at first. He felt his stomach was sick, his heart fluttering, his skin became covered in goose bumps and he realized it was all fear. He feared this woman.

Tanner rushed her. He never let a woman take him, so sir. He was the male, the dominant and all women were submissive. They fell to him, not the other way around. He was so blinded with anger that he didn't realize she still held the hammer and when it came up and smashed him in the face he fell down at her feet. His beautiful face was now a bloodied mess of smashed meat. He tried to function but everything was moving so fast. He was dizzy from the blow. She knelt down and with the hammer she continued to smash in his head. She smashed until the skull cracked open with a sickening sound and the grey brains fell out like bloodied cauliflower. Chad didn't move, he was mesmerized by it all. He was taken back.

The woman raised from Chad's corpse, this woman naked and covered in bodily waste and blood. Her jaw hung useless from thin strands of muscle, toothless and shattered. Her right eye was missing. Blood poured from her mutilated pussy, her tits were black and charred. Her right hand was gone and all that remained of that arm from the elbow down was about eight inches of splintered bone. The woman didn't scream, didn't yell, and didn't laugh; she just stood there and breathed. This woman had already killed two of the nation's worst modern serial killers.

"I've been looking for you." Tears began to flow from Chad's eyes. He smiled and wiped them with a shaking hand. "For a long time I looked. I thought I'd never find you. Please, go ahead and do it."

She dropped the hammer. She looked at the pathetic man as he blubbered before her. He wanted to die. She would oblique. The corpse like woman screamed and ran toward Chad. He closed his eyes and opened his arms as if he was accepting the lord into his life. The animalistic woman dove on him, knocking him over and onto the ground. Like a savage beast sent from hell she used the splintered bone of her right arm to stab the man. She screamed as blood soaked her body and she manically continued to rip him open with her broken bone.

Chad never once screamed, he welcomed the death; finally feeling peace.

John Putignano

John lives in North Carolina with his wife and three kids. He has written the books Torture Porn, Torture Porn 2, Pleasures in Putrefaction, God is Drunk and Malkuth: The Demon.

Visit online

www.entheogeniclab.com

Printed in Great Britain
by Amazon.co.uk, Ltd.,
Marston Gate.